What others have said about *A Tangled Web*:

"A persuasive study in criminal character that is a model fusion of the suspense story and mainstream fiction."

—*The New York Times*

"Fine characterization, moving treatment."

—*San Francisco Chronicle*

"The story is compelling and the quality of the writing is often delightful . . ."

—*Times Literary Supplement*

Also by Nicholas Blake

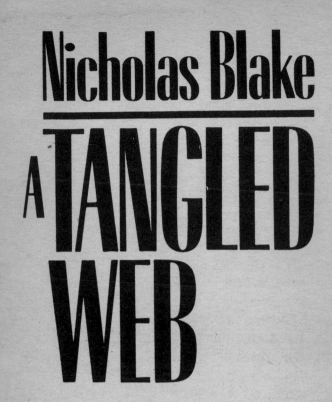

Nicholas Blake
A TANGLED WEB

Carroll & Graf Publishers, Inc.
New York

First Carroll & Graf edition 1987

Carroll & Graf Publishers, Inc.
260 Fifth Avenue
New York, New York 10001

Manufactured in the United States of America

ISBN: 0-88184-292-3

To

A. D. PETERS

Contents

This story follows in broad outline a criminal *cause célèbre* of the early years of the century. The color, detail and interpretation, however, are largely my own, and the characters are wholly imagined.

N. B.

Part One

1 Last Scene But One

"Why did he do it? Why did he do it? I just can't understand."

Daisy Bland's lover, the father of her child, had been sentenced to death for willful murder; but it was not her lover whom she referred to. The tears were flowing down her cheeks, welling up from an inexhaustible misery; yet in a way, thought Bruce Rogers, they did not seem to belong to her—they were like rain streaming down the face of a statue. The most beautiful face he had ever seen. She cried easily. She was a creature who would cry easily, laugh easily, make love easily—a child of nature. Even now there was a sort of luxury in her desolation.

For the hundredth time in these last months, Bruce Rogers felt out of his depth. His eye roved round the familiar office, seeking for reassurance, normality. The files, the deed boxes, the papers on his desk contained a wealth of human emotion, but abstracted—dehydrated, as it were; they could not shake the heart with this almost intolerable compassion, or cause it to shrink into itself, hiding away from its own inadequacy. It was humiliating, he thought, that tragedy should make one shrivel when one met it face to face.

"How could anyone be so wicked?" Daisy said. "How could he do it?"

A spasm of irritation shook Bruce Rogers. Women! Always asking rhetorical questions which nevertheless they expect you to answer. Emotion forever running molten into words. And *that* question of all questions! Goddamn it, he thought, I am neither a psychoanalyst nor a priest—nor am I William Shakespeare. I am a solicitor, whose business is conveyancing, testaments, briefs, not the exposition of the morbid psychology of an Iago.

3

"Now, my dear, you must try to be brave, for Hugo's sake," he heard himself saying, and was at once nauseated by the feebleness, the futility of it.

At the sound of her lover's name, the tears ran free again.

"They won't let him off, will they? I know they won't," she wailed. Yet her face was still calm, undisfigured by grief. Bruce had an instant picture of his own pretty wife's face, when she wept over some trivial setback—swollen, blotched, grimacing. He was still young enough to be horrified by the disloyalty of the comparison. He felt an appalling impulse to say to this girl Daisy, *No, they won't let him off. And it was through your evidence, and your evidence alone, that Hugo will hang.*

Poor girl, he thought, as if you don't know it! You're not particularly bright in the head, but you know that all right.

"We must hope for the best," he said. "Sir Henry is convinced that there are sound legal arguments for—good reasons why the appeal should be successful."

"It's like a game," the girl unexpectedly said.

"A game?"

"Two sides playing with a man's life. In Court, I mean. Scoring clever shots off each other, with a man's life. And so solemn about it, like men playing cricket."

Bruce opened his mouth, then shut it again. What was the point in trying to vindicate to this girl the workings of English justice? the beautiful firmness and flexibility of the Law? Three months ago he might have attempted it; but he had lost his starch on the battlefield of the Chesterman case. Had he lost, too, his belief in the Law? Even if Hugo Chesterman *had* shot the police Inspector, there was every doubt in the world—even the unsentimental Sir Henry proclaimed it—whether Justice would best be served by hanging him. At the Court of Criminal Appeal today, Bruce suspected, Law and Justice were fighting on opposite sides.

He glanced involuntarily at his wrist watch, then at the telephone on his desk. To his tired mind its impersonal, vulcanite mouthpiece became the mouth of the Lord Chief Justice, opening to give the Court's ever so learned, ever so impersonal judgment. The telephone lay there, like a time bomb, between them. Any time now it would ring—Daisy's hands were already clenched, as if against the imminent shock of an explosion—and Sir Henry would tell them how it had gone.

"I've always hated the telephone," said Daisy Bland. "In the shop I tried not to answer it—people were so rude on the telephone—you can't imagine."

How can she chatter like this, thought Bruce resentfully; but at once he realized she was doing it to ease the strain, for both of them. A wonderful girl. A nonpareil girl. No wonder that bold young spark Chesterman had fallen for her. For her, he might even have gone straight—only she was so madly in love with him that she did not really care whether he went straight or not.

In the Magistrates' Court, and later at the Assizes when she was in the last weeks of her pregnancy, this girl's beauty had magnetized the onlookers. It, and the Raffles-like character of the prisoner, had made a *cause célèbre* of a sordid, commonplace story. Beauty in distress—more beautiful in distress. The shining blue of the eyes (speedwell? forget-me-not?), deepening with a change of mood or of light to violet; the tumble of corn-colored hair; the glow on mouth and cheek which even her extreme distress could hardly quench: Bruce took them in again now while she talked, sitting upright on the edge of the black leather armchair as if she were being interviewed for a job. The voice, with its rough, boyish, countrified tone—he had heard it, in and out of Court, for so many hours; heard it give the evidence which condemned her lover, heard it so dramatically retract this evidence.

As she talked now about the enormities of the customers at the shop where she had served, keeping up conversation like a ring of fires to hold at bay the worse things prowling in the darkness beyond, Bruce was struck again by her lack of resentment. Even when she had exclaimed, "How could anyone be so wicked?" there was no bitterness in her voice, only a kind of sad curiosity. Daisy Bland, he judged, was a passive character; it was both her weakness and her strength—the weakness that abominable man had played on, and the strength, the yielding, accepting strength which would bring her, more or less whole, through this last ordeal.

On an impulse, he interrupted: "You'll make a wonderful mother, Daisy."

She turned the shining, sad blue eyes upon him. "Yes, perhaps I will," she said slowly. "I could have made a good wife too, Mr. Rogers."

"Think of the baby. It's a marvelous baby."

"Oh, he's all right. He's got ten of everything," the girl listlessly replied. Shading her eyes from him, she turned to the window. "Where's the harbor?"

"The harbor? Well, you can't see it from here. Over to the right. About half a mile." Bruce was flustered again. Wherever one stepped, it led to dangerous ground. The harbor; the sea; the beach; the revolver buried under the pebbles and dug for by Daisy in full view of the plainclothes man on the esplanade: the unescapable, unforgivable trap into which she had been led.

"We were so happy here," murmured Daisy, her face turned toward the distant sea. "It was romantic."

The purity of her feeling redeemed even that cheap, soiled word. Bruce made another effort.

"It's something to remember. The happiness. They can't take that—"

"Yes, they can," she said strenuously. "It's gone. I can only remember I *was* happy. I can't remember what it was like, feeling happy. All I know is, one moment we were on top of the world; and then he came back, half an hour later—I was still sitting on the front, like he'd told me—and I knew somehow it was, well, the end of the world. For me."

"You feel like that now."

"I'll always feel like that. Unless—" She could not go on. Her eyes, avoiding the telephone, sought refuge anywhere. "What a lot of books! Have you read them all?"

"Yes. A fair time ago—some of them. For my examinations, you know."

A thin finger, wearing the wedding ring to which it was not entitled, rubbed along the top of one row.

"Oof, they're dusty. Haven't you anyone to clean up this place for you?"

"Yes, my dear, but—"

"Got a duster?"

"I—a duster?"

"That's right."

Bruce, rather bemusedly, rummaged through the drawers of his desk till he found what she wanted.

"But really, Daisy, you mustn't—"

"Oh, don't you see?" she broke out, in a tone of passionate desolation that Bruce was never to forget. "Don't you see? I must be doing something. For someone."

She was vigorously dusting the tops of the books when, three minutes later, the telephone bell rang. In one swirling movement she had dropped the duster, turned, was standing by the desk, her hand outstretched. Then, with a little renunciatory gesture, infinitely pathetic, she took back her hand, leaving it all to him.

Bruce Rogers reached for the receiver. . . .

2 Lovers' Meeting

IT WAS on a spring day, some twenty months before, that Hugo and Daisy had first met. The pavements were wet after the night's heavy rain, and flowers of cherry blossom, shaken down by the storm, lay stuck to them like pink paper rosettes. Now the morning was calm and fresh. Along the St. John's Wood terrace pear blossom, cherry blossom, prunus sent up their colored spray, and white clouds bloomed in the sky. A country-bred girl, who had only come to London the previous autumn, Daisy Bland sniffed the Maytime air, feeling a waft of excitement stronger than the homesickness which such a scene might have been expected to provoke. In the country, one hardly noticed the flowers and the decorated branches. It was only a few minutes' walk from the bus stop to Mrs. Chetwynd-Smythe's house, and Daisy had no complaint against Madame Ramon for not sending her by taxi, urgent though her errand was. The other girls at the milliner's shop would have nattered about Madame's notorious meanness. Daisy swung along, with her free country stride, dangling the hatbox by its ribbon and enjoying the fresh smells, the exhilarated color of trees and gardens.

A blackbird whistled a phrase overhead; as she turned the corner, Daisy was looking up into a tree, from which the crystal notes came, and collided heavily with a man walking fast the other way. The hatbox was knocked out of her hand, its ribbon slipped, and as the box rolled away, the lid came off and the hat slid out onto the wet pavement.

"Oh lor'," said Daisy, clapping her fingers to her mouth. "I'm terribly sorry."

"You've done it properly."

8

The young man was already retrieving the hat with one hand—even at this disastrous moment she was able to notice how fast he moved—and had thrust out a foot to stop the hatbox rolling into the gutter.

"Just a speck or two of mud," he said, brushing Madame Ramon's fancy creation vigorously on his sleeve. Daisy snatched it from him before he could do any more damage.

"Oh, it's ruined. What *will* she say?"

"Ruined? But surely—"

The young man broke off. In the flurry, he had not looked at her properly till now, not taken her in. Daisy was conscious of his eyes upon her. The consternation went out of her as she returned his gaze. Something flashed between them, like magnesium, and in that instant he was printed on her memory forever —the thin, swarthy face, the mouth arrested in a half smile, the eyes brown, alert, ready to dance, with a sort of wildness asleep behind their steady gaze. A poacher's face, she said to herself. She might as well have said, an angel's, the way she was transfixed in a pure passion of astonishment: an angel's, or a fallen angel's—she was never to care which.

They stood, facing each other over the ridiculous hat, for a few seconds, for long enough to form their destiny.

"Oh dear," he said at last, "your new hat. Is it really—?"

"It's not mine. It's— I was bringing it to Mrs. Chetwynd-Smythe."

"Mrs. Chetwynd-Smythe? What an appalling name! It's an outrage that anyone called Mrs. Chetwynd-Smythe should wear a hat like this. I shall certainly not permit it."

"But—"

"What's *your* name?"

"Daisy Bland."

"Ah, that's better. Daisy. It would suit you." And the astonishing young man removed the hat from her grasp, placed it on her head, and stood back to study the effect.

"No," he said, "I was wrong. Not with all that lovely hair. It looks like a tatty old bird's nest perched on a waterfall."

He removed it, and stood contemplating her, twirling the hat on the point of his middle finger. Between tears and laughter, she exclaimed: "Do be careful. I'll get into such trouble—"

"I'll buy Mrs. Chetwynd-Smythe another one like it."

"Oh, you don't understand. It's a model—Madame made it specially for her. And she'll be wild if she doesn't get it this morning."

The young man sucked in his lower lip, then cocked his head at her with a glance of pure mischief.

"Well, let's deliver this object to the repulsive Mrs. Chetwynd-Smythe. Where does she live?"

"Number 39. A few doors away."

He replaced the hat in the box, and secured the ribbon.

"Come along, Daisy Bland. You're from Gloucestershire, aren't you? My father used to—" He broke off, frowning a little. "My name's Hugo Chesterman, of no fixed address. Now we've got all the relevant facts."

It was, perhaps, Daisy's capacity for accepting things, for not fussing or deprecating or playing coy, which, after her vernal beauty, won Hugo's heart. She, for her part, followed his lead as if in a trance; she had not begun to think about him yet; she just, fatalistically and with a sensation of utter felicity, let him take command.

They rang the bell, they were admitted into the hall, and presently Mrs. Chetwynd-Smythe, a plump, overdressed woman with a discontented face, waddled toward them.

"Miss Bland, isn't it? You're very late. I was promised my hat an hour ago."

Daisy began to explain that a slight accident had befallen it. The woman cut her short and, throwing open the hatbox, took out its contents. Her face went red and she began to gobble, shaking the flimsy hat in Daisy's face.

"It's insufferable. The thing's ruined. Look at it, you clumsy girl. Do you expect me to wear this?"

Hugo gave one glance at Daisy's flushed cheek, then, turning to the woman, said: "Certainly not, Madam. It is too young for you."

"How *dare* you!" Mrs. Chetwynd-Smythe rounded upon Daisy, panting with outrage. "Who is this—this creature? You ruin my hat with your bloody carelessness, and not content with that you bring your—bring this insolent person into my house—"

"Madam, the misadventure to your hat was entirely my fault," cut in Hugo imperturbably, "and I came with Miss Bland to explain it. May I introduce myself? I am the Reverend Chesterman, Rural Dean of Amberley; and I must ask you to moderate your language out of respect for my cloth."

"You don't look like a clergyman to me."

"I am in, ah, mufti. A brief surcease from my pastoral labors, Mrs. Smith."

At this point Daisy gave vent to a lamentable giggle. The woman turned upon her, jowls quivering.

"I shall telephone instantly to your employer, and demand your dismissal. And now," her voice rose to a scream, "get out! get out!"

Hugo was replacing the hat in the box and tying the ribbon again.

"I take it you don't want the article of apparel?"

"Put it down instantly, and GET OUT! And take this sniggering little bitch with you!"

Mrs. Chetwynd-Smythe had the front door open, and was trying simultaneously to push them out and to wrest the hatbox from Hugo. At her last words, he went quite rigid, and a look came into his face so dangerous that Daisy shrank back for a moment, torn between fear and a delicious excitement.

"I wouldn't use that word, if I were you," said Hugo. Then, turning his back contemptuously, he took five quick, short, running steps, and punted the hatbox high into the air. It landed among the branches of a big laburnum. Before Mrs. Chetwynd-Smythe could find her voice, he called out: "Go climb a tree, Madam. Take off some of that superfluous fat."

Grasping Daisy's elbow, he walked her quickly but not hurriedly down the street.

For Daisy, that was the beginning of a period when her life moved with the automatism of a dream. After such an opening, nothing could greatly surprise her any more. Once you had accepted as a fact a young man with a poacher's face, who came upon you out of the blue of a May morning and kicked hatboxes into laburnum trees—once you accepted this extraordinary proposition, everything else followed with the inevitability of dream logic. So it was almost as a matter of course that Daisy found herself, an hour later, lunching with Hugo Chesterman at the Berkeley.

When he had chosen her lunch for her, he left her with a martini while he went out to telephone Madame Ramon. Daisy watched him thread his way past the tables, an alert, compact figure little taller than herself, with something wary, self-sufficient, ambiguous in the way he moved. He is like a cat, was how she put it to herself; but not a tame cat: more like one of those in the zoo, except he hasn't got bars round him. Absently, she rubbed her elbow where Hugo had gripped it, walking her away from Mrs. Chetwynd-Smythe's house. It felt bruised. How strong he must be. With a furtive, blushing delight, Daisy thought to herself, I'm glad I bruise easily.

"A penny for your thoughts."

It was his voice; he was back already. Daisy selected her last thought but one.

"I was thinking you walk like a cat."

An enigmatic look came into his eyes. Was he displeased at the idea? Was he going to streak away? She added quickly, "A tiger, I mean. Or a leopard. I've seen them at the pictures."

"We must go to Whipsnade one day, and I'll introduce you to my brothers and sisters."

"They wander about there, don't they? Not in cages, I mean. Sort of prison without bars."

He was looking at her very strangely. "There's no such thing

as a prison without bars," he said; then, abruptly changing the
subject, "Your Madame is not to be appeased. You've got your
cards, old girl. I'm sorry."

"Oh dear."

"You don't sound so terribly put out."

"Well, I expect I can get another job."

"Without references from old Ramon?"

"My auntie got me that job. I expect she could find me another.
I'm good with my hands."

Daisy knew, and knew that he knew, that all this meant
nothing. Nothing mattered to her now, except him and her.
Without anxiety or misgiving, she awaited what, sooner or later,
was bound to happen. In the meantime, there was this lovely
feed.

"I do like to see a girl eating hearty," he said. "How old are you,
Daisy?"

"Nearly eighteen," she replied, with a smile so radiant that a
higher Civil Servant lunching two tables away, who caught the
overflow of it, made a mental note to read again *A l'Ombre des
Jeunes Filles en Fleurs.*

That afternoon they went to Kew. Summer had arrived over-
night: everything bloomed, and the air was warm as lovers'
whispers. Lying on the grass, her limbs heavy with indolence,
Daisy—a healthy girl who had never had an illness since childhood—felt like a convalescent, weak, passive, dazzled by the vivid
sounds and colors of life returning. The stuffy, scented hat shop,
its ritual and frivolity, the mirrored slow motion of its salon and
the tension behind the scenes, might have been years away, faint
memories of a delirium she had passed through. But this new
world into which she had moved was unreal too as yet—a truant's
world, delicious, yet disquieting and precarious. Its axis was the
young man sitting beside her, with arms clasped round his knees;
and she felt at times that her slightest movement might cause
him to vanish as abruptly, miraculously, as he had appeared. She
wanted to stay here forever like this, not even touching him. She
wanted to run away into the trees, and be pursued, and caught.

The sense of deferring what would happen lay heavily upon her, like the scent of white lilac from the bush beside them, making her breathless. She knew she should be considering plans, deciding how to break to her aunt the news of her dismissal, how to set about finding another job, how to face Madame Ramon and demand her week's pay. Yet she knew none of this was important; it will all straighten itself out, she thought vaguely, and rolled over on her side to look at Hugo.

He was threading a daisy chain. His fingers were often restless —she had noticed that already; they seemed to have a life of their own. Now, although they still worked deftly, they were trembling; and this gave her a sharp, novel sensation which she was too artless to understand as the sensation of power. After all, he had hardly touched her yet, and had not spoken a word of love. The notion that so confident, self-sufficient a man could be shy did not occur to her. She accepted him, without any desire as yet to explain him. He, for his part, had shown the liveliest interest in her background and her past. She had told him about her childhood, as the oldest of a large family, in the Cotswold village. Her father, a small-owner, had suddenly pulled up his stakes and left them when Daisy was twelve, so she had looked after her younger brothers and sisters while her mother went out to work. The local lady of the manor discovered in the girl a flair for millinery; and last year she had come to London as an assistant in Madame Ramon's shop, at the recommendation of an aunt, her mother's sister, who worked for a fashionable dressmaker in the same street.

Daisy told him about her room in Pimlico, the money she sent home every week, the feuds and foibles of the assistants in the shop. She talked without self-consciousness; yet as she talked, she became gradually aware how lonely she had been in London till now. She had no idea, though, of the way her beauty had contributed to her isolation, creating a barrier between herself and the other girls at Madame Ramon's. As for men, she had been no more touched by their hot glances than Daniel by the fiery furnace. Lacking the nervous vitality of town-bred girls, she was too tired at the end of the day for dancing or gallivanting.

"No young men?" Hugo had said. "Well, well, you amaze me."

He was piqued, though she did not realize it, by her incuriosity about himself. She seemed to take it for granted that a well-dressed young gentleman—for that was how she must see him—should come round a corner into her life, lose her job for her, and carry her off to Kew via the Berkeley. Hugo had never met a girl like this. One couldn't think of her in terms of pick-up and bed-sitting-room. The usual veiled sex banter, the perky, pathetically thin self-assurance of the girls he had stalked from time to time, when more interesting prey was not available—these were utterly foreign to her. She attracted him all the more because he was a little frightened of her—frightened by the potential of passion which he felt in her.

Now, reaching up, he placed the daisy chain round her neck. His hand brushed her neck, and she shivered a little, but never took her eyes off his face. The chain hung down over her simple, cornflower-blue dress. The sounds of children, playing nearby, seemed infinitely remote.

"I'm a bad hat, Daisy." Hugo's voice was not quite under control.

"Are you?" Her tone was like a slow caress. "You've been very kind to me."

"And you're the Queen of the May." Hugo felt half relieved, half troubled, as one does when an issue has been deferred which is bound to become more loaded with difficulty the longer one defers it.

"That's a poem," Daisy was saying. "She died, didn't she?"

"I won't call you that, then." Hugo gazed down at her where she lay on her back, open to the sun, the sweet smell of grass coming up as if it were an emanation from her innocence. "I'll call you Demeter."

She smiled vaguely. "Who's Demeter?"

"Mother Earth. A goddess. That's one of the things I learned before I was sacked."

"Sacked?"

"From my expensive public school."

"So we've both been sacked. Goody."

Hugo twisted a tress of her corn-colored hair round his finger. "The point is, what are we going to do about you?"

"Oh, it's such a lovely afternoon. Don't let's spoil it." Seeing his expression, uneasy and overcast, she added, "You mustn't worry about me. Really. I shall be all right."

There was a silence between them, and the sounds of children, birds, distant traffic, came back again. He wants to kiss me, thought Daisy: why doesn't he? Presently she heard him say, with a note almost of desperation, "You don't know anything about me."

"You'll tell me sometime."

He looked at the blue veins on her eyelids, the dreamy smile of her half-opened lips, and tenderness shook him like an agony.

"Come live with me and be my love."

He hardly knew he had said it aloud. But her eyes opened, shining up at him like dew ponds, like gems of midsummer blue.

"Do you want me to?" she murmured, stirring, arms wide, her fingers twining round tufts of long grass. She was his for the taking, and she exulted in it.

They lay, kissing. Past and future mercifully withdrew for a while, leaving them alone with the consuming present.

3   A Happy Time

Two months later, Daisy Bland was sitting alone in their Maida Vale lodging house, darning Hugo's socks. They had come here five weeks ago, when Hugo's money ran out. Brought up in thrifty ways, she sighed now to think how they had squandered it; but her sigh was half of pleasure, as she remembered the fairy-tale sequence of those first three weeks.

They had returned from Kew Gardens, Hugo in tearing high spirits, Daisy drugged and expectant with passion. They went first to a car-hire firm near Victoria, where Hugo was evidently a well-known client. He filled in forms, and paid the deposit with a handful of £1 notes which he produced, as he was to produce so many more during the days that followed, from his trouser pocket. She hardly had time to wonder how often this had happened before, with other girls, when he whisked her off to her Pimlico lodging. Then he left her, saying he must pick up his own belongings (he did not say where), and would return in half an hour. She packed a case, then filled in the time by writing postcards to tell her mother and aunt that she was off for a holiday with a girl friend. After posting them, she paid off her landlady and, with a dazed sense of burning boats, said she would not be needing the room any more.

She saw the little car draw up in the street below. She ran down the stairs as if the house was on fire. He had changed his suit; but he looked just the same, she thought with a new access of happiness—as though that had been almost too much to expect. Soon they were driving out of London, out of her old life.

"Where are we going?" Daisy asked.

"Where would you like to go?"

The way he said it made her feel as if he had all England, the whole universe, at his disposal. She laughed, deep from her heart, and laid her head on his shoulder.

"Anywhere," she said. "The country. Somewhere we can be alone together. Not—"

"Not a roadhouse or a flash hotel. You bet your life not!"

"I was going to say, not where you've taken your other girls. But I don't mind, really I don't."

He took her right hand, pressing his nails gently into the knuckles. "There aren't any other girls. Not any more. You can take that for gospel, sweet Daisy."

She believed it, in the mounting glow of her happiness; and she was never to regret believing it.

They landed up at an inn in an Oxfordshire village, which Hugo liked the look of. Daisy smiled secretly to herself now as she recalled that first evening, when they faced each other in the low-windowed bedroom, she rubbing between her fingers a geranium leaf she had plucked in the courtyard below, and Hugo saying, "Shall we go down to dinner now?"

"If you like," she replied, tilting her head back, the blood thrumming in her ears. He gazed at her a moment across the little room. With a rush of excitement and terror, she saw his dark face change. His eyes, piercing bright, seemed to pin her against the wall where she stood. She felt impaled, powerless yet wildly acquiescent. He was a stranger, he was a hawk hovering to swoop down upon her. They came together as if whirled by a clap of wind out of a cloudless sky. She was naked, staring up at him transfixed, an animal in a snare shamming dead under the poacher's hands, then quivering and struggling. But the pain was good, the surrender and fierce abjection were wonderful; and presently she heard him say, "There's no one like you, my love."

She went down to dinner with him in a dream. She did not know what she was eating or what she was saying. They sat in the bar afterward, watching a darts match. Then Hugo joined a game; he was a good player, she could see, serious, entirely absorbed; whatever he did, a sort of natural grace and featness came through. Once or twice he looked over toward where she sat, like a child demanding his mother's admiration, and something new stirred in her, quite different from the other feelings he had roused. At the end of the game, he was challenged to a return. He took up the darts again, raising an eyebrow quizzically at Daisy. Hardly knowing what she did, she rested her eyes upon him in the crowded, smoky room, with a look neither shy nor bold but deeply searching, which drew him to her like an invisible thread. Laying down the darts, he said to his opponent, "Not now, thanks. Tomorrow night, if you're here."

They were upstairs again; and this time Daisy came into full possession of her womanhood. She could not have enough of him. "Master! Master!" her peasant blood cried out. She went to sleep, still sobbing with pleasure, a scent of wallflowers from the window boxes blowing into the room.

Daisy would have liked to stay there for days, forever. But on the third day Hugo suggested they should move on. She agreed, sensing a restlessness in him which even his love for her could not appease. And so it went on for three weeks, the little car tracing a random course through county after county. Hugo drove fast, though he would always slow down if she asked him, so that at times she had the fancy that they were fugitives, twisting and doubling on their tracks to escape some remorseless pursuer. The absurd notion was exhilarating, yet remotely disquieting. One day she said to him:

"It feels as if we were running away, being chased."

"So we are, darling."

"What are we running away from?" she asked dreamily.

"Real life. We're escapists."

He said it lightly; but, responding to him as she did, she felt as if her question had touched him on some too sensitive spot; and for some little time after, he was unusually silent. To distract him from himself—they happened just then to be driving past a long, high park wall—she said: "I wonder what's on the other side of that."

He stopped the car at once. "Let's see." He got out, looked up and down the road, listened for a moment, then ran straight at the wall. She thought he must have gone mad, for the wall was nearly twelve feet high. But he leaped up at it, smoothly as a wave, one foot stretched out before him making contact halfway up, and the impetus carrying his body above it so that his hands reached the top of the wall, and flexing his arms all in the same swift movement he drew himself up to sit astride it. There seemed no effort at all in the proceeding: he just went up like a bubble.

"It's a knack," he called down to her, not the least out of breath. "Anyone can get up any wall, if it's not more than twice his height. Come along."

He hauled her up—she knew all about the strength in those slender wrists and fingers—then gave her a glance, at once reckless and queerly challenging, which she could neither interpret nor forget. Thinking about this episode afterward, when she had discovered the truth, she realized that he had given her a hint which he had not dared—or was by nature too evasive—to put into words. She could remember other occasions also, when he had as it were acted his secret in dumb show, half defying, half wanting her to guess it; and times when, with the mischievous expression of a schoolboy giving a dare, he had allowed his talk to tremble on the very edge of self-betrayal.

Ah, she thought, taking up another pair of socks to darn, I should have guessed. He was trying to tell me something; he was afraid to tell me—afraid, yes, of losing me; that was why; or afraid of spoiling our honeymoon. Silly boy.

"You're a funny girl," he had said one day, twisting upon her finger the wedding ring he had bought for her on their way out of London. "You've never asked me to ask you to marry me."

"Well, ask me then."

They were lying in a wood, high up on a Dorset hillside. The whole floor of the wood smoked with bluebells, as if the earth below were on fire, and the song of willow wrens tossed and dwindled through the long afternoon. Hugo turned on his back, speaking up to the trees whose leaf shadows shifted over his face.

"Would you want to marry a man, whatever he was really like, just because you loved him?"

To Daisy, this seemed an absurd question; but she had gained enough wisdom not to say so.

"I know you're—not bad," she ventured.

"You know damn-all about me, my love." His tone was harsh; but she replied gently:

"You could tell me. But not if you don't want to, sweetheart." Then, as he was silent, she went on, "I know you are twenty-eight, your father is a clergyman, you were sacked from your school, you went out to Australia, you fought in the war and were taken prisoner, you're a commission agent—whatever that is. And you're the most wonderful man in the world."

"Quite a dossier." He looked up at her searchingly. "What did you think about me the first time we met?"

"I thought you looked like a poacher."

"A poacher? In St. John's Wood? Well!" Hugo laughed shortly. After a pause, he said, "I hate the idea of being trapped. That's the one thing I'm really frightened of."

"Trapped into marriage, do you mean?"

"That might be part of it. I'm not cut out to be a domestic animal."

"Well, we won't get married then."

"Oh, darling, don't talk like a nurse humoring a fractious patient, for God's sake!"

The easy tears flooded her eyes, but he was not looking at her now. In a tight voice, Hugo said: "Would you marry me if I were a—a murderer?"

"Yes," she answered simply. "If you wanted me to. But—"

"I'm not, actually. Except for killing chaps in the war. Listen, Daisy—if you were a man, and a bad egg, a criminal type, would you ask a girl you loved to marry you?"

"*I* never started this talk about marriage," she replied, baffled and still feeling hurt by his rejection of her sympathy.

"Well, would you?" he pressed.

"I suppose criminals do get married. Why shouldn't they?"

Hugo pursued it no further. She felt she had failed him, but she did not know how. The whole conversation had seemed to her crazy, unreal. Criminals were people one read about in newspapers—cosh boys, Teddy boys, masked burglars, murderers—or the narrow-eyed men one saw standing about in groups in the little streets off Shaftesbury Avenue: thugs, riff-raff. Daisy could not begin to associate Hugo, who was so obviously a gentleman, a civilized person for all his streak of wildness, with that underworld. He might as well have said he'd dropped into St. John's Wood from Mars. Why must he go on as if he had some guilty secret? Perhaps, she suddenly thought, he is a traitor, a Communist agent—something like that. Then she felt his hands upon her, the brushing of cool air against her skin as he took off her clothes. He was saying how beautiful she looked; the only woman on earth; Eve stretched out in the woods of Paradise: and like a leaf in the fire, she twisted, curled up, was consumed. Nothing else mattered. He was her man.

Toward the end of those weeks, they arrived at a little seaport in the southwest. There was a fair on, and after dinner he took her there. He had been moody, withdrawn, all day; but now—she was getting used to the ebb-and-flow of his temperament—he suddenly burst into sparks like a stirred bonfire. The shouts of barkers, the snap of rifles in the shooting gallery, the blatant music from the merry-go-round, seemed to affect him like a fever, which communicated itself from his blood to hers. Dragging her from booth to booth, throwing for coconuts, shooting at ping-pong balls dancing on jets of water, careering and colliding in the bumper-car arena, he was like an overexcited child who will run himself to a standstill rather than miss anything. Daisy noticed how the girls eyed him and the stallholders winked at him. "Come on, you lovely great stook of corn," he exclaimed, and she was tossed onto the back of a wooden horse before she had time to protest that merry-go-rounds made her sick. Lights were spinning and splintering; the fair whirled round her like a room round a drunk man, rising and falling. When the thing stopped at last she felt so giddy-sick that, alighted from the horse, she swayed, staggered, fell to the ground.

A meaty young man in a platypus cap, standing nearby, said to his companion, "God, another drunk! Look, she's absolutely plastered."

Hugo, who was telling Daisy to put her head between her knees and keep still for a while, straightened up instantly and stepped in front of the man.

"What did I hear you say about this young lady?"

"Young *what?*" sneered the man.

Hugo had hit him thrice—a left jab to the stomach, a right and left rattling his jaw—before the man had time to realize he was in a fight. However, he was as big as Hugo was fast, and he rebounded from a tent against which Hugo's blows had sent him reeling, put up his hands, and made for his much slighter opponent. Daisy, feeling a different kind of sickness, scrambled to her feet; the young man in the cap—it was still glued to his head—looked dangerous, a giant. The light of a flare showed her Hugo's face, intent, malevolently grinning. He seemed to move in and out on castors; he ducked a haymaking right swing—then the crowd closed round the fighters and Daisy could see no more. But she heard cracks of fist on face which made her wince, and then a voice shouting. "Police! Police coming!" The crowd heaved, frayed out. Hugo was darting toward her, had seized her hand, was pulling her away, between two booths, out onto open ground, running with her toward the sea.

"Are you hurt, darling?" she asked when they had reached the esplanade. He shook his head vigorously, as if to clear it, and moved her on from under the lamp where she had stopped, looking up at him in anxiety.

"It's all right. I'll have a thick ear tomorrow, though. Did you see any police, or was it a false alarm?"

"I don't know."

"I could have killed that chap." Hugo's arm was trembling in hers.

"Don't, love. It doesn't matter."

A little farther on he halted, and stood listening. Daisy could hear nothing but the leisurely thump of waves on the sea wall, and a more distant sound of merry-go-round music braying above the confused noises of the fair. She became aware that she was still clutching a flaxen-haired doll which Hugo had won for her at the shooting gallery.

"What is it?" she said.

"Just listening for the hue-and-cry. Force of habit." He seemed to be talking to himself.

"What do you mean?"

"Oh, prisoner-of-war days. I tried to escape, once or twice."

"But the police wouldn't—"

"I don't want the police mixed up with our holiday, my darling." His bright eyes glanced away from her. "Suppose they ran me in for assaulting that bastard—well, you'd be dragged into it, and it'd come out that we weren't married. Endless fuss and bother. You don't know what it's like."

After a few minutes' silence—they were approaching their hotel now—she asked, "Would you rather we left here? went somewhere else for tonight?"

"Well . . . No, to hell with them. It's too late. We'll start earlyish tomorrow."

They did not start as early as he had intended, however. That night Daisy was awakened by his voice, muttering louder and louder, then crying out in a nightmare. It was a terrible sound, like a dumb man trying to utter his agony—quavering, bellowing sounds wrenched up from his inmost being, and at last achieving words— "Let me out! Let me out! Let me out!"

She shook him awake, her hands slipping on his shoulders, which were drenched with sweat.

"It's all right, love. I'm here. It's only a dream. Wake up, sweetheart! Poor Hugo, poor Hugo."

She pressed his head convulsively against her breasts. For a moment he struggled worse than ever; then, coming fully awake, gripped her so hard that she whimpered.

"Oh, God, what an awful dream!" he cried, shaking as if the heart she could feel thudding against her would knock his body to pieces.

Daisy turned on the light, and when she had soothed him, got out of bed to fetch a towel.

"You're soaking. I'll dry you."

He looked up at her like a child, an exhausted child, his lips still quivering; followed her with his eyes, as if the sight of her was almost too good to be true.

"That's better," she said briskly. "What *were* you dreaming about? You made an awful noise."

"Sorry, nurse. It shan't happen again—let's hope. What did I say?"

"You kept yelling, 'Let me out!' "

His eyes changed their teasing expression, and darkened. "I did, did I?" He fell silent for a little, holding her hand. Then he gave her that look, enigmatic, measuring, obscurely challenging, which was becoming familiar to her. "I was buried alive once."

"Oh, my dear! In the war?"

"And once, at school, some chaps shut me up in a locker. I half killed one of them when I got out. That's why I was sacked."

"But that was cruel. Shutting you up, I mean."

"People *are* cruel. Haven't you noticed it?" His fingers touched the red marks they had left just now on her body. "Because they're frightened. Frightened people scare me stiff—run a mile from them—including myself. When I was a kid, I was the timid type. So I used to dare myself to do the most hair-raising things. And I did them, as often as not. Showing off to myself—and to anyone else who was around: that's what they *called* it, anyway. So I got into the habit of it."

He went on talking in this disjointed way for nearly an hour, as if a floodgate had been opened. Daisy did not understand half what he was saying: his mind moved too fast for her. What is he trying to tell me, she thought. How can I help him? I wish I wasn't so young, I wish I knew more about people. Women are supposed to know by instinct.

She felt that it was a stranger lying beside her in the bed, a foreigner speaking out of that familiar body. The sensation was both bewildering and exhilarating; the strangeness of it gave her an almost sensual relish. She tasted her power over him, even while her weakness—the failure to follow his erratic, hurrying words—troubled her. A phrase repeated itself in her mind— "buried alive for twelve months": had he said it just now, or?— No, it was absurd, nobody could be buried alive for twelve months.

Scraps of what he had said then kept recurring to her during the days that followed; but she could never piece them together so as to make a whole of them; a pattern was missing. And at that time she was still too much absorbed in her own responses, finding out too many new things about herself, to leave much room for curiosity. Besides, the peasant blood which made her fatalistic also gave her the wisdom of letting well alone: you did not stir up hornets' nests for the satisfaction of proving to yourself that hornets can hurt.

The next morning they overslept, and did not leave the little seaport till nearly midday. A few days later Hugo said to her, out of the blue, "We must go back now, darling."

"Back to London?"

"Yes. No more money. Finito. I'm broke. Truly."

Daisy watched the hedgeflowers rushing by the car, streaming into the past. "Stop a minute," she said impulsively; then, as the countryside slowed and came to a standstill, "I want to say good-by properly."

"To me?"

"To our holi—our honeymoon." Opening the window, she reached out and pulled a spray from the hedge. He watched her silently. Not looking at him, she said: "Are you—am I to leave you, when we get back?"

After a pause, he asked, "Was it worth it?"

"Oh, yes. *Yes!*" she cried, her eyes like morning glories.

"Then don't talk nonsense about leaving me, my beloved."

"But how can you afford?—"

"I can't afford to do without you." The merry, reckless look returned to his face. "And I can always lay my hands on some money."

4 Evening in Maida Vale

HER mind still echoing with these memories, Daisy put down the last pair of socks and went to the window. Leaning out, her elbows on the sill, she might have been a castaway searching the horizon for some sign of human life. Her horizon was a row of detached houses, large, seedy and secretive, their ground floors screened by groups of laurel or privet which seemed to be putting their heads together furtively like men planning a dirty deal, the stucco of the façades peeling and discolored as if they had caught a skin disease from one another. Some of these mansions were still tattered and boarded up, a bomb having fallen nearby ten years ago; but even those which were occupied gave no evidence of it—one might have supposed their tenants to be persons who, having come down in the world like their houses, were ashamed to show their faces in it.

It was a neighborhood without neighborliness. The country-bred Daisy felt her isolation, not acutely, but like a permanent, pervasive ache. She missed the girls in the shop; she even missed the garish, clattering life of her old Pimlico street. Here, little traffic came; the few passers-by seemed intent on getting somewhere else as rapidly as possible; there were no lines of washing, no heads at windows, no gossiping in the street below. Even the other occupants of her own house might have been in a conspiracy of silence. They passed her on the stairs, the colored students with a polite "good morning" or "good evening," the others without a word; thin though the ceilings and partition walls were, few sounds of life percolated through them; and what one could hear was spasmodic and somehow meaningless—unrelated to the normal noises of domestic activity.

This vague, muffled existence going on around her had already begun to infect Daisy with its strong suggestion of fecklessness, raffishness, hand-to-mouth living. Her girlhood had trained her to be tidy, economical, a good housekeeper; but here, in the prevailing atmosphere of sluttishness, her standards were relaxing. And Hugo, though she would not have admitted it, was no help. Untidy as a small boy, he would leave his underclothes, shirts, towels, littered over the floor of their poky bedroom; he stuffed his belongings into drawers anyhow, and if he wanted one of them, he threw everything else out in the search for it, and put nothing back. These habits filled her with affectionate exasperation. She had remonstrated once, upon which he replied, gently but firmly, "You mustn't try to make a *tame* cat of me, my girl."

She did not want to try. She had enough domesticity for them both. It not merely passed the time but still gave her positive pleasure to follow behind him, righting the disorder he left in his wake; to wash the underclothes he would always have worn far too long; to press and brush the suits which were the only things he had obviously taken care of before they met. No, it was not his rather lordly carelessness over possessions which had begun to influence Daisy, but something deeper—a rootlessness in their life together which, strangely enough, was even more noticeable now, when they had settled down in Maida Vale, than it had been during those first weeks of flitting over the English countryside. One cannot have a home, Daisy obscurely felt, without some prospects; it is not the past but the future into which one puts down roots.

Daisy had the normal woman's need for the routine which is an emblem of security. But from her life with Hugo it was impossible to compose a routine. One day he would be out for hours—"looking up his contacts," as he put it; the next, he might lie in bed all the morning, reading the papers, lazily watching her as she cleaned the room, then pulling her down on the bed beside him. Or, in a sudden access of gaiety, he would take her off for a jaunt somewhere—as often as not, just when she had begun preparing a meal. Such things were delicious to her; but they made life seem more than ever ephemeral, and opened no predictable road into the future; so Daisy was beginning to be adapted to her environment, living for the present hour as well as in it.

She still had a little of the money saved from her employment. The rent was paid, Hugo had told her, for the rest of the year— he kept these rooms permanently, as a place of retreat for times when his funds ran low. Where these funds came from, she still did not know. Every now and then Hugo gave her a few £1 notes for the housekeeping; and, so wildly was she in love with him, it seemed like a present. It was enough that the money came from *him*. She had asked him once, less out of curiosity than out of a woman's simple pleasure in talk, what a "commission agent" did. "I just organize a deal between two chaps, and take a percentage," was his reply, which left her as much in the dark as ever. Daisy was still the village girl, for whom the "gentry" are a race apart, their foibles and failures the subject of cozily malicious gossip, their sources of income always taken for granted—amateurs of life, who move round the villages in an outer orbit, romantic, envied, but never taken quite seriously. Hugo was clearly "one of the gentry": so Daisy did not find his eccentricities at all surprising, and assumed that his cavalier way with money—spending it lavishly when he had it, then doing a bit of work when he needed to "lay his hands" on some more— was quite the normal thing for high-spirited young men of his class. It fitted in with the notions of "society" life she derived from gossip columns, which she assiduously read with a vague idea of preparing herself for the time when he might introduce her to such glittering circles.

For the present, however, she was content to stay as she was. Even her isolation, though it irked her at times, could be cherished as a necessary part of the wonderful dream in which she was living. Soon after returning to London, she had gone to see her aunt—gone in a flush of joy which the stony reception of her news, frankly and freely offered, that she was living with a

man, could not dissipate. The aunt had grumbled rather than
threatened; a good deal was said about the bad blood which
Daisy had clearly inherited from her runaway father; but it soon
became evident that this aunt was more concerned with her own
reputation than with her niece's—she could not recommend the
girl to any of her connections in the trade so long as she persisted
in this disreputable association. "You're throwing yourself away
on this young man," she kept saying. Only at the end of the interview did her grudging tone alter, as, looking again in her sidelong, flustered way at the radiant girl, she came out with "Well,
it's your life, not mine. He seems to be making you happy. Yes,
you only live once, Daisy my dear"—and then, as if regretting
such a lapse from her own respectability, "But it won't last, my
dear. These things never do, take my word for it! You should get
him to marry you." And Daisy, feeling infinitely wise, profoundly
sure of him, had replied, "We couldn't be more married, Auntie;
not if we'd been wedded in Westminster Abbey."

Hugo did not get back till after nightfall. Daisy heard his
rapid step on the landing outside, and flung herself upon him
when he opened the door.

"Sweetheart! I thought you were never coming."

"Supper spoiled again?"

"Well, it *has* been in the oven rather a long time."

"Never mind. Your burnt offerings have a sweet savour in my
nostrils, saith the Lord. And here's my contribution to the shrine."
Withdrawing a hand from behind his back, he held out a great
bunch of carnations.

"*Oh*, how lovely! Hugo, you shouldn't. Wherever did you get
them?"

"Well, I happened to be passing your Mrs. Chetwynd-Smythe's
garden and I saw them. Her carnations needed thinning out—
she's got far too many—such a vulgar display. So I did a little
gardening for the old basket."

"Oh, Hugo, you *are* a fool!" She beamed at him over the top
of the flowers. "I know what happened. You went without your

lunch to buy them for me. You're a very naughty boy, and I love you."

He sent his hat spinning like a quoit at the peg on the door, waltzed Daisy round the room, then collapsed laughing into the rickety basket chair. "Yes, I am hungry. Bring on the grub, slave, or I'll eat you, you succulent great morsel."

Daisy retrieved his hat from the floor where it had fallen. Infected, as she always was, by his gay mood, she showered the carnations over him and ran out into the tiny kitchen before he could struggle up. When she returned with their supper, he had arranged the flowers in a vase, and there was a card stuck in among them.

For my darling Daisy's 18th birthday, she read, unable to speak for a moment.

"I meant to smuggle them in and keep them for tomorrow. But—"

"Oh! How did you know? Fancy you remembering—"

"Of course I remembered. Don't cry, sweet. Nothing the matter, is there?"

"No. It's just—" she buried her face in his shoulder, on her knees beside him. "You make me so happy. You've no idea. I feel like—like an old married woman." She glanced up at him, and was surprised by a shadow on his face. "No," she went on quickly, "it's not—I don't want anything more, you give me everything I want."

The shadow had passed. As they began to eat supper, he told Daisy he was on the point of putting through a big deal. This was why he had been out so much lately. He must go out again, later tonight, to clinch it. If it came off, she would get a real birthday present.

"And we can clear out of this dump for a bit. How would you like to stay at the Ritz, pet?"

"Oh, but I couldn't. I haven't any clothes."

"That will be arranged. Not that you wouldn't knock them sideways, just as you are."

"Are you tired of—don't you like living here?" she asked, gazing round the shabby, cluttered room with a feeling of loss.

"Who would?" he said carelessly.

"I do." She could not keep a hurt tone out of her voice, and he responded to it at once:

"But it must be so dull for you, living here, never seeing anyone, while I'm chasing around."

"I don't want to see anyone but you. And I've plenty to do."

"That's not healthy, love." His brown eyes sparkled. "A young woman needs suitable companionship of her own sex. Or she starts going broody."

"Well, I never meet your friends," said Daisy, who was not always at ease with his gentle mockery.

"*My* friends? Oh, I wouldn't—"

"You mean they're too good for me?" It came out before she could stop it, but Hugo did not appear ruffled.

"Quite the reverse," he said equably. "They're a low lot of characters. I wouldn't trust them an inch with you. Except old Jacko, of course."

"Who's Jacko?"

"Very good bloke. Ran into him after the war. Medico of sorts. Looks like a tortoise. Tell you what—suppose we have him to supper tomorrow; celebrate your birthday."

"But I—"

"Don't give it a thought. I'll victual up at Fortnum's in the afternoon."

"I wasn't thinking about the food. It's just—it'd be nice to have dinner alone together, as it's my birthday."

Hugo prodded his fork in her direction. "Now look, my pet, you complain of never meeting my friends. I offer to produce one, and you turn round and—women baffle me."

"No, I didn't mean that. Of course let's have him. What's his name?"

"Jacko. Oh, Jaques—John Jaques."

"And he's a doctor?"

"I'll brief you on him tomorrow. Let's have a game of draughts after supper. Must steady my nerves for the big moment."

Daisy was aware of a tension in him—a subdued excitement different from the kinds she had known before. The next hour passed agreeably enough, though. Shortly after eleven, having beaten her several times at draughts, Hugo got up, saying he must collect his documents. Their rooms, which were on the top floor, had a small length of attic above them, where Hugo kept some trunks. She heard his feet moving about overhead. Presently he locked the door behind him—he always kept the attic room locked—and descended the ladder. He was wearing a dark, belted macintosh she had not seen before, and black gloves.

"Don't wait up for me, Daisy. I may be quite late."

"It's a funny hour to—"

"Oh, these big chaps are difficult to get at, you know. Got to suit one's timetable to theirs."

As Hugo moved to embrace her, the macintosh fell open a little.

"Oh, darling," she cried. "You've still got your old suit on."

"Old suit?"

"Oughtn't you to change? I mean, as you're meeting an important—"

"Suppose I ought. But there simply isn't time. I'm late already. Now, keep your fingers crossed for us, and mind you go to sleep. Bye, love. Over the top."

Hugo's tension must have communicated itself to Daisy, for she was not able to go to sleep; she lay awake, random thoughts passing across her mind, full of an uneasiness she could not explain. Saying good-by to Hugo just now, she had felt some knobbly, flat object, a case or a satchel, in the poacher's pocket of his suit. It had been a joke between them—that poacher's pocket. She remembered how, during their holiday, he had taken a fancy to some beer-mug mats at a pub, and suddenly whisked three of them into this capacious pocket; half amused, half shocked, she had told him to put them back. "But they get them free from the brewers," he had said, in an almost puzzled voice, as he obeyed her. "I thought you looked like a poacher, the first time I saw you," she said. The fancy tickled him: next day she found him making a catapult, and from time to time he took potshots at pheasants or rabbits they came across while wandering in the woods. But no game found its way into the pocket. "I always was a rotten shot," he grumbled, absurdly dashed by his failure, like a small boy who has been trying so hard to impress a grownup.

For some reason, Daisy could not take her mind off that pocket now. Businessmen, men who brought off big deals, carried brief cases: the world of "business" was a complete mystery to Daisy, but she did know that. And the case in Hugo's pocket, though flat, had not felt as if it contained documents; it was more like— she groped for a resemblance—more like the kit of tools they had had under the dashboard of their hired car. But the idea of Hugo's going to a business conference with a kit of car tools was silly. Ah, now she had it!—they must be samples, like a commercial traveler's; he was going to sell an idea—some industrial process, perhaps—and those objects would enable him to demonstrate it. Then why had he talked of "collecting his documents"? It must be very secret—something he could not mention even to her. A secret process.

The phrase touched off in her mind an old disquietude, which had been forgotten for weeks: the notion which had occurred to her in the Dorset wood, that Hugo was some sort of spy—a traitor, a Communist. Was he selling a secret to the agents of some foreign power? Judging by the films she saw, this sort of thing was going on all the time nowadays. But it was always documents, papers, top-secret formulae which passed from hand to hand in those films, not cases of tools. Daisy knew herself quite out of her depth in such matters, yet the dreadful thought kept nagging at her. One wouldn't carry such vital papers in a brief case: one would "secrete them about one's person"; one could conceal them, for example, inside some harmless-looking spanners or screwdrivers, hollowed out for the purpose.

The idea slid into her mind, irresistible and unexpected as an assassin's knife. And then she had to turn the knife in the wound, torturing herself for such disloyalty to the man she loved, such mad, poisonous suspicions. Hugo a traitor? She deserved to be shot like a traitor for imagining it.

Yet she knew she had to find out. And she knew she dared not ask Hugo point-blank; how could he ever go on loving her if she gave him the slightest hint of these horrible suspicions? The image of him as a wild creature recurred: she had got the creature eating out of her hand; but one false move, betraying her own uneasiness, her own fears, would send him streaking back into the darkness from which he had come. She was only his mistress. She had no hold upon him except by the leash of her love; to speak out would be to snap it; yet, if she kept her suspicions to herself, the cord would be gradually frayed and frayed.

There was only one thing to do. She must kill these venomous doubts. And only one way to do it—find out the truth for herself. If Hugo had a guilty secret, it was hidden up there in the attic he kept locked even from her. Her eyes, which felt graveled with sleeplessness, turned up to the ceiling. He had never forbidden her to enter the attic; it wasn't a Bluebeard's room; he just kept it locked, and kept the key in his pocket. On the one occasion she had asked about it, he did not start like a guilty thing, did not blush or bluster—merely turned off her inquiry with, "Oh, I just have some old lumber up there. It's a filthy little hole. I wouldn't bother with it."

I'll take his keys one day soon, and if he finds out, I'll say I wanted to clean the place, she thought, and was instantly appalled by the duplicity of it, the bitchy scheming stranger who had spoken in her own mind. "How could you?" she muttered to the darkness. This was what happened when you stopped trusting—this stain spreading over your mind like some galloping disease, disfiguring it so that you could no longer recognize yourself. "You'll do nothing of the sort, you bad girl," she murmured, and with a feeling of relief, as though her conscience had been somehow cleared, turned over to sleep.

She must have been sleeping lightly, for she was awakened by the sound of the front door closing. She heard Hugo call her name, quietly and tentatively, as if not to awake her should she be asleep. Something—a hangover perhaps from her own guilty thoughts—made his call sound stealthy to her, conspiratorial, and she did not immediately answer it. Then she was unable to, for she was listening with strained attention to a sound from the next room—a sound she soon identified as that of a clothes brush vigorously applied. Hugo was brushing his suit. A few minutes later she heard his steps in the attic overhead. Her mind, still dazed with sleep, registered some objection which she could not precisely pin down.

When he came into the bedroom, Daisy pretended to wake up. Hugo switched on the light. With a little sob she held out her arms to him, inexpressibly relieved to see the familiar face of the man she loved, not the face of the monster her imagination had been conjuring up. Hugo regarded her affectionately. Yes, he looked just the same: a little tired, perhaps—the gentle but pale and withdrawn look she had seen so often on his face after they had made love.

"Did it go well?" she said.

"Yes. All according to plan, love. Happy birthday."

He went to sleep in her arms at once, like an exhausted, trusting child. Just before she went off herself, she drowsily grasped the thing which had eluded her—the oddness of Hugo's brushing his suit *before* going up into the dirty attic, not after. You darling gormless lad, you do need looking after, don't you? she thought, and fell asleep.

5 Enter Jacko

LEANING out of the window, Daisy waved to Hugo in the road below. He blew her a kiss, flourished his hat, and walked quickly away, a dapper, decisive figure with that effervescent vitality in his gait, looking strangely out of place against the background of slatternly houses and grimed shrubberies. Daisy turned back into the room, fingering the brooch he had given her after breakfast. It was a pretty brooch, old-fashioned—Georgian, he had said; but its value to her was not in its age or delicate workmanship. Deliberately she put off thinking about it till she had finished her morning chores. As she washed up and made the bed, her mind played luxuriously with the feeling of being married to Hugo: she imagined him going off to work every morning, waving up from the pavement below, returning at 6:30 P.M. to slippers, a fire, supper, gossip. Daisy knew it was make-believe; but why should not make-believe come true? With her, might he not settle down, make a real home? Perhaps today was the start of a new life: she was to meet, for the first time, one of his friends; and she had the brooch.

Daisy made herself a cup of tea and settled down in the basket chair. Now she could take out her delightful memory, examine it at leisure. As they finished their breakfast, Hugo had said, "I want to give you something for your birthday, something special. Come along." Taking her by the hand, he led her out into the tiny hallway, then hooked in position the ladder which gave access through a trapdoor to the attic. Her heart beat faster, between anticipation and guilt.

"Are we—am I to come up there?"

"Yes, if you're not too fat to get through the trap."

"But I must—isn't it terribly dirty?"

"Oh, never mind that," he said impatiently. "I'll buy you a new dress." He had scrambled through, and was reaching down a hand for her. She found herself in a cramped, gloomy space, with a cistern in front and a low door on her left which Hugo was unlocking; then she followed him into the attic room. There was just enough light coming through its grimed skylight to show her a sloping ceiling, a floor with several planks missing, and a clutter of trunks and suitcases at the far end.

I must be going mental, she thought, ruefully recalling her disordered fancies of the previous night. Sheer relief at finding this Bluebeard's room so innocent—but what, she wondered, had she expected to discover here—made her say: "What *do* you keep in those huge trunks? The bodies of your wives, darling?"

"Actually, no. Relics of my checkered past."

Kneeling beside a trunk, he unlocked it and threw back the lid. Daisy moved across to peer over his shoulder.

"What are all those notebooks?"

"Oh, nothing. I used to keep a diary when I was a kid."

"Can I read them?" she asked eagerly. "And there are some photograph albums." Her eyes shone at the sight of this treasure trove, the idea of reading up the back numbers of a life so dear and mysterious to her.

"They're just adolescent maunderings. You'd be bored stiff."

"I wouldn't. Who is C. H. A.?" Daisy pointed to the gold initials on one of the albums. Hugo had taken out of the trunk an old cricket cap, a club scarf, a glass-topped box containing butterflies, a notice adjuring gentlemen to Adjust their Dress before Leaving, a ship in a bottle, a fretsaw, a revolver, a pair of running shoes, a tattered brochure on How to Develop Self-Confidence, a boomerang, and an opera cloak, with torn red silk lining. Now, rummaging deeper, he brought out a small jewel case.

"Who's C. H. A.?" Daisy repeated.

"Friend of mine. He disappeared." Hugo glanced at the box in his hand, then up at the lovely, intent face of the girl watching

him. Straightening himself up, standing curiously rigid now and
with his eyes averted from her, he went on, "To be quite precise,
it stands for Chester Hugh Amberley. . . . That used to be my
name. . . . I changed it a few years ago." He looked at Daisy
again, painfully but intently. "Chester Hugh Amberley has disappeared for good. Sunk without trace. Lost and totally forgotten." His expression changed, as almost roughly he thrust the
box into Daisy's hands. "These were my mother's jewels. I want
you to choose one, sweetheart, for your birthday."

Holding in her palm now the little brooch she had chosen,
Daisy drifted into a daydream. Hugo's gift gave her a pleasure
all the more exquisite because it seemed to admit her into the
inner circle, the hitherto closed circle of his family life, his past.
Though he had sometimes talked to her about them, what he
said never made her feel that she knew them. His father—a
country clergyman still alive, somewhere in Somerset now; the
mother who had died when Hugo was eight; the one brother,
with whom he had quarreled ferociously as a boy—these figures
at last took on some reality in Daisy's mind. Hugo had always
talked about his early life as an exile might talk about his native
country—painfully, allusively, with bitterness at times, giving the
impression that it had somehow rejected him and that, for revenge, he was seeking to obliterate its values in his own heart.
Yet he talked about it jealously, too, grudgingly, as if the sharing
of it with her would create between them a bond he might resent.

All this was over now, the simple girl reflected. Today was the
beginning of a new life, a fully-shared one, without reserves or
secrets. She pinned on the brooch again, a badge of respectability
far more reassuring than the gold ring on her finger: a symbol
of his trust. Surely he was committed to her now, absolutely, as
she was to him? "Chester Hugh Amberley," she murmured
several times, as if the knowledge of his true name gave her a
strong magic over him.

At four o'clock Hugo returned in a taxi, with a hamper of food
from Fortnum's and a case of bottles. He looked so boyish in his

excitement, as she opened the hamper, that she could not re-
proach him for such extravagance.

"No cooking for my Daisy on her birthday. All you'll have to
do is sit still and turn the glamour on old Jacko."

Daisy had almost forgotten that Hugo's friend was invited to
supper. But her nervousness at the prospect was soon dissipated
by Hugo's announcing, in his whirling way, that he had just
booked a room for them at the Ritz, and tomorrow they would
buy her a lot of new clothes—everything she wanted—he was in
the money again.

And when Jacko arrived, there was nothing about him to
revive her nervousness. He created at once the impression of
being an old family friend who was always dropping in for meals,
yet he treated Daisy with a deference, a respect which put her all
the more at ease with him and with herself. She had expected to
be patronized, made allowances for, or politely ignored. But John
Jaques went out of his way to show interest in her, plied her
with questions about her domestic arrangements, her neighbors,
her own family; it was more like talking to another woman. He
was certainly no oil painting. His clothes, which were good,
hung loosely about him as though he had shrunk inside them; his
face was all folds and wrinkles, the head poking forward over a
scrawny neck—Daisy could see why Hugo had said he looked
like a tortoise. With that baggy face and white hair he might
have been any age; but the eyes, large, limpid, almost girlish,
were not those of an old man. Spaniel's eyes, she thought, catching them fastened upon her with an attentive, imploring sort of
look, as if willing her to take him for a walk or give him a lump
of sugar.

"You mustn't mind my staring at you," he instantly said. "I
don't see the likes of you every day. Why, Hugo my lad, she's a
great beauty, a Renoir. You've been keeping her to yourself too
long."

"I'm keeping her to myself for keeps," said Hugo.

"Oho. Good for you." Jacko's voice was high, rather throaty,
with a croon in it. "And when is the happy event to take place?"

Hugo, for once, was quite put out of countenance. "Oh well, I—"

Daisy rescued him from his floundering. "We're not thinking of getting married just yet, Mr. Jaques."

"How right you are," he said, beaming at her. "What's the hurry, after all? You're still so young. Both of you. Marry in haste and repent at leisure." It was adroitly done—the temporary embarrassment at once smoothed over. Jacko's whole attitude was so cozy, so solicitous, that Daisy could not understand why she began to feel a faint uneasiness, as if a sore spot had been deliberately probed.

"Well, it's a nice little hide-out you and Hugo have," Jacko was saying. "I like these seedy bits of London myself. And have you ever thought what a beautiful name it is?—Maida Vale." He crooned the name again. "Maida Vale. So pastoral. Just the spot for an idyllic romance. Daphnis and Chloë. You really ought to have a flock of sheep, Miss Bland. Or was it goats?—you should know, Hugo old boy, with your classical education. I wonder is there any law against keeping sheep in Maida Vale. Wouldn't they be useful for drawing wool over people's eyes?"

Daisy laughed. She had not followed much of this; but a swift glance at Hugo showed her that his silence was not a disgruntled one. He looked happy, approving—the smaller brother proudly showing off the big brother to an admiring audience. She gazed at the thin, swarthy face, the eyes that could communicate to her such a current of recklessness, and was contented because he was. With Jacko here, she seemed to be seeing Hugo afresh, from another angle: this is what he is like when I'm not there, she thought. It was like getting another birthday present—this new picture of him, and she felt a little rush of warmth toward his friend.

"Smoked salmon!" cried Jacko, as she brought in the first course. "My favorite food. How clever you are!"

"It was Hugo's idea," she said in her forthright way, smiling at him. "But I *can* cook."

"I bet you can."

"A good plain cook, Daisy is," said Hugo.

"*Plain* cook? My dear chap! What do you call a beautiful cook, then?" Jacko rubbed his hands in glee. "Don't you realize you've got a treasure, a pearl, you base Indian?"

"Oh! Hugo's not an Indian, are you, pet?"

"But I know a pearl when I see one."

"I should hope so," chuckled Jacko, with a flick of a glance at his friend. Hugo found this an excellent joke. He was laughing a lot now, and Daisy realized that, unusually for him, he was getting a bit tiddly. What with all the gin and French before supper, and the champagne now, Daisy herself felt muzzy enough. Jacko kept refilling their glasses, having appointed himself, as he said, wine waiter to the snowy-breasted pearl of Maida Vale. He raised his own now.

"The time is ripe for a toast. To Daisy! Many happy returns. You're the luckiest chap in the world, Hugo!"

She saw her lover's eyes, full of tenderness, regarding her over the rim of his glass. "Don't I know it," he said, to her alone. For a moment they were enclosed together, the two of them, in the circle of their love. Then, flushing, Daisy turned to Jacko. She wanted desperately to do justice to this moment, draw him into it, express her gratitude for everything; but it overflowed any words she could think of. With a little, self-conscious toss of the head, in a voice shy and quaintly dignified, she said:

"Thank you very much. It's very kind of you. To come here, I mean, and"—she tried again—"I don't deserve—it's really Hugo you ought to—"

"No, I mean it," said Jacko, in an earnest, confidential way, his large soft eyes beseeching her. "You're obviously wonderful for him. I've never seen him look so well and happy. The whole thing's perfect."

"I'm glad you're the first—the first of Hugo's friends—"

"Am I really?" He took the point quickly, eagerly. "I say, old boy, you *have* been keeping her close." Hugo frowned a little, and Jacko went on, "Quite right too. One shouldn't put temptation in people's way."

"Don't worry. I won't."

"I see I'm even more privileged than I'd thought."

"Oh, she's safe enough with you, Jacko."

"Thank you kindly, sir, for those words. Those famous last words. But not in this case."

Jacko's tone remained light and droll. Daisy thought she must have imagined the momentary change of expression on his face just now; too much champagne was playing tricks with her eyes.

"I think the wine must be going to my head," she remarked, with somewhat owlish grandeur. "Will you have some more game pie, Mr. Jaques? I do beg your pardon—Dr. Jaques, I should say."

"Mister is correct," said Hugo. "He's a surgeon, you see. Sort of."

"Oh, good," she remarked vaguely, beginning to clear away. "Can you eat iced pudding, Mr. Jaques?"

"I can and will. If it kills me." Jacko's hand sketched a distended stomach in front of his own.

"Not that it'll be very iced," Daisy went on. "Hugo brought it back hours ago, and we haven't got a fridg."

"Anent which," said Jacko in his droll manner, as she took the plates out, "did you see Paula Lamerle lost her ice last night, Hugo?"

"It's terribly runny," said Daisy, when she returned with the pudding. "We'd better pretend it's soup. Who is Paula Lamerle?"

"Cabaret star," said Hugo shortly.

Jacko was watching him with an expression which, under other circumstances, might have been described as an egging-on look. Since Hugo vouchsafed no more, Daisy asked: "What d'you mean, 'lost her ice'?"

"Ice means diamonds, in the circles Jacko moves in," Hugo explained.

"Someone, to put no finer point on it, pinched them." Jacko enlarged upon it, gazing interestedly at the girl. "While she was doing her cabaret turn. Midnight last night."

"Oh. Do you know her?" Daisy asked him. "Is she very famous?"

"I've met her."

"Jacko could probably get you her autograph. He has attended her professionally."

Though she could not have put her finger on any reason for it, the girl felt dimly that the two men were ganging up on her. She was accustomed to being teased by Hugo, but this was somehow different: they were like two schoolboys with a private joke, using it to unnerve a third. Rather miserably, she turned to her liquefied ice. Hugo was spooning his up, and at the same time reading the account of the burglary in an evening paper which Jacko had brought.

"One advantage of being poor and humble nowadays," the latter remarked to her affably, "is that one is spared the visitations of these burglarious gentry."

"I suppose so," Daisy replied, feeling stupid and inadequate.

"No doubt, like artists, they feel the world owes them a living." The little man's tortoise head turned and poked forward at Hugo. "Do you do any painting nowadays?"

"What? Me? No."

"I never knew—" Daisy began.

"Oh, Hugo's a versatile chap. Turn his hand to anything."

Daisy, needing comfort, got up and stood behind Hugo's chair, leaning over him. His hands made the beginning of a movement, as if to close the newspaper, then desisted. She read it over his shoulder. Cabaret Singer's Flat Burgled. Paula Lamerle in an interview with our crime reporter said . . . on returning after the show I found my bedroom had been ransacked . . . £5,000 diamond necklace stolen . . . the thief must have entered by climbing . . .

The print jigged in front of Daisy's eyes. There was a photograph of the block of flats, a dotted line indicating the burglar's supposed route up the back wall, along a ledge, then using a drainpipe—the sight of it made her feel dizzier than ever, and she suddenly gripped Hugo's shoulders.

"Steady, old girl! What is it?"

"He might have broken his neck."

Hugo laughed. "Served him right if he had."

Jacko's face, swimming before her as she looked up, for an instant resembled that of a woman she remembered at an all-in wrestling match to which Hugo had taken her—mouth open, eyes drinking in the sweat and pain.

"A glutton for punishment," she heard herself incredibly saying. "Oh dear, I *have* drunk too much."

"Go and make some black coffee, love. We all need it."

"All right. I hope they don't catch him."

"Catch whom? Oh, the burglar. Don't you worry about him. Off you go." Hugo slapped her smartly on the bottom.

Jacko said, "Criminals always get caught, sooner or later. They're so damned stupid, most of them."

"They get caught because they can't keep their traps shut," said Hugo, "and because they won't vary their methods. Leave the same old trademarks every time, silly mugs."

Daisy heard Jacko chuckle, as she went into the kitchen. She put the kettle to boil and set the cups on a tray, aware of the men's voices through the door, which she had not quite shut behind her, as a confused burble. She wondered what they were talking about. What did men talk about when they were alone together? Hugo's friend was very nice to her, really—not a bit stand-offish or disapproving. But did she like him? Why didn't she like him?

Daisy warmed the jug, spooned in the coffee, poured boiling water over it slowly, stirred. When she had finished, the sound of conversation from the next room came back, amplified but still blurred. Perhaps they were talking about her. What would Jacko be saying about her? On an impulse she moved to the door. Jacko's voice: ". . . give you a sweet alibi."

"No, I wouldn't drag Daisy into it. Not on your life."

Hugo's voice, though he had spoken not much above a whisper, sounded unnaturally loud in her ears, like a noise heard at the moment of waking. And Daisy had awakened. At last. The wheel stopped whirling and the balls fell exactly into their slots: yes, everything that had puzzled her, disquieted her, intrigued her—everything fitted in. The pattern was now clear, but she dared not yet look at its detail. She was beyond any emotion—fear, resentment, pity, shame; beyond mortification at her own blindness or the way he had consistently deceived her. She was, quite simply, stunned. The dream had fallen about her ears; and like a survivor picking her dazed way over the rubble, she walked into the other room, set down the tray on the dining table, held out her hand to the guest, and said:

"I'm very sorry, Mr. Jaques, but I must go and lie down. I'm not feeling very well. No, you mustn't think of going yet. Stay and talk to Hugo. No, it's all right really—I'll just take some aspirin. I'm not used to so much drink."

She moved like a pale sleepwalker past Hugo, who had risen from the table, his face full of concern, and walked carefully over the debris into her bedroom.

6   The End of Innocence

Daisy lay on the bed, still dressed, in the dark, sensation coming back to her. She lay on her back, quite rigid, and steeled herself to probe the wounds. The superficial wounds first—her own blindness, stupidity; she felt Hugo's deception, poor girl, as a wound not to her pride but to her love. If I'd loved him truly, I'd have guessed, known the truth. I knew he was trying to tell me something, yet I never helped him out with it. "I'm a bad hat, Daisy" —that was at Kew, our first day. Then paying for everything with £1 notes: crooks always do that, so the newspapers say. And my funny feeling, on our holiday, that we were running away, being chased. Perhaps the police were after him then. And running away from them at the fair ground. A woman's instinct is always right. But when you love a chap so much, it goes to sleep. He tried to confess, to make me guess his secret. Running up that wall. Cat burglar. Like last night. And, afterward, in the bluebell wood, "Would you marry me if I was a murderer?" and "If you were a criminal type, would you ask a girl you loved to marry you?"

It helped, to remember that. He's got some decency left. Oh, you nasty wicked thing, to think of him like that, when he's always been so loving and considerate.

Blank incredulity returned. It was impossible that he—her wonderful Hugo—could be a common crook. The talk she had heard just now between him and Jacko must mean something else. But it could not. Poor sweetheart, with your nightmares, your fear of being trapped—"buried alive"—perhaps he was in a real prison, not a prisoner-of-war camp: "There's no such thing as a prison without bars." . . . Then trying to swipe those beer

47

mats; he didn't even seem to understand it was wrong; there
must be something missing in him. Oh God, those flowers he
brought back for me last night: he said he'd pinched them, and I
thought it was a joke. How can I believe anything he says now—
anything he ever said? Stuffing me up with tales about his business deals. He must have had a good laugh, the way I swallowed
it all. Having a good laugh with that Jaques chap now, I
shouldn't be surprised. Don't be a bitch, he'd never laugh at you,
not in that way; don't you see, he's been trying to protect you all
along.

And he might have killed himself last night, climbing up to
. . . Brushing the old suit when he got back, in case I noticed
marks on it, dirt; the suit with the poacher's pocket, and the
knobbly satchel inside it: burglar's tools—what do they call them?
—jemmies, skeleton keys and such. I wonder is he frightened
when he breaks into places. Worth it, for a diamond necklace,
and . . .

Daisy winced away. This was the mortal wound. Then she
forced herself to examine it. The brooch was on her dress still.
It had made her birthday and seemed to mark a new stage in
her life with Hugo, admitting her into the mysterious, precious
circle of his past. Why did he have to tell her it was his mother's?
That was a gratuitous insult, a piece of cruel mockery. She could
have forgiven him for being a thief, for any other lies; but to
have passed off as his mother's a jewel case he had stolen—that
was a cheap, rotten thing to do. It made him utterly unreliable,
made nonsense of his love. You could never again trust a person
who did that.

The girl fell into a passion of sobbing. She tore the brooch from
her dress and hurled it into the darkness, with a spasm of physical loathing, as if it were a scorpion. It struck the door and fell
clinking on the floor boards. Ten minutes later, when Hugo came
in, he trod full upon the brooch, shattering it.

"What the devil?" Harsh light from the naked bulb overhead
violated the room. Hugo bent down from the switch. "Oh, Christ,

it's my mother's brooch! What's it doing here? It's ruined. Daisy, you've not undressed yet. Are you all right?"

"I threw it there."

"You *what?*"

"I threw it there."

Hugo stared at her, incredulity turning to anger on his face. She gazed implacably back, sitting bolt upright now in the bed, her eyes screwed up against the glare.

"*Threw* it? Have you gone mad?"

"Your mother's brooch! I suppose it belonged to that tart—"

He was at the bedside in two swift strides, and had struck her a terrible blow across the face. Without a cry or a whimper, the beautiful head slowly bowed forward into her hands, covered away from him.

Hugo stood for a moment irresolute, as if he might hit her again or fall on his knees beside her. Then he turned away, began to take off his coat and tie, and when he had mastered his voice, said coldly: "Will you please tell me what all this is about?"

"I heard what you and that man were saying." Her voice came out muffled from behind her hands and the thick hair drooping over them. "I know what you were doing last night."

"Oh?" Hugo sat down, and went quite still. The silence stretched between them till Daisy felt her mind must snap. Painfully she lifted her head, gazing full at him. He did not avoid her eyes, but he did not seem to be seeing her. She groped for the right thing to say, knowing that anything else would be the end for them. She felt too young, too tired, to manage this situation; yet it was in her hands—she must give the lead. Hugo's mouth twitched. For an instant it was not Hugo there but her little brother, the baby of the family, whom she had loved most and mothered. A shaft of compunction, compassion, went through her. He was a thief, and a liar; he was hers.

"Hugo. I love you," she said, holding out her arms.

He came stumbling into them, sightlessly. "I'm glad you know. I tried to tell you, but I couldn't. I was afraid you'd leave me."

"I know, my dear love, I know," she soothed him, recognizing, with a wisdom beyond her years, with a woman's tender, indulgent scorn, the tones of masculine self-pity—so facile, so sincere. "I understand," she said. "Don't you take on so, sweetheart. It's all right now. I shan't leave you." His body was shaking convulsively, as though some furious engine had broken loose inside it. She crushed his head tighter to her breast, desperately trying to bury thus her reproaches and his betrayals.

"I hurt you, darling," he muttered.

"I don't mind. That's over now."

And presently, when he had grown calmer and was stroking her bruised cheek, she let herself say: "It wasn't that that hurt me. Not hitting me."

"I don't—"

"You told me it was your mother's."

"My mother's? Oh, your brooch. But it was, darling. All those trinkets I showed you." He broke off, flushing painfully. "Oh, I see now. You thought I'd stolen it. You really believed I'd do a thing like that?"

"I was so miserable," she answered drearily. "How could I believe anything you said, after—"

"After—?"

"Well, those flowers you brought to me for my birthday."

"But I told you I'd pinched them."

Daisy sighed. "I thought it was a joke, and you let me think it was."

"Yes, that's true," he said ingenuously. "But the brooch was different. I'm not all that of a clot. I do draw the line somewhere. Don't you believe me, love? Look, I can prove it. I've got the letter my father sent, saying mother wanted me to have—"

"I don't want you proving things to me," Daisy broke in. "I want to be able to believe what you tell me."

"You're rather like her, you know. She never nagged me; but she never suffered me in silence, like a martyr. Funny, because she was just a doormat to my father. I hated him as a child—the way he treated her. Made me miserable. I used to run and hide under a table when he started bullying her."

Daisy undressed quickly, bathed her face, and got into bed. Hugo was still sitting on the edge of it, his arms hanging down between his knees.

"Well, what happens now?" he asked, not looking at her.

"That's for you to say," she wearily replied. "Can't we leave it till tomorrow?"

"You want to make conditions?"

"Conditions?"

His lips twisted. "If I reform, you'll stay with me? That sort of thing?"

"I never—"

"No, but that's what was in your mind, my pet. I'll have another shot, if you like. But I warn you, it won't work. I've tried before. I'm no good at anything else, and I'm rather keen on my present profession: it suits me. Besides, it's hopeless trying to get a job once you've been in stir. Can you see me, anyway, touting soap flakes or sitting in some god-awful office? Why—"

"Oh, Hugo, do listen to me. I *don't* want to make conditions. I just want us to trust each other—never to have to wonder if you're telling me the truth, or putting me off with some clever story. You could do that so easily, because I'm not clever and I love you. I'd hate to feel suspicious of everything you said. It'd be the end of our loving each other, don't you see?"

Hugo took her face between his hands, and gazed deep. At last he whispered: "You're too good for me. I always knew it. I'll try to be someone you can trust. But you ought to find someone better—"

"I don't care what else you do! I don't mind your stealing!" she cried, in an abandonment of gratitude and relief. Her eyes shone with an unearthly, sacrificial light; then, as his hand moved on her breast, they misted over, and she was trembling, calling to him in a weak, harsh voice, "I want you. I want you. Quick. Kill me if you like."

Their love-making that night had a new sensuality of violence. They tore at each other, struggling, like animals in a net, as though each had something to take revenge for and something to expiate, or as if their bodies were an area unpacified, exasperated even, by the reconciliation just now of their minds. One way and another, it was the end of innocence between them.

It left her pale and flaccid as a drowned corpse, her lips cold, her head hanging back over the edge of the bed.

"Have you had enough?" he said; but she could make no sound.

Later he was talking to her, gently and remotely. "I have to work alone. It's safest. That's why I didn't tell you. I didn't want to drag you in. The less you know, the better: the police might come asking you questions."

"But Jacko knows, doesn't he?"

"Jacko knows as much as I tell him. Which is damned little. What he guesses is another matter. He gets a kick out of it, you see. Sort of vicarious excitement. Like respectable citizens pawing at some of the Sunday newspapers. Not that he's such a respectable citizen himself."

"But isn't it dangerous?"

"Oh, well, it's mutual. I know a bit about him, too: enough to keep him gummed up all right. So we both go our own ways, more or less regardless. Besides, he's useful."

"Useful?"

"He does illegal operations." Hugo offered this in a purely factual tone. "He has rather a classy clientele. So old Jacko just mentions to me in passing, as it might be, that Lady Stinkeroo or Miss Gloxinia Can-Can owns some eligible sparklers; and we get talking; he knows where she keeps 'em, maybe, knows her goings-out and her comings-in. A nod's as good as a wink. Oh yes, he slips me quite a bit of information behind his back. Nothing open, of course. Nothing ungentlemanly about it. You can't pin anything on a chap for being—well, slightly indiscreet."

Daisy digested this in silence for a little. "But he said something about 'a sweet alibi.' I heard him. That means he must know—"

"Ah, you don't understand Jacko. A devious character. He likes a little game of cat-and-mouse. That's his substitute for a bit of slap-and-tickle. He was saying that *if* I ever elected to embark on a life of crime, and *if* the bluebottles came buzzing round with awkward questions, you'd be able to give me a sweet alibi. By God, he's right too! You'd have them eating out of your hand. You look so innocent and wholesome—they'd believe anything you told them. But I'm never going to put you in a position of having to tell lies for me. Be dumb, sweet maid, and let who will be clever. No, I'm not having you involved."

But I am involved, thought Daisy, lying awake beside him, after he had dropped suddenly, as was his way, into deep, unvexed slumber. She felt how totally she was now involved, not only with the Hugo who had said "I'll try to be someone you can trust," but with that other Hugo who could prattle of wicked things as lightly and knowledgeably as a woman talking hats.

The pattern of their life began to establish itself. First, there had been the reckless holiday, then the weeks in limbo at Maida Vale; now they were embarked on another gay fling into the world, buying clothes for Daisy, moving to the Ritz, theater going, all the fun of the fair. It was like living on a roller coaster, Daisy thought—a life of ups and downs so dizzying that you could only hold tight and hope for the best. She felt that it corresponded with something in Hugo's nature—the way he swung violently from wild high spirits to a sodden gloom.

Daisy had always been a suggestible girl, and Hugo brought out a strain of wildness in her which almost equaled his own. Seeing the pair dining in a restaurant, one might have taken her at first for a fashion model, or perhaps a deb with bohemian inclinations; closer scrutiny might discover a freshness, an unexpected lack of self-consciousness, behind the bloom and poise of her personality. But no one could have guessed that this exquisite apparition concealed a village girl whose heart was bubbling half the time with "Oh, what a lark it all is! What a lark!" Still less would they have supposed that the dark, sleepy-eyed athletic young man escorting her (a gentleman rider? a racing motorist? a cricketer?) was a hardened criminal, and that his glances were appraising, not the women, but the jewels they wore.

At first Daisy had been apprehensive. She thought it was mad to be throwing money around like this and making themselves conspicuous so soon after the robbery. And indeed it was mad. But Hugo had, at this time, an ebullient belief in his own luck— the luck Daisy had brought him; and when he was on top of the world, his confidence was irresistible. After serving his first sentence, some years ago, he had changed his name, changed his sphere of operations from a Midland city to London, and changed his methods. Since he seldom entered the criminal underworld now, and always worked alone, he had little to fear from informers. The fence he dealt with was the only person in a position to give him away, apart from Jacko and Daisy herself; and each of these had good reasons for not doing so.

Hugo, besides, lacked the criminal's obsessive vanity. What vanity he had was satisfied by showing Daisy off, being seen with her, and by the mischievous pleasure he took in gulling the world at large. He would often talk to Daisy now about his past exploits —though he never talked about his future plans—and this gave him the safety valve most criminals need, requiring both to confess and to be admired. Daisy received these confidences as a mother might receive a boy's boasting about his audacities: she was shocked, but secretly excited; she felt she should disapprove, but she could not resist him.

One thing became more and more evident to her—Hugo's genuine contempt for society, his hatred of the settled, the humdrum, the respectable. Jacko was to explain this to her one day; but she already associated it vaguely with Hugo's childhood, his father's treatment of him, and more particularly with the prison term which still haunted him in his occasional terrible nightmares. As time went on, she gradually and unconsciously came to identify herself with this part of him, to feel that society was her enemy too. The first seed was sown when she got a letter from her mother, returning some money Daisy had sent her. Daisy's aunt must have written to tell her sister that the girl was living with a man, and Mrs. Bland now announced that she would rather die in poverty than share the wages of her daughter's sin. Daisy, after restraining an impulse to take the next train down to Gloucestershire, accepted this fatalistically: she had heard her mother say too often that those who make their bed must lie on it; and she did not want to lie on any other bed—not she.

But the seed was sown. And, a week after they went to the Ritz, something occurred which was more forcibly to make her feel an outlaw, and in due course to affect their fortunes disastrously. At the theater one night, looking round before the curtain went up, Hugo suddenly remarked: "Good God, there's my brother!"

"Oh, where? Shall we go and talk to him in the interval?"

"Lord, no. I can't stick him."

"But he's your brother."

"That's why. No, on second thoughts I couldn't stick him even if he wasn't my brother." Hugo grinned at her amiably. Then, with his occasional capacity to read her thoughts, said, "You really want to meet the family? All right then. But don't say you haven't been warned."

7 An Intellectual Tea-Party

FROM her brief meeting with Hugo's brother in the foyer, Daisy derived no very clear impressions. Mark Amberley was evidently disconcerted at the encounter: his small eyes swiveled this way and that as though he might bolt off any moment into the crowd. Hugo, however, had a firm grip on his elbow and performed the introductions with mischievous aplomb.

"Mark, let me introduce you to my fiancée, Miss Bland."

"Oh. How do you do. I didn't know—er, congratulations, Hugh —Hugo, I should say."

"It was very sudden. I'm afraid we didn't put it in the *Times*," Hugo affably remarked. "Gertrude with you?"

"Gertrude? Oh, er, yes. Yes. She should be somewhere about." Mark looked round desperately. "No. Of course. She's still in her seat. She didn't come out with me. So crowded and noisy here in the foyer. Are you enjoying the play, Miss—er—Bland?"

"Yes, it's ever so funny, isn't it." Mark Amberley's embarrassment, communicating itself to Daisy, made her revert to an idiom she had almost lost. She blushed a little.

"Funny? Well now, I suppose from certain aspects one might —but the underlying feeling is hardly that of comedy, surely? Of course, they were playing that first act very broad; too broad, wouldn't you say?"

"My brother is an Extension Lecturer," said Hugo, winking at Daisy over Mark's shoulder.

"An Extension Lecturer?" Daisy was hopelessly at sea.

"Yes. His lectures extend indefinitely."

Mark gave his uneasy laugh. "My brother's a great wag, as I

expect you've discovered, Miss Bland. But I do in fact lecture. London University, you know."

"You must be very clever," said Daisy, meaning it.

His head shied away from her—he's really rather like a horse, she thought, with that long face and that neighing voice—then turned back, and he seemed to be seeing her properly for the first time.

"Why don't you bring Hugo to tea with us one day?"

"I'd love to."

"Do I smell fatted calf roasting?" inquired Hugo. "If fatted calf is the word."

"Bourbons," Mark unexpectedly came out with. "You always used to like Bourbon biscuits. I'll see if Gertrude can acquire some. Still Maida Vale?"

Hugo nodded, frowned and was silent. Shortly afterward, the bell rang for the end of the intermission. As Daisy and Hugo went back to their seats, he said moodily: "Now you've done it."

"But it was very nice of him—"

"Oh, there's no vice in old Mark; he's just a bore. But Gertrude's a real stinker. Just you wait."

"He'll probably forget."

"Not a hope. I know him. He thinks you're going to reform me. A great chap for lost causes, Mark is."

And Hugo was right. An invitation duly arrived for the following Sunday afternoon. It had been difficult for the girl to see the desiccated and nervous Mark as Hugo's younger brother; but their encounter had at least broken new ground, and Daisy looked forward to the next, feeling that the acquaintance would give her a fresh hold on normality. At this period, in bars, on race courses, and at the club cricket matches to which he once or twice took her, she did meet other young men and women of Hugo's acquaintance; but, though she was sociable enough and enjoyed such meetings, they were too brief and accidental to mean anything. With Mark it would be different. Daisy looked forward to cozy, womanly chats with Gertrude. Mark, and presumably Gertrude, knew about Hugo's prison sentence: since

then, so Hugo told her, his relationship with them had been
confined to an occasional request for a loan when he was on his
uppers; they had no knowledge, whatever they might suspect, of
how he made a living now. "As far as I'm concerned, they keep
their heads in the sand," he said. "They're just bloody intellec-
tuals."

Daisy was not in the least alarmed at the prospect of entering
this strange new world. She saw no reason to shrink from "intel-
lectuals," having met none. The complacence of the well-loved
woman, superimposed on her own naturalness and zest for life,
prevented any apprehension that the meeting would be an ordeal.
She had held her own with Hugo's smarter acquaintances; why
should she worry about a harmless couple living respectably in
the Vale of Health?

Their "respectability" was what Hugo seemed most to resent.
He fired off a number of satirical comments on it as the tube
conveyed them northward that Sunday afternoon. For Daisy, the
word meant what it means to any village girl—lace curtains,
chapel on Sundays, primmed lips, and scandalized whispers. So
she was thrown off her balance, on entering the Amberleys'
drawing room, to be confronted by a stark, staring nude on the
wall above the mantelpiece.

"She's rather a pet, isn't she?" said Gertrude Amberley, inter-
cepting Daisy's open-eyed gaze at the picture; and shaking hands
briskly without any more formal greeting, she turned to give
Hugo a peck on the cheek. Thoroughly rattled, Daisy stood dere-
lict in the middle of the floor till Mark fussed her toward a chair.

"Well, Hugo, how are the ungodly flourishing nowadays?
Pretty well, judging from appearances."

Gertrude's voice, light and rather girlish in tone, articulated
her words with a precision which came near to pedantry. Her
talk was like shelling peas—neat, efficient, automatic. Daisy
wondered if she was a schoolmistress: that clicking, rapid talk,
cleanly gutting each subject; the smack of the lips at the end of a
sentence; the high, narrow forehead, with the hair drawn severely

back to a meager bun; the trick of conducting conversation through a series of questions.

"And what's your job, Miss Bland?"

"I haven't got a job. I used to work in a hat shop."

"Did you like that? What sort of hours do they work you?"

After this catechism had gone on for some time, Daisy felt she must show some reciprocal interest in her hostess.

"Are you a schoolteacher, Mrs. Amberley?"

"I teach, yes. W.E.A., actually," came the brisk and, to Daisy, incomprehensible reply.

"Enlightenment to the masses," Hugo murmured. "T. S. Eliot for bank clerks."

"Rather suitable," whinnied his brother, "when you come to think of it. In my end is my beginning."

"Eliot is finished," Mrs. Amberley stated. "Nothing more to say. We must look to the neo-classicists now. Don't you agree, Miss Bland?"

"Well, I—"

"I simply can't agree with you there," said Mark. "I admit Harry Grutch is doing some quite promising work; but the rest of them—they're just dogs returning to someone else's vomit."

"Well, of course, if you really see neo-classicism as a return to the thirties, there's nothing more to be said. Auden and that lot have been dismissed long ago—" Gertrude laughed shortly— "*Scrutiny* settled *their* hash all right. But the point I'm trying to make is that, although they haven't produced any very remarkable work yet, the neo-classicists are on the right lines. They do at any rate understand what Leavis wants."

"The neo-Parnassian group at Reading," suggested Mark, "are on the same alignment, perhaps. I don't know if they've come your way, Miss Bland?"

"All that's come Daisy's way, from Reading, is biscuits," said Hugo, smiling at her.

The smile caused Daisy to make a valiant effort. The name of T. S. Eliot had been the one clue she could grasp in the otherwise unintelligible conversation.

"You write poems yourself, Mrs. Amberley?" she timidly asked.

"Those who can, do; those who can't, teach," murmured Hugo.

"Gertrude is too severely self-critical," said Mark hurriedly. "She is, er, concerned with the setting and maintaining of the highest standards. She could never be satisfied with anything she had written."

"I can imagine that," Hugo ambiguously remarked.

"No, I don't write poems," said Gertrude, her intonation picking out the last two words for inspection, distastefully, as it were in a pair of tongs. Daisy was made to feel as if she had insulted Gertrude by the suggestion. "Why should one?" Gertrude continued. "This is an age of criticism. All the best work is being done in criticism." She continued for some time, tossing the ball to her husband over Daisy's head, and catching it from him. Whether or no it was done to show her up, it made Daisy rather miserable and flustered: it was too like that childhood game of He-in-the-Middle. Mark, to give him credit, did try to draw her into the conversation, but his attempts only emphasized her ignorance. Hugo, as Daisy could see, was beginning to smolder with rage.

Things went a bit better at first over tea. Hugo, appeased by chocolate biscuits, started teasing Gertrude about her male pupils, and she responded more readily than Daisy would have thought possible. The girl relaxed, half her attention occupied with the room where they were sitting. Its walls were color-washed a thunderous shade of pink, which rendered corpselike the flesh tones of the nude above the mantelpiece, and clashed stridently with the copper and white stripes of the curtains and chair covers and a couple of saffron velvet cushions on the sofa. The tea set was in thick Italian pottery. Magazines littered a low round table, and the wall opposite the window was lined with bookcases of different heights. The window looked out upon a small neglected garden. There was a gramophone, but no television or radio set. The square of shabby carpet left a narrow strip of naked floorboard on one side, where it failed to meet the staining. No ornaments at all, but ashtrays everywhere; yet cigarette ash lay in patches, like scurf, all over the carpet: Gertrude smoked incessantly, puffing away as if for dear life, and knocking the ash brusquely in the direction of the nearest ashtray.

There was something nerve-racking, unco-ordinated, schizophrenic almost, about this room, as though a number of total strangers had each, at different times, contributed to it. Neither elegant nor cozy nor agreeably eccentric, it could have been pathetic but for its aggressive disregard of harmony and grace. Its occupants, one might have supposed, either lacked all taste or despised it; an acute observer would have seen that both these predicates were true—indeed, that the latter was, with such people as the Amberleys, a consequence of the former. The room whined a sort of doctrinaire puritanic sermon against the mere enjoyment of life, condemning charm as frivolity; it was a machine, not for living, but for partly living.

None of these considerations occurred to Daisy. She felt oppressed here, certainly; she thought her hostess's color scheme very odd, but assumed it to be artistic in the most up-to-date style. The whole atrocious lack of decorum about this room, the perverse and supercilious flouting of the visual decencies, which even turned the nude into a body one would not be seen dead in a ditch with, passed, like the Amberleys' talk, over Daisy's head. She was thinking, this is a home, where two people live together, Hugo's relations. The unreality of her life with Hugo came over her like a suffocating wave. She wanted to scream out, "It's all wrong! What are we doing here? Why don't you ask Hugo where his money comes from—you who ask every other question?" It was like in a dream, standing red-handed beside the corpse, when the tongue cannot utter the confession and the passers-by will not notice the deed.

Unconsciously Daisy clasped her hands over her breast, and her eyes turned upward. She was struggling to release herself from the nightmare. Gertrude, like ill-cooked food, had been its accidental cause; but its core was Hugo—the criminal secret which put a barrier between them and the rest of the world, and might even infect their love with its false pretenses.

"She's just like 'Lady Hamilton at Prayer.' Do look!"

It was a rasping whisper from Gertrude, which at last penetrated Daisy's unhappy reverie. She looked about her vaguely, a little wildly, wondering what they were talking about now.

"What?—I'm sorry."

"I was saying you looked just like 'Lady Hamilton at Prayer.' Didn't she, Mark?"

"Oh, er, yes. Yes."

"I don't understand," faltered Daisy, trying to smile.

"It's a picture," Gertrude explained, clicking out the vocables like a string of beads. "By Romney. At Ken Wood."

Recollection of a history lesson, years ago, came to Daisy.

"Is that Nelson's?—" the girl found herself unable to utter the next word, which was readily supplied, however, by Mark.

"Nelson's mistress. That's right." He beamed encouragingly at Daisy. "A very beautiful creature she was, too."

"I think Romney got her essential flooseyness quite perfectly, don't you, Mark? In *that* painting. It's genuine criticism."

"Unconscious, I take it."

"Oh, naturally. One wouldn't expect critical awareness from a Romney. Dear me, no. No doubt she fooled him to the top of her bent. She was a professional *poseuse*, after all, the absurd creature. And artists are very naïve. That's really the whole point. He painted exactly what was there—a glamorous, milkmaidish ninny putting on an act of prayer. And because she wasn't even a very good actress, the floosey emerges from behind the prayerful pose."

"But couldn't she have been praying?" Daisy said on an impulse. "Praying for Nelson? She loved him."

"That's the last thing that would ever occur to Gertrude," said Hugo.

"She *could* have been"—Gertrude ignored him—"but in fact she was putting over her sex appeal on Mr. Romney, and posterity."

Daisy remonstrated, "I don't see how you can be so sure of that."

"I've seen the picture. You haven't, apparently." Gertrude snapped the words like dry biscuits, and Daisy realized that the woman was suddenly, inexplicably furious; this talk about Lady Hamilton was directed against herself. Though ductile and placid enough in temperament, Daisy could be roused; she was not overawed by Gertrude any longer, now she saw her ill-suppressed venom for what it was.

"You think I'm a floosey, like this Lady Hamilton?" she said, laughing.

Mark, without performing the action, gave the impression of one wringing his hands. "Oh, come now, Miss Bland, Gertrude really never suggested—"

"Why so shocked?" his wife cut in crisply. "You are Hugo's mistress, presumably? For all I know, you pray for him too—as well as serving him in other capacities."

Mark began to flap his hands, looking as if he were about to burst into tears, but Gertrude paid him no heed.

"I've no objection to Hugo's bringing his mistress to my house— it's hardly the first time. But I despise this tawdry camouflage of being his fiancée."

"I do believe you're in love with Hugo yourself," Daisy was startled to hear herself say—and at once bitterly ashamed.

"No doubt you do. Sex is all that moronic shopgirls ever think about." Gertrude positively spat the words into Daisy's face. Hugo leaned back, speaking with a measured calmness which frightened Daisy:

"Gertrude, nature made you a bitch, but you needn't be a vulgar bitch. You've done your best all the afternoon to make Daisy feel ill at ease. I'll pass that over, because you can't help waving your intellectual pretensions under people's noses. But you will apologize for what you've just said."

"Oh, look now, Hugo. Steady on. That's damned offensive," Mark began.

"Shut up, Mark," said his wife, beside herself now, and turned upon Hugo. "How dare you talk to me like that! You're a waster. I know you. A jailbird. You go round sponging on people—d'you know how much you owe us?—throwing your famous charm about. You make me sick. You're diseased with vanity. I don't know what keeps you alive, except basking in the admiration of a string of cretinous creatures like—"

"Don't splutter at me, Gertrude. You're just adding to the list of things you've got to apologize for."

"Please, Hugo! Let's go," said Daisy urgently, pulling at his sleeve.

"Not till my dear sister-in-law has apologized."

"If you think I'm going to apologize to you—"

"Not to me. To Daisy."

Gertrude's grin was a rictus. "I'm not one of your tarts. You can't bully me. And if you had any brains in your head, you'd know that."

"Aha, my fearless little highbrow critic, don't you be so sure," said Hugo; and before Daisy could anticipate his next move-ment, he had drawn a revolver from his pocket and pointed it at Gertrude. A muddy flush came over her face and went, leaving it dead pale.

"No, no!" she whimpered, pushing at the air in front of her eyes. It was not the revolver which had done it, so much as Hugo's expression. Daisy had seen that expression once before: a bleak, cold recklessness; a look of almost ecstatic surrender to the violence within.

"Please, Gertrude, please apologize," she cried imploringly. "He means it."

Mark had shrunk back against the wall. Daisy feared that, if she herself stirred, it would pull the trigger. The revolver struck forward a foot toward Gertrude, as if of its own volition. She began nodding her head violently, the eyes staring at Hugo, like a woman in a fit. Her teeth chattered, and at last the abject words came out.

8 "He'd as Soon Be in Prison"

ONE evening, a fortnight later, Daisy set out to visit John Jaques. The fling of high life was over, and Hugo had taken her back to the rooms in Maida Vale. They had seen Jacko several times during that period. Daisy's first doubts about him were set at rest by these meetings: he was attentive to her, and he jollied Hugo along in an easy, impish way that made her warm to him. He was in any case a more solid figure than the chance acquaintances of bar, night club and race meeting—young men who made difficult conversation or facile passes at her, young women whose eyes lingered upon Hugo—a drifting, brittle society with no more relationship than matchsticks swirling together and apart in some back eddy.

Jacko represented something more permanent. And it was a measure of Daisy's need for such stability, now the first flood of passion had subsided a little, that she should seek it in him. Jacko was an abortionist, according to Hugo, and a sort of pilot fish for his own criminal activities, yet Daisy could not feel any moral abhorrence for him. He's like—like an uncle to us both, she thought as the underground train rattled her toward Kensington High Street. Perhaps I'm just a naturally wicked girl—taking to this sort of thing like a duck to water; I don't seem to be able to feel shocked any more. She took out her compact. A face pure and dreamy as the dawn gazed at her from its little mirror. So there I am, a burglar's moll, on my way to visit a doctor who . . .

Hugo was out this evening. He would not be back till late, he had said. He said no more than this, but she knew—as she was always to know now—that something was in the wind. He had looked taut this morning, withdrawn from her, as if he must

listen attentively to something tuning up within himself. But
there was the tacit compact between them that he should not tell
her his plans, nor she inquire. A lowering, foreboding sensation
oppressed her; it was like when the sky came down and sat for
days upon the wold above her village in Gloucestershire. Outside
the station, some impulse made her ask a policeman the route to
Albert Grove, though she did not need his directions; he looked
at her steadily, in the policeman's way, but without suspicion or
curiosity. As she walked on, Daisy thought how strange it was
that the police should not have troubled them yet; disquieting
too, and heightening her sense of isolation, as if They knew all
about her but were biding their time, waiting maybe for some
sign, some crucial, irretrievable error, before They took action.

Albert Grove was a crescent-shaped terrace, lined with plane
trees, of early-Victorian houses, which one could imagine in-
habited by the widows of deans and Indian civil servants, by sere,
punctilious bachelors devoted to stamp collecting or archery, by
distant cousins of county families. In the small double drawing
rooms there would be Benares brass, amateur water colors, a
goldfish bowl, a solitaire board—relics of a civilization which had
never been fighting against time. The brass plate at John Jaques'
door repeated the note of unobtrusive smugness. He came to the
door himself, an image of discreet professional respectability,
and, taking her by the elbow, led her into a parlor on the left of
the hall, its window darkened by ferns and muslin curtains.

For a while, as she sipped the dry sherry he had poured out,
they talked on indifferent subjects. Daisy felt both nervous and
relaxed. In the dim little room she could only see him as a feature-
less face surmounted by white hair, outlined against the window.
She found herself gradually sinking into this new environment,
whose greenish light suggested an aquarium—an impression
heightened by Jacko's slow-motion gestures as he poured out
more sherry from a Venetian decanter. His light, throaty voice
curled like slow arabesques of smoke in the close air: it was a
consoling sound. A phrase swam into Daisy's head—"bedside
manner"— and involuntarily she shivered a little. At once, though

how he had noticed it in the gloom she could not imagine, Jacko said with solicitude:

"Are you cold, my dear? Shall I light the fire?"

"No, it's all right," she replied, in some confusion. "I'm not—it's very dark, though, isn't it?"

"Restful for the eyes. People talk a lot about the effect of noise in our city life; but I believe modern lighting has a more adverse effect on the nervous system—all these high-powered street lights and neons, and 100-watt bulbs in private houses—it's against nature." His voice went soothingly on. Daisy, following her own thoughts, was suddenly arrested by a phrase . . . "our instincts. We are still creatures of the dark. We ignore the dark element within us at our peril."

A not very obscure association made Daisy say, "We had an awful scene at the Amberleys'. Did Hugo tell you?"

"No. But I'm not surprised. It was Gertrude, I suppose. What happened?"

As Daisy recounted the lamentable scene, she began to shake uncontrollably. Jacko now came to sit on the arm of her chair, and was stroking the hair over her temple with a rhythmic movement she found quite hypnotic. A car, passing in the street, sounded distant as a memory. The window blurred before Daisy's eyes; she felt weak, convalescent, comforted.

"Probably do her good, in the long run," Jacko was saying. "That sort of woman needs shock treatment. But old Hugo doesn't normally carry a gun about with him, does he? Was it loaded?"

"I don't think so. I really don't know," said Daisy, answering both questions. "But I was terrified. Hugo's face. It scared me dreadfully. I'm afraid what he might do if—"

"That's a price you must pay—"

"I mean, he really might kill someone. He seems to lose all control."

"Oh, come now, my dear, I can't quite believe that. Anyway, it's what Hugo is like. You've got to accept it. You can't just choose the things you like about a person and say that is the

person you love. Though nearly everyone does. You must take
him for better *and* for worse."

"Oh, I do, I do! But I wish—"

"Wish you could change him?"

"No, understand him. His moods."

"Hugo's not all that difficult to understand, surely. He's a
straightforward manic-depressive type, and—"

"Oh," the girl cried, "he's not—you don't mean he's, well, not
right in his head?"

"Of course I don't. A manic-depressive is simply someone who
swings between two extreme states of mind, exhilaration and
apathy. Most of us are like that, up to a point. It's perfectly all
right, as long as you don't swing too far."

"I see." Daisy was partly reassured, and pressed Jacko's hand
in gratitude. He patted her shoulder; and a forgotten memory
rose momentarily from the past—of her father, that dour, silent
man, comforting her over some childhood misadventure.

"Nothing gone wrong between you two?" he presently asked;
his voice in the gloom sounded strange to her; if it had been anyone but Jacko, whose sympathy she had come to take almost for
granted, Daisy might have imagined something in his tone
beyond the usual attentive interest—a kind of eagerness.

"No, nothing at all," she cried. "But it *is* difficult. We live such
a funny way. The insecurity."

Even with Jacko, to say more would be, she felt, a kind of disloyalty to Hugo. However, he took it up briskly. "You worry
about Hugo's antisocial tendencies?"

Dumbly, gazing down at her hands, she nodded.

"Well, you've either got to accept them, or make a break,"
Jacko went on. "Unless you plan to reform him."

"I just want to do what's best for him," she replied, put on the
defensive by his last words.

"Don't misunderstand me. I'm not being censorious, not being
nasty. If anyone could reform him, it's you. But you must understand what you're up against. Old Hugo hated his father—you
know that—when he was a boy. Now that hatred is deeply en-

grained in his character. He's simply transferred it to a wider reference: authority, respectability, society—whatever represents the father figure he violently reacts against. It's not his fault. He can't help being a rebel, an outlaw. Do you see what I mean?"

"Yes, I think so." Daisy sighed. "You think I ought to let things go on as they are?"

"Does it sound very immoral advice to you?" Jacko chuckled in his friendly way.

"I don't know," she replied.

"Put it this way—do you really want Hugo different, even supposing he could be changed?"

Daisy bowed her head, feeling suddenly confused and unhappy. They had gone so far in confidence, yet the word "criminal" had not once been used. The vague, subaqueous light in this room, Jacko's fingers gently stroking her upper arm now, seemed to have put a spell around her. It was on an almost desperate impulse to break free of it that she said:

"Doesn't it ever worry *you*, living the way you do?"

She was aware at once that Jacko was taken tremendously aback. Glancing up at him, she saw his face overhanging her, like stone, like a gargoyle. His fingers had left her arm.

"Not in the least," he said, after a pause. "And what way *do* I live?" Abruptly rising, he switched on the light, as if to illuminate the early-Victorian respectability of the room.

"Well, Hugo told me—"

"Yes?"

Daisy took a plunge at it. "—told me you did illegal operations."

"Like a good many other doctors. Are you so shocked?" There was something like a jeer behind the usual crooning tone of his voice. The planes of his lumpy face seemed to have altered their relationship, so that it resembled for a moment, under the glaring light, a dead lunar landscape.

"I'm beyond being shocked at anything," the girl drearily replied. "I just need help."

"Oh, I see, my dear. You're pregnant, is that it?"

Daisy flushed, in her turn disconcerted. "No, John, of course

I'm not. It's the way we live—Hugo and I." She began to flounder in her mind, unable to find words for the sense of unreality and isolation which so oppressed her. She was aware of Jacko scrutinizing her; and something wry, dispassionate yet expectant in his regard made her once more uncharacteristically aggressive. "Don't you feel any responsibility for Hugo?"

"Responsibility?" His voice had a humoring upward inflection.

"Well then, guilt," she said forthrightly.

Jacko lit a cigarette, his first of the evening; then, apologizing, offered Daisy one. "I don't quite understand you. Do you mean I should feel guilty because Hugo is my friend and Hugo's way of life is—er—rather unconventional?"

"Oh, do let's stop pretending," she cried. "You know perfectly well that Hugo is a burglar."

Jacko's nostrils flared, and one side of his mouth twitched.

"All right then. He's a burglar. Ought I to feel guilt about that?"

"About helping him—what's the word?—tipping him off."

"Tipping him off?" The man's voice became almost falsetto. "My dear child, what are you dreaming about?"

Daisy had gone too far to draw back. She told him what Hugo had told her—how Jacko let fall bits of information which were useful to Hugo. As she spoke, Jacko looked at first amazed, then tickled.

"Oh, my goodness me," he said, with a chuckle. "The old boy was pulling your leg. He's a desperate romancer, you know."

"He doesn't tell lies to me, really he doesn't." Daisy was wounded, and Jacko's voice at once became solicitous again.

"I'm sure he doesn't. Not about important things. But as a joke, a tall story—don't you see? You mustn't take everything he says too seriously. It's a sort of game with him, to invent discreditable fantasies about his friends; haven't you noticed? Though I must say this is a new one to me. You can see, my dear, that a doctor in my position has to watch his step extra carefully. It would be madness for me to talk about my patients, to anyone."

"Isn't it dangerous for you to—well, associate with Hugo at all?"

Jacko had an embarrassed look. "One doesn't drop one's friends for the sake of one's reputation."

"I'm sorry I—" Daisy squeezed his hand. "You're a good man."

"And you're a very very good girl. And a beautiful one," said Jacko, smiling at her. "Now what about some dinner? You're not expecting Hugo back till late, are you? It'll cheer you up." Jacko chuckled again. "I take it he's on the tiles again tonight, in a manner of speaking?"

Overwrought, Daisy began helplessly to cry. Jacko watched her in silence for a while, then said, "You must try not to worry. If he thought you were worrying, it would be bad for his nerve."

Daisy nodded, miserably. But it was not the thought of Hugo's danger which had made her cry: it was not knowing what to believe. She could have sworn that Hugo had been serious when he told her about Jacko. But now Jacko had convinced her, or nearly convinced her, that the idea was fantastic, impossible. So Hugo must have been lying to her then, quite wantonly. And she could never talk to him about it: he would be furious if she told him she had discussed it with Jacko—equally furious whether it was a joke or the truth. The thing would weigh upon her mind, unresolved, like a malignant lump.

Presently Jacko rang for his housekeeper to take Daisy upstairs. The housekeeper was an elderly woman with a non-committal expression, natural or cultivated, who proved, however, unexpectedly talkative. It was nice for the doctor to have company—they didn't often have visitors, except professionally of course—she hoped Miss Bland could fancy a chicken omelet and a trifle—watch the step down into the bedroom, it could be dangerous. It soon became evident to Daisy that the woman was putting out feelers to discover whether she was a prospective patient of the doctor's; and Daisy, who had glanced timidly about her in the hall below, wondering which of those doors led to the surgery, felt an acute shame—an apprehension, almost, as though the place were haunted by the furtive desperate shades of women who had been here to have the life within them destroyed. While the housekeeper hovered inquisitively beside her,

it came to Daisy, with all the force of a great discovery or a
great decision, that if ever she were pregnant by Hugo, however
difficult it might make things for them, she would have the baby.

"Why, that's better," Jacko exclaimed, when she came downstairs again. "You look as if someone had given you a million."

From time to time during dinner she noticed his eyes upon her,
a puzzled look in them she had never seen before. She was used
to his reading her like a book: she could not imagine that this
new page might be in a language he did not understand. Her
heart was so lightened by the simple discovery she had just made,
she felt like hugging it to herself for a while, not sharing it—
even with Jacko. From a round mirror above the sideboard her
own face gazed at her dreamily, complacently, with an expression
which almost duplicated that of the Piero della Francesca ma-
donna reproduced on the wall to her right.

"Don't go broody on me," Jacko said.

"I'm sorry. I was thinking."

"A penny for them." His eyes followed every movement of
hers, like a dog's waiting for a tidbit from the table. It seemed a
shame to disappoint him, yet she could not come out with it
point-blank; instead, she murmured: "I can't understand a
woman wanting to get rid of her baby."

Jacko dabbed his mouth in a finicky way with his napkin. "It's
need, not want, with most of them. And of course some women's
maternal instinct is completely dormant till after a child is born."

"It must be horrible for you," said Daisy.

"You mean, *you're* horrified by *me?*"

"Oh no, no!" Daisy was distressed. "I'm sure you don't like
doing—well, it is taking life, isn't it?"

A strange expression, which she was to remember afterward,
passed over his face and was gone. It reminded her of the impish,
"dare-you" look which Hugo sometimes had; yet it was different,
more secretive.

"It's only a small part of my practice, you know," he answered
mildly.

"You are nice. You never tell me how young and inexperienced I am."

"Why should I? You're wise beyond your years. Like any child of nature. I hope Hugo realizes it." Jacko's eyes were upon her steadily again, like fingers feeling a pulse. "I'd never forgive him if he hurt you."

"Oh, one can't be truly in love without getting hurt," she gaily proclaimed. "That's how you know it's the real thing."

"Well! You little masochist! You'll be telling me next you want Hugo to beat you. Or perhaps he does." Jacko leaned forward, his eyes brightly interrogative.

"I'm black-and-blue all the time. Silly! Of course he doesn't." Daisy blushed, thinking of the love bruises, and went on quickly, at random, to conceal the thought, "I wonder would Hugo be a good father."

Jacko leaned back again, neatly skinning an orange with his dessert knife; he did not reply at once.

"My dear," he said at last, "if that's the way your mind is working, I must warn you. Hugo travels light. He'd never let himself be saddled with a family."

"But—"

"Remember, I've known him some time. He's a fine chap, but he's not cut out for responsibility. Can you see him as a family man—nappies, regular hours, life insurances? Bless your heart, he'd as soon be in prison. . . ."

Jacko's words were still tolling in her head when Daisy got home. The Maida Vale flat seemed a poor place after the spruce, spinsterish little house in Albert Grove. Daisy set herself to tidying up the sitting room, a leaden depression weighing on her mind. If only Hugo would come back soon! It was so silent here, so desolate.

She went into the bedroom, and switching on the light, gave a little cry. Hugo *was* there, lying full length, fully clothed, on the bed, his eyes staring at her, past her, with a lack-luster expression.

"Hugo! What's the matter, darling? Didn't you hear me come in?"

"It was a flop," he said in a bitter, dead voice. "A proper bloody washout. All I've got out of it is a sprained ankle. Managed to find a cab, and save myself from the wreck. For Christ's sake, love, don't look as if I'd raped you or something!"

9 Journey Through the Underworld

Hugo's sprained ankle kept him inactive for several days. At first he was docile, submitting to Daisy's cold compresses and fussing, following her with his eyes like an injured child who is not yet sure whether he will be blamed for the accident which has caused his injury. Hugo was evidently mortified by his failure, and Daisy's instinct told her that just now he needed very careful handling. He would say nothing more about his failure than that he had fallen fifteen feet from a window ledge: such a drop was nothing to him; but he had landed with one foot on a paint pot in the yard below, and this had turned his ankle.

The girl could not help remembering what Jacko had said last night: "If he thought you were worrying, it would be bad for his nerve." Hugo had never slipped before, he told her, almost apologetically; he must be out of practice or something. And she avoided his eyes, feeling guilty.

At least there had been no alarm given. The occupants of the house were on holiday, and the nearest neighbors presumably asleep, so Hugo felt no apprehension about inquiries being made of taxi drivers; after lying doggo for five minutes, he had managed to hobble a hundred yards, then caught a taxi in the main street, pretending to be drunk and blearily explaining to the driver that he had fallen down some steps after a party.

Hugo's *piano* mood that first day made it all the more of a surprise to Daisy when, as she ate her supper off a tray by his bedside, he suddenly said: "What's up, old girl?"

"Nothing," she replied, conscious of his eyes upon her—the eyes that could be so evasive, but sometimes, as now, so disconcertingly shrewd.

"You're cherishing a grievance. I know you," he said, amiably teasing, but searching too. She shook her head.

"The breadwinner failed to bring home the bacon?"

"Oh, it's not *that!*" she cried, with a self-betraying emphasis. "You know I don't blame you for—"

"Then what *do* you blame me for? You're bottling something up. You've been keeping your distance."

Daisy had not been aware of this; but she knew now it was true. There was nothing she could hide from Hugo.

"Why did you tell me Jacko was sort of an accomplice—I mean, tipped you off—?"

"So he does. In his back-handed way." A wariness in Hugo's voice made her feel a little sick.

"But he absolutely denies it. He was staggered when I—"

"You brought *that* up with him last night?" Hugo's tone was almost hostile now, but she had to go on.

"Well, he's our friend, isn't he? He wasn't angry. He just said you were pulling my leg, romancing."

"You don't really suppose he'd admit it to you, do you? My poor, simple-minded girl—why, he hardly admits it to himself."

"But I don't understand—"

"Keep your nose out of it then," he flashed up at her.

"I *won't!* Why should I be kept in the dark all the time? Don't you see I want to share your life—all of it, not just the dainty bits you decide to dish out?"

"I'm sorry, love." He took Daisy's hand, gazing at her thoughtfully. "I shouldn't have told you that about Jacko."

"Was it true?" she asked.

"Yes. Perfectly true. But why?"

Daisy sighed. Could she never make Hugo understand that, if they did not tell each other the truth, their life together was meaningless?

"Jacko's a queer fish," Hugo was saying. "He doesn't let his right hand know what his left hand is doing. But you can trust him to the limit: I've proved that all right."

"*You* certainly do," said Daisy, on a perverse impulse.

"How do you mean?"

"You don't seem to mind my going there alone at night."

Hugo burst out laughing. "Oh glory! You're angry because I'm not jealous? I really believe you are. Poor Daisy, wasn't she assaulted by her young man's wicked friend then!"

The girl dragged her hand away furiously. "I hate you when you talk like that!"

"My word, we are touchy today! Look, darling. I'm as jealous as hell normally. But not over Jacko. He's my friend, and anyway I suspect the poor old bastard's as good as impotent."

As always when Hugo talked about Jacko, Daisy felt herself excluded—a frantic little dot dancing about on the outside of a closed circle. She tried now to convey this to Hugo, and presently found herself telling him how unreal and isolated her life sometimes seemed. He listened patiently enough; he did not, as she had half feared, tell her that she could take it or leave it—this hole-and-corner life; nor did he indulge in self-pity of the I-always-said-I-wasn't-good-enough-for-you kind. Instead, a subdued gleam came into his eye, and with that boyish audacity, complicity, which always swept her off her feet, he said:

"Well, love, if you're on for it, shall we change our way of life?"

"Change our—?"

"Go and live where I belong. Amongst the publicans and sinners. We've hardly a bean in the kitty, anyway. I can sublet these rooms furnished till the end of the year." Hugo talked with the same enthusiasm as when he suggested a move to the Ritz, and Daisy was, as usual, infected by it. She would sell the clothes he had bought her, she would go out to work, she—

"Oh no, my pet, we don't *work* in the circles I'm introducing you to." Hugo made a shocked face. " 'Work' is a word you must never use there. A dirty word."

What Hugo's motive was in transplanting her to the underworld, Daisy never knew, nor indeed bothered to think about much. Some inhibition against doing so, some chivalrous desire to protect her innocence, must have been swept away. Or perhaps the self-destructive element in his nature impelled him to show

himself to her against his natural background. At any rate, as
soon as he could move about again, he went off to re-establish
contact with a man he had known when they were both working
the Midland city. This man, Tacker Fenton, he told Daisy when
he returned, had put him onto a lodginghouse off the White-
chapel Road where they could get a room cheap and no questions asked. Hugo had booked the room; and in the same whirl
of energy he sold most of Daisy's clothes—at a price which
astonished her—and found a tenant for the flat.

"Are you going to join a gang?" she asked, hesitantly. "I
thought you always worked alone."

"We'll see. Maybe I'll have to double up with someone. The
free-lance lark hasn't got me anywhere lately."

A schoolboy going home for the holidays could not have been
more gay than Hugo when, the next morning, he humped their
two suitcases and hurried Daisy through the early autumn air,
en route for the underworld, where they were to sojourn now,
off and on, for nearly twelve months.

Daisy's first impression of it, once she had acclimatized herself
to the lodginghouse room, the seedy cafés and the crowded,
babbling streets, was of a life curiously similar to their high-
flying days at the Ritz. Here was the same drifting, apparently
rootless society, easy come easy go, its members—like Hugo's
elegant acquaintances from the upper world—talking a language
of their own, allusive and slangy, living on their wits or their
parasitic powers, showily generous if they were in the money,
shamelessly cadging when funds ran low. Daisy's introduction
to these people, all of whom existed by crime or on its shady
fringes, was made easier by Tacker Fenton. Tacker, a squat,
broad, merry character, took to her from the first, nicknamed her
"the Queen," acted as bear leader and bodyguard. It was from
Tacker that she learned the gradations and snobberies of the
criminal world, whose aristocracy are the con men and the
burglars, where pickpockets are small fry. Himself one of the
aristocracy, Tacker deplored the postwar tendencies—crimes of

violence, Teddy boys, and the mob of leftovers from the rackets which had flourished under rationing and shortages. The profession, one gathered from him, was overcrowded, while half the operators were amateurs who ought to be condemned, for their incompetence, to do an honest job of work.

Hugo, having been out of touch with the fraternity for some time, took a back seat at first. But he was looked upon with respect as a solo operator whose reputation was secure; and Daisy soon observed how quickly he became at home here, like a born countryman returning to his old village after many years. He even seemed to take on the color of the environment, his appearance growing both jauntier and warier, his gestures adapting themselves to the nervous, slick stereotype of criminal freemasonry. It was partly a game with him, Daisy thought; but in playing this game according to its rules and conventions he took a boyish pride. This—his alert bearing and high spirits seemed, if a little defiantly, to proclaim—this is where I belong; I need not keep up appearances any more.

Such conscience or hankering after respectability as had remained to Daisy was soon dissipated by Hugo's new-found contentment. She realized that he too had felt isolated, often ill-at-ease, in their Maida Vale existence. She would always be happy so long as he was happy; and now, imperceptibly to herself and by gradual degrees, she was surrendering to the values of this new world, Hugo's world, where the honest citizen was honestly considered a mug, respectability a smear, and the Law a thing to be broken, evaded or suffered—one's natural adversary.

Hugo for his part, whatever uneasiness he may have felt at first on Daisy's behalf, soon lost it. For Daisy was a great success. Her malleability and her zest for life carried her with flying colors through an experience which would have degraded or broken any other kind of woman. Young toughs boasted to her about their girls, consulted her about their flash clothes; older lags reminisced sentimentally about the mothers whose hearts they had broken, and gave her tips for the dogs; and Daisy listened, offering admiration or sensible advice, a sort of White

Goddess amongst the savage tribe. The women were at first more suspicious; then, seeing that she had eyes for none but Hugo, they too accepted her. No one would have tried anything on with a girl who had Hugo and Tacker at her back; but the quality of innocence, which her beauty still emanated, made itself positively felt, so that the foul-mouthed restrained themselves in her presence and the cynical were temporarily softened.

Above all, she brought luck. To the criminal, superstitious and of low intelligence as he usually is, luck seems a kind of divine grace; he admires the lucky operator as a soldier admires the lucky general. Although Hugo and Tacker did not at this time attempt any big coups, they were uniformly successful in a small way: and this was attributed to Daisy, giving her the status of a mascot. It became the practice, indeed, among those of the confraternity who knew her, to seek her out before going to play the dogs or crack a crib, and to touch her dress as if touching wood. The queer loyalty she thus inspired—the nearest thing to affection and disinterestedness, perhaps, which these warped, egotistical creatures would ever feel—produced its own reward; treacherous as small boys, selfish as gold-diggers, they nevertheless were protective toward Daisy; to have let slip a word which might get her and Hugo into trouble would have been like betraying the tribal totem.

Theirs was a perpetually shifting community. Members would vanish into hiding, or prison; new faces would appear, to be greeted familiarly or with reserve. The associations, so rapidly formed—for criminals can recognize one another as easily as compatriots in a foreign country—were as quickly broken: to maintain them long would attract the attention of informers and busies; or the partners in an enterprise might quarrel over methods, distribution of the spoils, suspicion that one partner was itching to double-cross the others. These men veered frantically between devotion to the accomplice of the moment and a permanent rankling mistrust. Even the criminal argot was changing constantly, like wartime codes.

During that winter they moved eight times to new lodgings—

a precautionary measure on Hugo's part. The association with Tacker was dropped, also for safety's sake, after the pair had made a killing which enabled Hugo to take Daisy into the country for Christmas. Then, their money nearly exhausted, they returned to the round of cheap rooms, fried-fish suppers, pin-ball arcades, the mooching from day to day, the furtive recognitions in pub or dance hall. This desultory, aimless life, varied only by hours of tension when Hugo was out on a job, had not yet begun to pall upon Daisy. She loved the crowds, the animation of the East End; Hugo was a perfect companion, who could make a jaunt out of a stroll down the street; and knowing she was in it up to the neck with him now gave Daisy a deep contentment. They were at war with society; and criminals, like fighting soldiers, live in the moment.

How long this might have gone on, nobody can say. But toward the end of April Daisy found herself pregnant. For some days she did not dare tell Hugo. Then one night, while he was reading aloud to her—a habit they had recently formed—the cozy domesticity of it encouraged her to speak. Hugo's reaction was not at all what she had expected. His face lightened with surprise, and then a shadow came over it.

"Oh, Daisy," he said at last. "My poor Daisy. *Now* what have I done to you?"

"Are you angry?" She could still be timid with him.

"Silly girl. It was bound to happen, wasn't it?"

Sitting on the arm of her chair, he gently kissed her. His face was darkened with a sadness which seemed like remorse.

"It's all right, darling," he said, but more to himself than to her. "Don't worry. I'll stick by you."

"I'm not worrying."

His eyes glanced round the sordid, untidy little room, with a look of repudiation.

"You needn't worry. Jacko will look after it."

Daisy could not help stiffening, shrinking away from him. As if expecting a blow, she hunched her shoulders.

"Oh *no*, Hugo. I won't—I want to have your baby." It came out

more loudly, defiantly than she meant. There was a brief silence.
Daisy felt his gaze upon her averted head, felt he was making
some mental adjustment. His voice did not ring quite true when
at last he said:

"Why, of course, love. What did you think I meant? Of course
we'll have it."

He went on to explain that Jacko could do the prenatal treatment and wangle her a bed in some hospital. How lucky they'd
got a tame medico on a string: it would obviate all the embarrassment of Daisy's having to declare herself to the National Health
Service as an unmarried woman.

It was an embarrassment Hugo could relieve her of, any day
and more simply. But such was her gratitude to him for not
opposing her about the baby that, at the moment, the idea of
marriage hardly entered her head. Entirely confident of his love,
accustomed so long to living with him as wife with husband,
Daisy had no need of the formal reassurance of marriage lines;
they could never mean more, now, than a practical convenience.
She did not even ask herself why Hugo failed to suggest it; and
she had her reward for this when, later, he said:

"You're a marvel, Daisy. Any other girl would have jumped at
this chance for putting the screws on me."

"But we *are* married, sweetheart," she replied simply. "Mar-
riages aren't made in registrars' offices."

"I would, if you really want it," he blurted out.

"Oh, there's plenty of time. What do we care?"

"Young Thomas will care."

"Young—who?"

"The baby, love. Thomas Bland-Chesterman. Blue eyes and
gold hair, just like his beautiful mum."

"No, I want him to be like you."

"Good God, that's a crazy sort of wish," he replied, half
seriously. "Give the poor little brute a chance."

"He's going to be the image of you. You're my ideal."

"Now you look like 'Lady Hamilton at Prayer' again." Hugo's

words were lightly teasing, but his voice was unsteady; and suddenly he knelt down, burying his head in her lap.

Two days later, having made an appointment, Daisy went to see Jacko. They had kept up with him during the last six months, going to dinner from time to time at Albert Grove, and occasionally, when they were at rock bottom, borrowing money, which Daisy was always scrupulous to repay. Jacko—in her presence, at any rate—never showed curiosity about their new way of life. "Still slumming?" he would ask quizzically, then turn the conversation.

"And what can I do for you, my pretty maid?" he said now, leading her into the dusky, veiled little house. "You were very mysterious on the telephone."

"I want to consult you, professionally." Daisy had thought up this form of words on her way here, and brought it out with a stilted air which made the man smile. He opened the consulting-room door for her, however, motioned her to a chair, and sat down at his desk, regarding her gravely; it was all done with a sort of ironic exaggeration, as though he were an adult playing a doctor-and-patient game with a child.

"I'm—I think I'm going to have a baby." She spoke at once, breathlessly. "Hugo said you would help."

For a few moments Jacko was silent. His lips moved, as if he were savoring something, some new sensation, rather dubiously.

"Well, well. And you want me to—"

"I'm going to *have* the baby," she put in, forestalling what she feared he would say.

"Good for you," he smoothly replied. "The father is reconciled to the idea?"

"Oh, Hugo's delighted. We've decided it's to be a boy, called Thomas." Daisy prattled on, unaware of a hardening in the speculative gaze of his brown, hang-dog eyes. She talked on, as it happened, to bury from him—perhaps from herself too—a sudden realization that she did not wish to be examined by him; she averted her eyes from his hands, her mind from what they had done to other women. Yet she was also a little discountenanced to find, presently, how correct, remote, clinical he became. It might have been a strange doctor, not their best friend, who fired questions at her, outlined plans for prenatal treatment, performed the physical examination and tests.

"I'll let you know the result in a couple of days," he said, as she put on her clothes behind a screen. "No doubt we'll get a positive reaction. You're a strong, healthy girl, and I don't anticipate any complications. Any physical complications, I mean. But come and see me again in a month's time."

"Will it—cost a great deal?" Daisy asked, as she prepared to go.

"Now don't you start worrying about that. Leave it all to old Jacko."

He had become human again—the man she knew. Gratefully, she learned forward, putting her cheek to his. His arms went round her; then his body was clinging to hers, softly, strangely, like a twining plant or a cobweb, with a kind of brittle, weak tenacity. And after a few moments he had released her, given her an unfathomable look and a brisk pat on the shoulder. She left the house, feeling obscurely sorry for him, so lonely there, so unloved.

10 Tragedy at Southbourne

DAISY said something of this to Hugo after she got back.

"Poor little Jacko? Don't you believe it," he replied, in the half-admiring, half-contemptuous tone he so often adopted when talking of his friend. "He likes living that way. Probably gets a kick out of terminating little embryos, too. He's as hard as nails, really."

"Oh, Hugo, but he can be so sympathetic!"

"Emotional frigging, that's what it is. The female patients love it. Oh, you've got to hand it to him."

"I think you're absolutely beastly about him."

"So *you've* fallen for that bedside manner too? Ah, what hopes it has raised in the girls! But it's the nearest he ever gets to—"

"Don't be so foul, Hugo. It's not like you. And why do you keep on with him if you despise him so?"

"I don't. I rather admire him. He's damned good company, and he's useful. He'd never let you down once you're really in with him. Why grudge him his vicarious pleasures?"

Their talk blew up to a row. Daisy had often felt the relationship between the two men as a closed circle, from which she was excluded, a freemasonry into which Hugo escaped from her; and this made her aggressive. But it was the last quarrel they were to have. As that chilly spring merged into a wet and doleful summer, Daisy throve on her pregnancy, growing ever more placid and self-possessed. During this period, Hugo continually astonished her by his tenderness, solicitousness. He insisted on their moving away from the East End and the circle of tough customers where he had been so much in his element. He found them furnished rooms in a relatively respectable street near

Russell Square, and his old restlessness hardly ever showed itself there: he seemed quite content to sit at home with Daisy, or take her walking in the parks when one of the rare bright days encouraged them to go out. They would talk endlessly about the baby, spinning plans for him as though the whole world would be at his feet. How strange, thought Daisy, for Jacko to have said that Hugo would be hopelessly irresponsible as a father; and Jacko's misjudging of him made her feel indulgent toward Jacko himself, no less than she was touched by this new Hugo, so that when the three of them were together she felt completely at ease.

Where the money came from to support their present way of life, whether it was borrowed or stolen, Daisy did not know; for it was part of Hugo's solicitude that she should not be worried by his affairs, and if he had any criminal enterprises afoot, he did not talk to her about them. From time to time he went out alone, telling her that he was looking for digs or a small flat where the landlord did not object to children. After the lease of their Maida Vale rooms terminated, Hugo had given her £50, the proceeds from the sale of his furniture there, and this money she kept to provide the necessaries for the baby. Fatalistic as she was, her condition made Daisy still less anxious about the morrow. Her life was concentrated upon the life within her, so that everything else, except Hugo, seemed remote, unreal, un-urgent, a dream which demanded nothing of her; but this unreality was different from the oppression she had experienced during her first months with Hugo; it was comforting, enveloping her like a cocoon.

So the weeks drifted by. In the first days of September, London drew breath again after a stuffy, overcast August. Asters, like children's windmills, spun their colored rays in the gardens, and the clouds, as if some celestial traffic jam had at last been broken up, bowled cheerfully across the sky. On one of these blowing days, about the middle of the month, Hugo returned in high excitement to the room where Daisy was knitting.

"We're going for a holiday, love. A second honeymoon. How do you like that?"

"Wonderful! But we can't afford it, can we?"

Hugo tugged a roll of notes from his trouser pocket and scattered them over her head.

"Danaë in a shower of gold! Where do you think these came from?"

The girl shook her head, laughing up at him.

"Old Jacko," he said.

"Oh, darling, ought we to be borrowing money from him?"

"It's not a loan. It's a free gift. Or rather—"

Hugo gave her one of those merry, crafty glances which never failed to enchant her—"or rather, it's conscience money."

"I don't understand."

"Well now, hold tight and I'll divulge all." Hugo sat down on the floor and laid his head on her knee.

"Do I look different?" he asked, gazing up at her.

"You look jolly pleased with yourself."

"The witness must confine herself to answering the question. Yes or No?"

"No."

"Hell's bells! I suggest to you that I look like a reformed character."

"Sweetheart, what *is* all this about?"

"My poor great beautiful nit-witted cluck, I'm *telling* you. You may have noticed my occasional absences from our residence recently. I was not, curiously enough, about my unlawful occasions. I was looking for a job."

"A job?" Daisy breathed incredulously.

"Yep. A humble post in the great army of mugs."

"Hugo! But why?"

"Aren't you pleased?"

"Ye-es. Yes, of course. But—"

"All that sort of thing"—he made a sweeping gesture, as if to include the East End pubs, the wide boys, the amusement arcades, the shifting, feckless, raffish life they had lived—"well, it suited me. And you were angelic about it. But it's not good enough for young Thomas."

The girl began to cry.

"Extraordinary, the effects of paternity," Hugo went on. "Sort of throwback to my lily-white origins. Never thought I'd have a relapse like this. Anyway, I got a nibble of a job the other day—selling advertising space. Nearly got it on the strength of my forceful and winning personality alone. Unfortunately the twirps came out from under the old spell just in time to ask for references. Which is where Jacko comes in."

"Jacko?" Daisy had quite forgotten how the conversation had started.

"Yes, Dopey. I needed two references. My company commander gave me quite a hot one, years ago of course. So, Jacko being the only other respectable ha-ha type I know well enough to ask, I applied to him. But the old bastard wouldn't play."

"Oh, darling! Surely he couldn't be so mean?"

"He could, and he was. One sees his point, of course. He's got to be damned careful about preserving his façade; if it came out that he'd recommended a bloke who'd been over the wall, it'd do him positively no good at all. Actually, he *was* a bit abashed at refusing. Hence these smackers." Hugo began to collect the notes off the floor. "And hence our holiday. Where shall we go?"

"But oughtn't you to have another go at the job first, sweetheart?"

"Jacko said you were peakish—though I must say you look blooming to me—and you ought to have some sea air. And secondly, this job thing needs a bit more organizing than I realized."

Hugo explained how difficult it was for a man with a prison record to get honest work—about as hard as entering a foreign country without a passport. There was a society for helping discharged prisoners, but he had not availed himself of its services, and it was a bit late in the day to do so now. Any employers would ask him what work he had been doing, and almost every employer would demand proof of it. "Can't get anywhere nowadays without bumf," said Hugo disgustedly; this meant, in his case, forged references, and someone to answer for them should an employer decide to take them up. The whole thing was a bind.

If there was any wrong in Hugo's working out a scheme of false pretenses in order to go straight, the simple-minded girl did not see it. At the moment, her feelings were confused—indignation with a world which made it so difficult for a man to reform, gratitude to Hugo that he was aiming to do so for the sake of their child, and a certain bewilderment at the idea of being uprooted from a way of life she had come to accept. Her old phantasy of Hugo as the honest breadwinner, now it looked like being realized, seemed less unequivocally desirable. He was such a volatile chap: if he went through with it, her instinct warned her, might he not tire quickly of dull, respectable work, and unload his resentment upon herself and the child, as if they had trapped him into a situation intolerable to him?

Such doubts, however, did not trouble Daisy for long. Her will had always shaped itself to his, and in her present condition she was only the more acquiescent. Like water, she reflected his moods, sparkling or glooming, rippling or sullenly congealed. Just now it was all light and movement; and if there was something feverish in Hugo's gaiety, she had felt that too often before to be disquieted by it. As they went down to Brighton, huddled together arm in arm at the corner of the railway carriage, Daisy knew she was the luckiest girl in the world.

They spent a few days at Brighton, then moved on to Southbourne. It was Daisy's idea to go there: she had a vivid memory of a picture postcard which her aunt had sent her from Southbourne many years ago. It was now the first week of October, and they found lodgings without any difficulty. Making amends for that dismal summer, the sun shone day-long, day after day. In a trance of quiet happiness, Daisy sat with Hugo on the esplanade, looking out over the great half moon of the bay, the golden sands, the long pier pointing toward the horizon. She imagined her child playing among those children on the shore one day; they would come here again, they would come every year when Hugo got his annual holidays. The Town Hall clock calmly chimed their hours away; a freshness of autumn and the sea mingled with the smell of asphalt drawn out by the sun's heat. It was all such worlds away from the greasy squalor of those London back streets, Daisy felt she had slid from one dream into another.

Some evenings they would stroll along to the harbor, whose narrow waterway ran deep into the town under two bridges, then broadened to a lagoon. Rusting hulks reclined groggily on the mud; there were yachts and paddle steamers laid up for the winter, and on the lagoon itself a sprinkling of small boats rode at their moorings. The little streets leading from the harbor offered a number of snug small pubs, patronized by longshoremen, the crews of rescue tugs, liberty men from the naval harbor which lay on the far side of the headland, sailors off the Channel steamers.

"It's romantic," sighed Daisy, leaning on Hugo's arm as they watched the lights of the night steamer recede toward the harbor mouth. "I'd like Thomas to be a sailor."

"Suppose it's a she?" Hugo teased her. "I don't fancy having a stewardess in the family."

"Well, she could be an air hostess. Flying all over the world. Must be a wonderful job."

"Why not marry her to a millionaire? Then she could have her own airplane."

"Silly! If she could marry a man just like you—that's all I'd ask."

They turned into one of the little pubs near the quayside, and Hugo ordered Hollands for them both. The bar was divided up into snugs by high-backed settles, as in an old-fashioned restaurant. Woodwork and brass shone like a naval pinnace's. The bar was already fairly crowded, but most of the company were regulars, playing dominoes, talking quietly and intermittently, so that Daisy was able to hear a conversation taking place behind the settle where she and Hugo had established themselves.

". . . Don't give me Princess. You want to know what I think? I'll tell you then. She's a spy."

"If she's a spy, you're Marilyn Monroe."

"What she come to roost for in a dead-alive hole like South-bourne then? If she's a bona-fide resident, why does she hang about the pubs this end of town?"

"All right, you tell us."

"I'm telling you. Because it's handy to the naval harbor see, and the navy lads talk when they're in these pubs. She come from Rumania, didn't she, and Rumania's Red, isn't it? Trouble with you, matey, you couldn't recognize a hammer and sickle if little old Malenkov walked in and stuck it under your nose."

"Wait a minute. Look. Spies don't make themselves con-spicuous. They don't want anyone to notice them. Now the Princess—well, I ask you! Those hats she wears, and talking in broken English, and—"

"Double bluff. Where does she get her money from, then? You answer me that. You know what the rent of those houses in Queen's Parade is? Well I do. Here's a woman who's supposed to have escaped just in time from the revolution over there—a refugee—the Commies take over her family estates. Why isn't she broke, like any other D.P.?"

"I can answer that one." It was a third voice, mellow with liquor and authoritative. "She got out with the family jewels. Worth a king's ransom. The Popescus were one of the wealth-iest—"

"You *seen* these jewels?" broke in the first speaker skeptically.

"No, but my niece Alice did. She was working for the Princess. The old girl took a fancy to Alice, and showed them her one day. That was some years ago, mind you. She must have popped a few of 'em by now. But she told Alice they'd last her out her time all right."

Daisy stole a glance at Hugo. He was sitting quite still, gazing into his glass of Hollands. She put out a hand, in what might have been a restraining gesture; and when Hugo felt it on his wrist, he started.

"Want to go, love?" he said.

The girl shook her head. Hugo gazed at her more attentively.

Then he whispered: "Don't you worry. That's all over and done with now. . . ."

The next evening, Daisy was not feeling so well. She decided to go to bed early, and Hugo went out for a drink alone. He returned, an hour or so later, in high excitement. At the bar of the Queen's Hotel, he told her, he had met an old acquaintance, a trainer, who had a horse running in the local races tomorrow—an outsider which simply could not lose; it was a red-hot tip.

"And, do you know, love, it's called Autumn Daisy! If ever there was a sign from heaven! Shall we have a real splash on it?"

"Oh, darling, you know we haven't much money."

"But the odds, my pet. Twenty to one. Think of it. Come on, say yes."

She could never refuse him when he was in this boyish, extravagant mood, for it filled her with his own recklessness. She was a little dashed, the following morning, to find that he did not intend to take her, but was quickly comforted when he said: "No, love. You get a rough crowd at these local meetings. Too much bumping and boring—might be bad for young Thomas."

She sat out on the sea front all that afternoon, making clothes for the baby, sunning herself, and basking in the thought of Hugo enjoying himself; it was good for him to get away from her now and then.

So, when Hugo got back to their lodgings that evening, the sight of his face, tight and haunted, was all the more of a shock.

"What's the matter, love?"

"The bloody brute fell down on me," he flung out. "Beaten by a head. I could kill myself."

"Never mind, precious, it's only a horse."

"A horse? A God-blasted, spavined cripple. It had the race in the bag, and then—"

"How much did you put on it?"

Hugo's expression changed, from black rage to a kind of childish mutinous guilt. Looking away from her, he sullenly muttered: "Fifty quid."

"But where did you get fifty—?"

"You agreed we should have a real splash, put our shirt on it."

"Oh, Hugo! You didn't take the money I was keeping for the baby?"

"Yes I did take the money we were keeping for the baby!" he exclaimed furiously. "Where the hell else would I get fifty pounds?"

It was her heartbroken tones, Daisy knew, which had stung him into this cruel violence. What Jacko had said once—"you must accept him for better *and* for worse"—came into her mind, and she made a superhuman effort to conceal the grief, resentment, dismay which she felt.

"Never mind, darling. We'll manage," she said at last.

"I am to be forgiven?"

Daisy fought down her temper, which had risen at the sneer behind these words. She spoke quietly: "There's nothing to forgive, my sweetheart. It was your money."

At once, with an impetuous movement, he was beside her.

"Oh, Daisy, Daisy, I'm sorry, I am sorry! I'm utterly worthless. I even have to steal from my own wife and child."

Her heart lifted, hearing him call her "wife," and she began to soothe him. She hated his self-pitying mood, anyway—hated, or feared, anything he did to humiliate himself. But he went on brokenly: "I did it for young Thomas, for you both. It would have given him a proper start in life. And it was a certainty—an absolute certainty. It'd have won us £1,000, given me time to look around for a decent job. You could have had a nurse for the baby. And now I go and muck everything up!"

"Darling, please don't. We can—"

"I'll make it up to you, I swear I will. I'll get that money back somehow."

"Yes, love, of course you will. It'll be all right, I promise you."

The next morning Hugo went out early. When he returned, he told her he had found cheaper lodgings nearby. He was determined that she should not miss the last few days of her holiday. As Hugo paid the landlady, Daisy heard him say they had been called back to London suddenly. "Well, I couldn't very

well tell her we were moving to other lodgings in Southbourne,
could I? She'd have been dreadfully offended," Hugo explained
when Daisy commented on this later. The new lodgings were
five minutes' walk away. When they arrived, Hugo registered
them as Mr. and Mrs. Bland; he had often used Daisy's maiden
name like this, and she thought no more about it.

The scene of the previous night had taxed the girl more
severely than she realized, so she was quite amenable to Hugo's
suggestion that she should lie down and rest after lunch. He himself went out, not returning till the late afternoon. They had
high tea together. Then Hugo asked her, if she felt better, to
come out for a blow with him. He changed into his dark green
tweed suit, put on a cap she had bought him in Brighton, and
tucking a brown-paper parcel under his arm, led Daisy out of the
house. He was very gentle with her, but subdued and withdrawn
—which Daisy put down to the shame he felt at having lost them
the £50. But she herself was still too numbed by that bitter blow
to react with her usual sensitivity.

They sat down in a shelter on the esplanade. Hugo clung to
her side, yet his mind did not seem with her. Presently, as if by
a hard physical effort, he detached his arm from hers.

"Wait for me here," he said abruptly. "I shan't be very long."

He flipped his hand at her, unsmiling, and walked away into
the dark, walking with that limber, self-contained gait which
always made him look alone, even in a crowd. "Come back,
Hugo?" To Daisy it sounded like a scream, but she had only
whispered the words, and he did not even glance back.

The girl was used to these comings and goings of Hugo's,
sudden and unexplained; but this evening it felt different. Her
eye lit upon the brown-paper parcel. Had Hugo left it behind by
mistake? She would have run after him with it, but he was
already out of sight and she did not know where he had gone.
The Town Hall clock chimed a quarter—7:15. Daisy opened the
parcel. It contained a length of rope, about twenty feet, with a
hook at one end. She gazed at it in a stupor. Her first thought—
she almost smiled at the absurdity of it—was that Hugo had gone

off to hang himself and forgotten to take the rope. But it could be used for burglary too. Her mind filled with vague misgivings. Carefully she did up the parcel again, then pushed it behind her as if to conceal from herself the riddle it contained.

The incoming tide crept up, a splash of sea upon the pebbled beach below, then the hoarse, bronchial, rattling sound, as of wounded lungs gasping hard for air, when a wave drew back, dragging at the stones. From time to time, strollers went past; but Daisy, wrapped up in her own foreboding, did not notice them. A fantastic notion had begun to pluck at her mind—that Hugo had gone forever, deserted her, and left her the rope to hang herself with. She thought she must be going mad. Getting up, she moved to the edge of the esplanade and gripped the iron railing. She was still standing there, peering seaward, when, half an hour after he had left her, Hugo returned.

Daisy flung herself upon his breast, sobbing, "I thought you were never coming." He comforted her, but in an absent-minded way so unlike himself, so mechanical, that she drew back and looked full into his face, and saw a fixed wild glare she had never seen there before.

"What's the matter, love? What is it?"

"Nothing. Come on, let's go back."

"All right. Oh, what about that parcel? You left it behind."

"You may as well throw it away now."

She flung it down on the beach below the esplanade, and took his arm. It was like walking with an automaton.

"Where's your cap, darling?" she asked. "Have you lost it?"

"It blew off," he answered, still in that dead voice. Petrified by this stranger who had returned to her, Daisy said nothing more, though she was hurt that he expressed no sorrow at losing a present she had given him.

When they got back to their lodgings, Hugo sat for a short while, still as a stone image except for his fingers ceaselessly tapping on the table. Then he jumped up again, saying he must go for a walk, and was out of the door before Daisy could stop him. Calling to him to wait for her, she put on a coat and ran downstairs after him. Daisy had known these moods of his before, which froze him into glum silence and made him at the same time edgy and restless; she knew from experience there was no talking him out of them. One had to distract him, as one would distract a child from a fit of grief by showing it some new object. She suggested now that they should go to a cinema, and listlessly he agreed.

The next morning, when the landlady brought in their breakfast, she was breathless with excitement.

"Terrible doings last night! It's all over Southbourne. A murder. A police Inspector was shot. Burglar trying to get into a house on Queen's Parade. Such a respectable district. But you're not safe anywhere nowadays, I always say. Poor man had a wife and kiddies, too."

Part Two

11   The Morning After

Hugo and Daisy sat up in bed, reading the local paper which the landlady had laid on their breakfast tray. The *Southbourne Echo*, like many of the older residents of the town it served, seemed a relic of more spacious days. Its layout was old-fashioned, its style formal: if any newspaper could have succeeded in making the events of the previous night sound unsensational, it was the *Southbourne Echo*.

Police Inspector Herbert Stone, of Southbourne, well known to visitors in the town for many years as the Parade Inspector, was shot last night by an unknown man who is believed to be a burglar. He died within a few minutes. The murderer made his escape, and up to a late hour the police search for him had been unsuccessful. The fatality occurred outside the residence of Princess Popescu, in Queen's Parade, which leads from the sea front, east of the Queen's Hotel, to the main shopping center. Little is definitely known as to the circumstances leading up to the crime, but it is established that about 7:25 P.M. a man was seen on the top of a porch, above the front door of the house.

On receiving a telephone call from Princess Popescu's companion, Mrs. Felstead, Inspector Stone proceeded to Queen's Parade. Entering the front garden, the Inspector was shot and severely wounded. He went out into the road, and was then shot again. One bullet entered his chest, causing a fatal wound. Several persons heard the report of the shots, and an alarm was at once raised. Subsequently a man was seen running down the road toward the sea front, and a cloth cap was found in the garden of an adjacent house.

Princess Popescu, who is a well-known local figure and related to the former royal family of Rumania, told our reporter that the unknown assailant had not succeeded in breaking into her house; but there is little doubt that his intention was to commit a burglary.

A keen bowls player, Inspector Stone, who joined the Wessex

Constabulary twenty-four years ago, was transferred to the South-bourne Police in 1940. He was a popular figure in Southbourne, and leaves a widow and three children.

"Well, that's torn it," said Hugo. "We'll have to get out of here double-quick."

Daisy sat rigid, her tea growing cold. She felt she could not breathe, so terrible was the oppression weighing upon her. There were so many questions she wanted, and feared, to ask; any of them would sound like an accusation. Why did you leave me last night? Where did you go? What was that rope for? How did you lose your cap? Why were you so strange when you came back? The questions tapped and tapped in her head, like hammers. She felt, even above her anxiety and bewilderment, an immense pitying love for Hugo, a passionate desire to help him. But there was no way to help him: except by silence, by holding back those questions which were all accusations.

He had got out of bed and was opening the gladstone bag he always kept padlocked. With affrighted eyes she stared as he took out a revolver and began to clean it.

"Hurry up and get dressed, love," he said, not even looking up at her. Automatically she started to obey, then sat down heavily on the edge of the bed, crying. "What is it, pet? Look, your tea is getting cold. Be a good girl and drink it."

"That gun!" she sobbed. "I can't bear it!"

"We've got to get rid of it. They'll be combing this town, and any chap with a police record they find—he's had it. I know them. How much money have you left?"

Daisy groped blindly in her bag. There were two £1 notes and a little silver.

He said, "We'll need more than that. My brother'll have to fork out. We'll put through a call on the way to the beach, and then bury this little old gun." As he spoke, Hugo wrapped the revolver in a handkerchief he had been rubbing it with, and stowed it in his trouser pocket. "Better get onto Jacko, too, while we're about it. He'll have to look after you for a bit, till this kerfuffle dies down."

"No, Hugo, please! I don't want to leave you!" the girl cried.

"It's only for a little, my pet. There may be some unpleasantness, and I'm not having you involved. I've got to be pretty mobile, and I've got to disappear till they've found the chap who did this: which means being alone."

Hugo spoke briskly, kindly, if in a preoccupied voice, as though the need for action had dispelled the nightmare stagnation of his mood last night. But his businesslike tone had only thickened the nightmare for Daisy. It gave her the feeling of being enclosed in a small box, blinded, suffocated, with no possible way out, shut off from Hugo and all hope.

She found she had got herself dressed, without remembering one single movement of the process. Hugo was saying: "Yes. Jacko's a good idea, if he can get down. You're his patient, after all. Patient taken poorly. Medico sent for—old family friend. Examines patient. Slight operation required. Perfect reason for sudden return to London. No suspicions raised in landlady."

"*Hugo!*" It was almost a scream. Daisy, half distraught, could stand no more. She controlled herself, and, in a voice roughened with emotional exhaustion, began again. "Hugo. *Please!* What am I to say if they ask me about last night? The police. Or anyone. Just tell me what to say."

"Sorry, love. I'm in a bit of a tiz." He came over, and, putting his hands on Daisy's shoulders, looked straight into her eyes. "You remember that chap who tipped me the sign, on the front, a couple of days after we came here? He was with another man, and a woman. He's a chap called Joe. In the profession. Well, I ran into him again in the bar at the Queen's Hotel. Actually, it was he who put me onto that bloody horse."

"Oh, Hugo, but you said it was the trainer."

"He *knows* the trainer," said Hugo impatiently. "I couldn't go into all that with you. Anyway, he told me he'd got a job lined up, and would I like to cut in. I said no, I'd finished with that lark. Then I lost the £50. I was desperate to get it back for you. So I went to see Joe again. He gave me that parcel of rope to keep, and said to meet him at the Queen's at 7:15—that was last

night—then we'd do the job together. Well, I wanted to and I
didn't want to. You know. I was worried. Expect that was why
I left the rope behind. Couldn't make up my mind to go through
with it. But it seemed the only hope; so finally I toddled off, as
you remember. I was only a few minutes late at the Queen's, but
Joe wasn't there. I waited nearly half an hour, and he never
turned up. Must have double-crossed me and tried to do the job
alone. The rope was a dumb idea, anyway. Those climbing ropes
with hooks are only good for houses that have verandas, which
the houses in Queen's Parade haven't. So now you know all, my
precious."

"You've got an alibi then." Daisy was smiling brilliantly with
relief. She believed everything he had said, because she wanted
to believe it, but also because it made sense—it was just like
Hugo. No wonder he'd been in such a state last night—utterly
deflated after having keyed himself up for a crisis which never
arrived, and in despair that the money for the baby's birth was
still lacking..

"An alibi?" he asked.

"Yes. Somebody must have seen you at the Queen's Hotel,
surely?"

"I don't know so much about that. Naturally, as I was up to a
bit of no good, and in the near neighborhood, I didn't make
myself conspicuous. Just sat in the hall lounge, where Joe was to
pick me up, behind a newspaper."

"But couldn't Joe—?"

"Give evidence that he'd made an appointment with me there,
to do a burglary, and then stood me up? Use your loaf, girl. Joe's
not a charitable institution. Who knows he didn't bump off this
copper himself, come to that? No, Joe'll be keeping himself out
of circulation for a while now. And so must I. Let's get cracking."

They went first to the General Post Office, where Hugo shut
himself up in a telephone booth. Daisy sat down on a bench and
waited, her eyes straying uneasily to the door whenever someone
entered. Half her mind was on what Hugo had just told her: yes,
it made sense; but something was missing, and she wearily
groped for it. In the telephone booth, Hugo's lips were moving.

He had got through—to his brother? to Jacko? Daisy saw him run his fingers through his dark hair, in a familiar gesture. Ah, the cap! It said in the paper a cap had been found near the scene of the crime. Oh God, said Daisy to herself, aren't there thousands of men with caps in Southbourne alone?

When they had left the Post Office and were walking toward the sea front, Hugo said: "That's O.K. Mark is coming down this afternoon, early. And he's going to ring up Jacko."

"What did you tell him?"

"Said I was broke. And in trouble. S.O.S. Old Mark isn't a bad stick. He rallies round."

They came out on the esplanade, near the bandstand. The sun was still shining, and it had brought out quite a few people to saunter along the front or read their papers in the shelters.

"Might as well be in Piccadilly," Hugo muttered. He helped Daisy down the steep stone steps onto the beach, and they sat with their backs against the sea wall. Hugo took her hand, giving her one of his quick, mischievous glances.

"Shall I make love to you, darling?"

"I'm not much use to you nowadays, sweetheart, am I?" she absently replied. Then he was whispering in her ear: "Lie down flat. Put your left arm round me. Dig a deep hole in the pebbles with your right hand. People will only see a couple of lovers, and they'll look away pretty sharp if we're locked in a passionate embrace."

The girl gave a shuddering little moan. It was a moment of such anguish as she had never experienced: it was all wrong, all wrong. Then Hugo was leaning over her, on his elbows, his body hiding her right arm.

"Go on, love. Dig. A nice deep hole."

She scrabbled at the pebbly shingle, in an ecstasy of embarrassment and fright, tearing her nails, only wanting to get it over quickly—this mockery of their sweet love-making, while Hugo's lips wandered on her face and his right hand played with her tumbling hair.

"Oh, this is horrible," she whimpered. "I can't go on."

"Don't be so soppy," he breathed, his lips against hers. "All in a good cause, love."

Finally it was done: the revolver transferred from Hugo's pocket to the cavity, and the shingle smoothed over it. He seemed disposed to linger here, but Daisy scrambled to her feet and went stumbling along the beach, as if fleeing from a crime. When Hugo caught up with her, he was quite annoyed for a moment.

"Do you *want* to call attention to us? Anyone who was looking would think I'd tried to rape you and you were running away from me. That's just asking for trouble."

Tears came to Daisy's eyes. "You're so cold-blooded about it all."

"*Some*body's got to keep their head. You don't seem to realize what a jam I'm in."

"But you're innocent!"

"Tell that to the dear constabulary. They'll be out for blood, and they won't be too particular whose blood it is. . . ."

Mark Amberley and Jacko arrived soon after lunch: they had traveled down to Southbourne together. Daisy, who had not met Mark since the scene at his house a year ago, felt a kind of social embarrassment which, under the circumstances, she knew to be ridiculous. Nor did he make things any less difficult for her. He was obviously ill at ease, kept sitting down then standing up again, and created in the drab little parlor the atmosphere of a station waiting room. When he had first come in, after nervously greeting his brother he had turned to Daisy, hand outstretched; then his short-sighted eyes took in her condition and swerved away from her. She realized that Hugo had never told him about the coming child. Jacko, on the other hand, was glancing round him interestedly and making affable small talk, as if this was a housewarming he had been invited to. For a few minutes, till Daisy could have screamed, they chatted about the weather, the train service, any triviality. Then Hugo broke the unnatural constraint.

"Mark, old boy, do stop fidgeting about. You look like a fly on a window pane."

Smiling uncertainly, Mark sat down again. Jacko stood with one elbow on the mantelpiece, regarding the hideous ornaments displayed there, while the other three were now round the table with its red baize cloth and dispirited-looking maidenhair fern in the middle. Mark made a great effort: "Well now, what's up, Hugo? You were rather secretive over the telephone, you know."

"You brought some money?"

"Yes, but—"

"Good man. And you've read today's paper?"

"You mean about the shooting of that—?"

"Yep. It's a bastard. I suppose Southbourne station was buzzing with bluebottles when you arrived?"

"Bluebottles?"

"Bogies. Flatties. Policemen."

"Well, yes. There seemed to be one at each barrier."

"Now look, old boy. With your stainless past you won't realize it. But anyone here who's got a prison record—"

Jacko gave a theatrical "psst," and moving to the door with exaggerated caution, flung it open. There was nobody there.

"Do cut out the play-acting, Jacko."

"One never knows, with landladies." Jacko gave his doglike grin, then sat down beside Daisy. "Carry on, my dear Hugo."

Hugo proceeded to explain his predicament. He spoke crisply, more like a staff officer than a suppliant or a potential suspect. He must get out of the town and go into hiding for a while. Which meant, among other things, temporarily separating from Daisy. Which meant that someone else must look after Daisy. Mark Amberley, who was flushing and fidgeting harder than ever as the enormity of the situation broke upon him, at last interrupted:

"W-wait, j-just a mi-minute, Hugo. Surely all this is quite unnecessary. You've got an alibi, I take it?" He pronounced "alibi" as if it were some novel and probably disreputable term employed by a rival school of criticism.

"Oh for Christ's sake, Mark! If you'd ever taken yourself out
of the cotton wool you're swathed in, you'd know better than to
go neighing about alibis."

"Hugo, please!" protested Daisy.

"I haven't got a sweet little alibi. I just happened to be somewhere else. But I doubt if I could prove it. And anyway, if a
bobby runs into a bullet, his chums don't give a sod for alibis.
Once the Law's got its knife into you—"

"I can't say I'm surprised." Mark's voice was suddenly high
and quavering with indignation.

"Can't say you're surprised at what?"

"Why should they treat murderers like—as if they were decent
people? It was a brutal thing, shooting that inspector. And the
chap who did it deserves what he'll get. You talk as if criminals
ought to be protected from the police. I can't share that point
of view."

"Be careful, Mark." Hugo spoke with dangerous calm. Daisy
had heard that tone before, and it terrified her—so much so that,
without thinking, simply in order to interpose something between the two men, she said:

"The poor chap had a family. I'm ever so sorry for them."

"Pipe down, Daisy, and let my brother finish his sermon."

"Exactly. But that doesn't occur to Hugo. 'If a bobby runs into
a bullet'! How awfully careless of him! No one to blame but himself for the misadventure! He should have dodged, I suppose, or
been somewhere else—not interfering with burglars who are
just inoffensively trying to make a living. The self-pity of the
average criminal makes me vomit!"

Hugo had listened to this, with lips compressed and his
swarthy face darkening. Daisy turned imploring eyes upon Jacko;
but he was sitting up, absorbed in the altercation, a bright,
anticipative, half-smiling expression on his face. Once again,
Daisy was reminded of the ringside spectator. But, almost as
soon as she gave Jacko that imploring look, he became aware of
it; his face changed, and he winked at her reassuringly. And as

Hugo, stung to fury by his brother's sarcasm, jumped to his feet, evidently intending to go for him, Jacko said lightly:

"Now, now, now! Don't let's get worked up."

"If you'd like to come outside, Mark, and repeat that sanctimonious rubbish—"

"Some other time," said Jacko, in his throaty, ingratiating voice, which took an edge on it as he added, "For one thing, it's not very good for my patient here to be involved in domestic brawls. Could we think about her for a moment?"

"O.K. Think away," said Hugo ungraciously.

"Would you agree to her staying with me, till things are straightened out?"

"As a matter of fact, I was going to suggest that."

"Oh, Jacko, you are kind. But—"

"That's all right, Daisy. My housekeeper lives in, you know. She'll be your chaperone."

"My God, how respectable we're all becoming!" Hugo was amused, but still a bit disgruntled. Mark had got under his skin properly.

"I'd offer to take your—take Daisy myself," said Mark. "But I don't know if Gertrude—"

"Very good of you, I'm sure," said Hugo brusquely. "We quite see your difficulty."

"Well, that's Daisy disposed of." Jacko looked round like a chairman of committee. "Now we come to Hugo. You're set on clearing out for a while, are you?"

"Of course. Why?"

Jacko moistened his lips. "Only that running away *might*, under certain circumstances, be interpreted as an admission of guilt." He said it with a slight upward inflection that made it sound like a tactful suggestion, or even a query.

"I've got to risk that. You don't expect me to hang about here, waiting to be picked up, just to demonstrate my innocence?"

Jacko gave his companionable chuckle. "No. But you could go back to London openly, with Daisy, and resume your normal life. As if nothing had happened."

" 'As if?' Nothing has happened, as far as I'm concerned."

"Nothing happened!" Mark broke out with a kind of bewildered, querulous violence. "We're all talking as if—" He gulped, and started again. "I've never been in a situation like this. It's a nightmare. Doesn't make sense. Of course, I want to help. I've brought you £20, Hugo—and I expect I can manage some more. But—" he dithered into silence.

"What's on your mind, old boy? I'm grateful for the cash. Really. Forget what I said just now. You know I always had a foul temper."

"It's not that." With a visible effort Mark forced himself to look straight at his brother. "I only want to know . . . Hugo, you *didn't* do this thing? You swear that?"

"If you don't believe me, there'd be no use my swearing."

"That revolver of yours, Hugo. I'm sorry, but I simply can't forget—"

Smiling, Hugo held up his hands, like a man about to be searched. "Take it easy, boy. I got rid of the nasty firearm. Quite a while ago."

Daisy had winced when the revolver was mentioned. She could not help it, for the burying episode had been so atrocious to her that she was still emotionally flayed. She hung her head, unable to meet the glance of amused complicity which Hugo had given her. She was unaware that one of the other two men had noticed her wince, and was now giving her a curious, covert scrutiny.

12 "We'll Get Him"

WHILE the four of them were talking in that lodging-house room, another conference had begun half a mile away. Early this morning, after a discussion with Chief Inspector Nailsworth, the Chief Constable had telephoned Scotland Yard, and Detective Inspector Thorne was sent down to Southbourne in response to his appeal for help. The three men, with a stenographer at hand, were now sitting round a table in Nailsworth's office at the police station. The Town Hall clock, on the other side of the square, tossed its golden chimes over the town, and a shaft of sunlight, striking through the dusty window, fell upon Nailsworth's hands, stretched out on the table before him. They were large hands, in proportion to his huge body; and the left hand, with a signet ring on its little finger, kept clenching and opening again.

The Chief Constable glanced up from his papers. Nailsworth's face, round, pink and smooth, surmounted with short flaxen hair, wore an implacable expression which Colonel Allison had never seen upon it till today. Normally a good-humored, easy-going man, the life and soul of police smoking concerts, Nailsworth seemed to have gone hard in a night. Allison was aware, unofficially, that his Chief Inspector was known to subordinates as "Elephant"—not only for his immense bulk but for an incredibly retentive memory. Nailsworth was too big a man, in character as well as physique, ever to have used that memory vindictively; neither the police force nor the petty criminals of Southbourne had any grievances on that score. But Herbert Stone, the dead man, had been an old friend and comrade, and today, "the elephant never forgets" bore a different meaning.

"A bad business," Thorne was saying conventionally. The

Detective Inspector was a peaky, colorless man, with one of those long, questing noses which seem made for poking into trouble.

"I saw his wife again just now. It's finished her." Nailsworth's face, so bland and pink, was momentarily convulsed; it startled the Chief Constable, as if a doll had suddenly expressed violent emotion. Nailsworth was taking it even harder than he had realized.

"Well, gentlemen, let's get down to it," said Allison briskly. "Will you put Thorne in the picture?"

Nailsworth flicked a fingernail over the reports which lay before him; he only had to refer to them once during the discussion that followed. Detective Inspector Thorne's long nose pointed at Nailsworth, as if he were listening with it.

"At 7:32 last night," began Nailsworth, "the sergeant on duty received a telephone message from 17 Queen's Parade, to the effect that a man had been seen lying on the porch over the front door. The house belongs to a foreign lady, Princess Popescu—she's lived in Southbourne some years now, and it was her companion, a Mrs. Felstead, who rang us up. The duty sergeant telephoned to Herbert—Inspector Stone; Herbert looks after the Parade district, you understand, and has—had a small office nearby. He said he'd go and investigate. Four minutes later we had another call here. The Princess herself. Said there was a man shot, and to send help at once. The sergeant detailed P. C. Bowyer, and got in touch with our Police Surgeon."

Without looking down, Nailsworth flicked a page from off the top of the sheaf and continued.

"Herbert—Inspector Stone was lying on the pavement outside the house. He was dead by the time they arrived. Dr. James's report: bullet wound between second and third ribs on the left-hand side; another on the edge of the left lung. Bullet had passed through the heart and lodged under the surface of the right lung twelve inches from the point where it entered the body."

"Fired from above and to the left," said Thorne, his thin nose twitching.

"Just so. By the chap on the porch. Now then. We have an eye-witness to the shooting. Princess Popescu's cabby—"

"Cabby?" broke in the Detective Inspector. "Do you mean—?"

"I mean cabby." Nailsworth's quiet, impersonal voice took on a slight edge. "We have a few horse cabs here still. Visitors seem to like them. And the Princess regularly uses one; she's old-fashioned. This particular cabby, Charles Poore, is about as old as his vehicle. And as slow. Which doesn't help. Anyway, he'd gone to Queen's Parade to drive the Princess and her companion out to dinner. He drew up outside the house and waited a few minutes. Then he noticed a movement on the porch over the front door—saw a man's head and shoulders."

"Can I just get these times right?" said Thorne. "You say the first telephone call came in here at 7:32. But, according to your local newspaper, the man was first noticed 'about 7:25.' Why the delay ringing you up? Or was the paper wrong?"

Chief Inspector Nailsworth nodded approvingly: this Scotland Yard chap seemed up to his work.

"No. There *was* a delay. The cabby looked at his watch when he arrived. It was a little after 7:20. Saw this bloke a few minutes later—he must have been up on the porch already, before the cab got there. The Princess was dressing in her bedroom—the window's directly above the porch—with the curtains closed and the light on. The burglar was presumably waiting for her to go out of the room."

"And what was the cabby waiting for?"

"Charles Poore did not give the alarm at once. He *says*, because he thought the chap might be a workman, or a guest—the porch top is a sort of balcony, with a low wall. Actually, of course, the old fool was scared the Princess might ask him to do something about it. Anyway, she and Mrs. Felstead came out presently, and the cabby drove off with them. About a hundred yards down the road, he got an attack of conscience or something—stopped the cab and told the ladies about the man he had seen. The Princess ordered him to go back. She's a queer old guy —what's the word—?"

"Flamboyant," suggested the Chief Constable.

"That's it, sir. But she's got nerve. Walked straight in, and her friend telephoned the police."

"Any maids kept?" asked Thorne.

"A cook-housekeeper. Italian girl. Her mistress had given her the evening out, though. Poore turned his cab round again, to be facing the way the ladies wanted to go—that's *away* from the sea front, north." Nailsworth tapped a large finger on the sketch map which lay in front of Thorne. "It was the Princess's idea—to make it look as if she'd just turned back for something she'd forgotten, and not frighten off the burglar. He saw Herbert come along on his bicycle, saw him go in at the front gate—there's a tablecloth of garden between the house and the pavement. He couldn't see the chap on the porch just then. But he heard Herbert call out, 'Come down, old man!'"

Nailsworth paused, to get control over his voice. His mouth quivered, then set into a line so thin that it almost disappeared. Inspector Thorne tactfully looked down at the sketch map.

"He didn't give him a chance," Nailsworth began again, in a tight, violent tone. "That b—— fired as soon as the words were out of Herbert's mouth. And if ever I lay my hands on him, God help him, that's all I say!"

"Let's stick to the facts, my dear chap, shall we?" said the Chief Constable gently.

"Sorry, sir." Nailsworth's face was wooden again, but his hand on the table still clenched and unclenched. "The cabby saw this chap's head and shoulders appear above the low parapet of the porch—as if he was trying to sit up, Poore said. Then there was a flash, a report, and Poore's horse started to bolt. He heard another report. He managed to stop the horse a few hundred yards up the road; but by the time he'd got back to the house, the murderer was away, toward the sea front, the opposite direction from what the horse had bolted in. We have a witness, though, who saw a man running down the road toward the front. This witness says he was a smallish man—five feet six or seven was his guess. And she and the cabby both agree that he was wearing some dark-colored suit."

"That the best they can do, between them?"

"It was getting dark, remember. And Poore's sight isn't up to much, anyway. He *might* be able to identify him, or he might not. The other witness only saw his back."

"What about the Princess?"

"She was looking out of a front window, at the left of the porch. She heard the first shot. Then Herbert, who'd been standing to the right of it, came into her view." Nailsworth's voice went utterly colorless; he fumbled for the typewritten sheets before him, and as if he could not trust himself to use his own words, read out a few lines. " 'The Inspector staggered away from the door. He was bent double, clutching himself and gasping. Then I heard another bang. The Inspector gave a shudder. He was reeling through the front gate, and he collapsed on the pavement. I could not look any more. I was hiding my eyes for a little time. Then I went to telephone again for help.' "

"Hiding her eyes when this bird jumped down off the porch, I suppose?" said Thorne sourly. "We don't seem to be in luck."

"Herbert wasn't in luck either." Nailsworth's upper lip curled back from his teeth, and he looked at Thorne as though he hated him.

Colonel Allison interposed: "Afraid we haven't got much to show you, Thorne. No fingerprints on the porch or bedroom window. We took casts of some footprints in the mold of the front garden, but they're probably Stone's. There's the cap, of course. Poore *thought* the fellow was wearing a cap, and we found one just inside the garden of a house, seven doors up the road, the way he ran. It's a pretty new cap. Name of a Brighton shop in it. Nailsworth sent a man there this morning, and he's telephoned the shopkeeper's information: the cap was one of a consignment that only came in a month ago; so far he's only sold four of them; he might be able to identify the purchaser."

Inspector Thorne scratched the end of his long nose. "This bird seems to have been in a hell of a panic," he said ruminatively. "You say there were no signs of his trying to break in?"

"No, but he was obviously waiting till—"

"I'm sorry, sir, but that's not my point. At that stage he could only have been charged with intent; yet he shoots to kill, twice, rather than be arrested on a minor charge. That's amateurish, panicky. Then he throws away his cap—"

"It could have blown off as he ran."

"I grant you that, sir. Yes, I dare say jumping down from that porch would have loosened it." Thorne studied the plan before him. "The porch is ten feet high, I see, and no side supports. He must be quite a climber. And no rope was found? That may give us a line." The inspector scratched his nose again. "How did he know the house would be empty that night?"

"I talked to the maid," said Nailsworth. "She swears that no strangers came round inquiring—anyway, the Princess tells me she only decided two days before to go out for dinner."

Thorne's peaky face looked sharper than ever. "There you are again! It's amateur work. A professional would have cased the house beforehand; he'd not climb up and lie over the porch, with the bedroom light on behind the curtains, on the off chance that the occupants were all going to be out presently. It doesn't make sense."

"What's in your mind, Inspector?" said Allison.

"Could there be a political angle? This Princess now—what do we know about her?"

"She's Rumanian. An expatriate. Escaped over here when the revolution broke out. Eccentric old girl, but quite harmless. Why?"

"There's a lot of cloak-and-dagger stuff going on nowadays, as you know, sir. This attempt at burglary wouldn't look so amateurish if it was an attempt at assassination, or to steal political papers, say. Foreigners get panicky—they're quicker on the trigger than us."

"Then why didn't he shoot the Princess the first time she went out of the house?" Inspector Nailsworth sat back in his chair, with the air of one who had made a crushing move at chess. Thorne was apparently undiscouraged.

"What's she got worth stealing, then?" he asked.

"Family jewels. They're what she lives on. In a tuppenny-farthing safe in her bedroom. She won't keep them at the bank, she says—you know what old ladies are like. Makes you weep, doesn't it?"

The two inspectors threw up their eyes to the ceiling, in sympathy at last over the folly of those who asked for trouble.

"Was it generally known in Southbourne, about these jewels?"

"Oh yes, the Princess is quite a celebrity here."

"More likely a local job then."

"We have thousands of visitors every summer. There's nothing to stop one of the wrong sort getting to hear about the Princess's little hoard." Inspector Nailsworth was frosty again; he had the provincial's touchiness about the good name of his own town. "Of course, we've got some bad lads here. But not the shooting kind —I'll take my oath on that."

"He *must* be a Londoner then," said Thorne dryly. "Well, we've got to find the weapon. The usual caper. A bird in that sort of panic is bound to get rid of it double quick. He was running toward the sea front—"

"Yes. He could drop it off the pier, or the harbor wall," said Nailsworth with ponderous sarcasm. "Or he could board the night steamer and toss it into the sea. Quite a job, dragging the English Channel."

"We're making inquiries, of course," said Allison, "in that direction. But—yes, what is it?"

A constable had come in, and was standing to attention by the door. There was a man outside, he said, whom he thought the Chief Inspector should see at once; it might have a bearing on the murder. This man proved to be one of the municipal cleaners, whose job it was to clear up litter from the beach. Early this morning he had found a parcel just under the sea wall, a few hundred yards from the Queen's Hotel. He had taken it, after finishing the rest of his work, with several other articles, to the municipal offices. There it had been opened; and in due course someone had put two and two together.

Nailsworth opened the parcel, whistling through his teeth when he saw what it contained—a length of rope with a hook at one end.

"You're certain this wasn't on the beach yesterday morning?"

"Quite certain, Inspector. I couldn't have missed it—not a parcel that size."

"Well, he's done everything except write his name and address on the wrapping for us," said Nailsworth, when the cleaner had been temporarily dismissed, and his find removed for finger-printing.

Thorne looked dubious. "Well, he *may* have left his dabs on the hook. But it's crazy to me. The hook's too small to grip the parapet of a balcony, for one thing. And even if he did use it on the house, he made off much too quick to have had time for unfastening it. And why leave it, neatly parceled up, where it was certain to be found?"

"You think he *wanted* it to be found?" asked the Chief Constable keenly.

"Well, sir, if it isn't just a coincidence. And I can't swallow that."

"You mean it's a blind? He wanted to fix our attention on burglary, when he was really up to something else?"

Chief Inspector Nailsworth gave a loud snuffle. "My youngest kid's a great reader of crime fiction," he remarked at large.

Thorne's mouth twitched. "In my experience, crime fact is a good deal stranger than crime fiction these days." He turned to Colonel Allison. "Well, sir, if there's nothing more you want to discuss, I'd better get down to the field work."

"What do you propose?" The Colonel was not accustomed to being dismissed, however tactfully, by junior officers. But he had worked for Military Intelligence during the war, and recognized brains when he met them.

"I'd like to see the spot where this rope was found, sir; then the scene of the crime. One can't quite get the hang of these things from maps and sketches. After that, I'll interview the Princess's household, the cabby, and the other witness—though I don't expect I'll turn up anything the Chief Inspector hasn't discovered. What we need is some more material evidence. You can't make a brick with only three straws—and one of them a broken reed."

"The shopkeeper in Brighton may be able to give descriptions of the men who bought that kind of cap."

"Let's hope so. But it's a rare thing, the gift for describing. Most people can't even see, let alone put it into words. Queen's Parade. It sounds like one of those high-class neighborhoods where everyone's far too superior to peer out between the curtains."

Rather unexpectedly, the Chief Inspector was tickled by this sardonic remark of Thorne's. "You're right there, my lad."

On this note of unanimity, the Chief Constable took his leave. Maybe the other two would stop getting across each other now; there always tended to be this initial *froideur* between the local man and the Scotland Yard expert; and besides, Nailsworth was badly cut up by Stone's death.

When Colonel Allison had gone, there was an uneasy silence for a few moments.

"A good man, the Colonel," ventured Thorne.

"One of the best." Nailsworth turned away toward the window. "So was Herbert."

Thorne moved to his side, a sparrowy figure compared with the huge bulk of the Chief Inspector.

"No use fretting, sir," he said; then, in a chilled, bitter voice, "I know what it's like. It was one of my chaps who had it in that Craig-Bentley business. Don't you worry. We'll get him."

13 "I Only Want to Help"

DAISY lay on the bed, her body hot and dry, exhausted with weeping. The child kicked in her womb, but she was beyond feeling it; she herself was imprisoned in a horror from which there seemed to be no way out. It was two days since Jacko had brought her back to his house, and the oppression of her misery showed no sign of lifting. Her mind kept turning and turning within the narrow orbit of disaster, trying every way to reach back to the girl she had been before Hugo left her on that seat on the promenade. But it was as if a fog had closed down between her and the happy past—a fog in which she was utterly lost, and which made trivial things loom large out of all proportion. Hugo's dressing gown, for instance; she had wanted to keep it—to have something of his she could put round her. But, in the bustle of departure, the agony of saying good-by to him, it had been forgotten. Hugo and his brother had gone off by an earlier train that afternoon, and he had packed the dressing gown in his own bag; and now it seemed like an extra, wanton cruelty —not to have even this to remember him by.

Daisy shut her eyes, trying to summon up Hugo's face. But it evaded her, she could not fix it; it started to form in her mind's eye, then turned into something monstrous—a figment of the fog which choked and mocked her.

"Not asleep yet, my dear? This won't do."

She had not heard the door open. Jacko came over and sat on her bed.

"Is it very late?" she muttered.

"Nearly midnight. I think I'd better give you another sedative."

118

"No. I don't want—" She gripped his hand convulsively. "You won't leave me? I haven't anyone else."

Jacko made soothing noises. The girl was staring at his face, with a wild, unfocused look.

"Haven't you heard from him yet? Is he all right?"

"No news is good news, my dear. You must try not to excite yourself."

"He might have written to me," she said in a quavering voice.

"He will. But it wouldn't be wise just at present. You do see that, don't you?"

"I suppose so." The girl lay back, closing her eyes. Jacko began to stroke her temples rhythmically; it was comforting. After a while she said: "Do you think I'm very wicked?"

"Wicked? What is all this?"

"Well, I'm being punished, aren't I?"

"Not for anything *you*'ve done." Some faint insinuation in his tone made Daisy start upright; her nightdress slipped from one shoulder, revealing a blue-veined breast.

"*Hugo* isn't wicked!" she cried. "You shan't say that! I know he—stole things. But he was going to give all that up. He told me. He's kind, and good. If he hadn't lost that £50 betting—and he only did that for me. You don't think he—"

"Look at me, Daisy." Jacko's voice had never been so gentle. She gazed at the ugly, pouchy face, deep into the brown eyes which never quite lost their imploring look. The faithful dog. The one friend she could trust.

"You know I only want to help you—you and Hugo. You know that, don't you?"

"Yes."

"Why don't you tell me all about it, then? It's not good for you, keeping it bottled up. I'm saying this as your doctor. You're heading for a nervous breakdown, and that won't do the baby any good, or Hugo. Things go bad when they're bottled up inside you."

"Not now," she sighed. "I'm so tired."

"Tired? It's not that. You're afraid, my dear."

Her body jerked, as if he had struck her. She gave him a startled, wary glance. "Of course I'm afraid. Hugo's in danger."

"I don't quite mean that. Be honest with yourself. You're afraid he really did it."

Daisy's first impulse was to get out of the room, get away from him. She scrambled to her knees, sobbing a little, but he bore her back and held her down by the shoulders, his thumbs kneading the plump flesh. Her head on the pillow rolled from side to side, as if to evade his eyes. He held her thus till she had grown calmer, then moved to the chair at her bedside. He was breathing hard. At last he said:

"We both want to help Hugo. I can't help him unless I know what really happened."

"But didn't he tell you, when you came down to Southbourne?"

Jacko's tongue flickered over his lips. He gave her a sidelong, speculative glance. "But was that the true story, all the story? Do you believe it yourself? If so, why are you afraid?"

"Oh, why do you torture me like this? I thought you were fond of me."

"You *are* afraid. What do you think you were trying to run away from just now? Me? Not a bit of it. You couldn't face the possibility of Hugo's guilt. And you've been feeling guilty yourself, for suspecting Hugo. You can't just shove all this dirty linen into a drawer and pretend it doesn't exist."

"Hugo never did it—not a cowardly thing like that. I know he couldn't have."

"All right, then, my dear. I don't believe he'd do such a thing myself. So, as we both believe in him, why can't we talk about it?" He gave her his engaging, rueful smile. "Or is it that you don't quite trust *me*?"

"I dunno. I'm proper mazed." Rubbing her eyes with her knuckles, like a child, Daisy lapsed into her childhood vernacular. "Proper mazed. I don't know where I'm to."

"Of course, if you feel you can't trust me, there's no more to be said."

"Don't *you* turn against me now, John," she said forlornly.

"I didn't mean to hurt 'ee. But sometimes—well, you can be ever so curious."

"Curious? How?"

"Asking so many questions. Sort of for the fun of asking them. It used to make me uncomfortable."

"You felt I was prying unwarrantably into your affairs?" he asked—not stiffly, but the girl felt his sympathy withdrawing like a tide.

"Oh, I don't mean you're a busybody," she said in distress. "But—I'm no good at words—it's as if you wanted to take people to bits and find what makes them tick. Like little boys do with frogs and insects and such. They don't know they're being cruel."

"Well, I must say, you're a pretty outspoken young woman. So I'm like a little boy tearing the wings off flies? You think I get a kick out of watching people squirm and wriggle?" His tone, even now, was more interested than affronted.

Daisy's exhaustion gave her a sort of clairvoyance. She saw that the answer to Jacko's last question might be "yes"; but she didn't quite dare to say that.

"Hugo told me once you liked having power over people."

"Who doesn't?" Jacko eyed her quizzically. "Be honest now. Don't you enjoy being able to make Hugo come to heel? Your sexual power over him?"

The girl flushed, rather shocked by the naked way he presented this truth. "It's different when you love someone. That's nothing to do with power."

The silence lasted so long that presently Daisy turned her eyes on Jacko and was disconcerted to see his face working and his whole body shivering violently.

"Are you cold? I'm so sorry. I oughtn't to be keeping you here."

"So you think I'm incapable of love? That's it?" The man's voice frightened her: it sounded like some explosive mixture, barely under control, self-pity, resentment, malice. How touchy men are, she thought—touchy and vain and difficult. But she felt she must make amends for whatever injury he imagined she had done him.

"I don't mean that at all, Jacko. You're twisting my words." She had another flash of clairvoyance. Smiling at him—she did not realize how maternally—she went on, "You know, I believe you keep things bottled up as bad as anyone."

"And, being a woman, you want to let the genie out of the bottle?" Gazing full at her, he said, "An attractive woman. I'm not your doctor all the time, my girl."

She blushed, in a confusion of feelings, of which a kind of shamed gratification was not the least.

"I suppose you assume you're perfectly safe with me," Jacko went on, in an almost petulant tone. If he intended to put her out of countenance, he had not reckoned with the element of country frankness in her make-up.

"Oh, I should think I'm safe enough with anyone just now," she replied, laughing. "Besides, you're our friend."

"Then why don't you treat me as a friend, not a convenience?" His voice became smooth and melting, like honey. "Why don't you let me help you and Hugo?"

"You've done so much already."

"There's plenty more to be done, if you'd really confide in me."

And so it was that the girl told him everything about those last two days at Southbourne. Emotional exhaustion had created in her the automatism which makes one go forward, as a man, at the extreme limit of fatigue, will go on walking, for if he does not he must drop down and die. Daisy heard this automaton within herself talking, talking; her tongue seemed to remember little things which her mind had forgotten. And, partly anesthetized though she was by exhaustion, she could still have the sense of being nearer to Hugo in reliving that time and repeating his words. But she said nothing about the burying of the revolver—not because she distrusted Jacko, but because the horror of that episode, as shameful to remember as if they had made love over a corpse, inhibited her.

However, when she had finished Daisy felt wonderfully re-laxed—floating and unharassed, as if she had given birth—and this filled her with gratitude to Jacko. She pressed his hand.

"Good girl," he said. "You feel better already, don't you? What did I tell you?"

"Yes. I do. But it will be all right for Hugo? Say it will. Now you've heard—"

"I don't see how the police could prove anything against him—"

"But, Jacko, it's not a question of—he's innocent. He must be," Daisy exclaimed.

"Provided he hid that revolver of his in a really safe place."

Daisy stared at him, aghast. "Revolver? I didn't—"

"You remember, his brother asked him about it, and Hugo said he'd 'got rid of the nasty firearm.' I just hope he got rid of it thoroughly," said Jacko in a light voice.

"Oh yes. We"—Daisy broke off, rubbing her fingers against her mouth—"we decided he mustn't have it any more—after what happened at his brother's house."

Jacko did not pursue the topic. They talked for a little longer, Jacko very brisk and encouraging; then, giving her a chaste kiss on the forehead, he left her.

Daisy slept late the next morning. When the housekeeper brought in her breakfast tray, there was an affectionate note from Jacko saying he had been called out of London but would get back in the evening and looked forward to dinner with her.

At Southbourne the Chief Constable was in conference with Chief Inspector Nailsworth and Detective Inspector Thorne. They had just come from the inquest upon their colleague, which had been adjourned for a fortnight. The three men were discussing plans, for the investigation had ground to a standstill. Thorne had spent a considerable part of the two days interviewing the occupants of houses in Queen's Parade, starting with Princess Popescu, her companion and her maid. But no further evidence had come to hand which could give them a lead to the murderer; nor was the cabby, Charles Poore, able to provide any further identification. Indeed, it had become plain to Thorne that none of the few eye-witnesses who had seen the murderer would be able to identify him with any certainty at all.

One trail, which at first seemed promising, had petered out. A crook called Joe Samuels was discovered to have been staying at the Queen's Hotel, with two friends, on the day of the murder. The party had checked out of the hotel at six o'clock that evening, however, and returned to London by car. It could have been a feint departure; but Joe's alibi stood up like a rock to the C.I.D. inquiries—he produced several witnesses, other than the man and woman who had accompanied him, to vouch for his arrival in London at a time which could not possibly have allowed him to commit the murder. There was nothing against Joe, except that he had served two sentences for jewel thefts. Nevertheless, one of Thorne's colleagues was checking Joe's alibi once again.

Nailsworth had detailed a sizable part of his force to the search for the weapon, with equal unsuccess. The foreshore was scrutinized at low tide, every garden in Queen's Parade searched and its street drains investigated. The search was continuing, and police officers were making a round of the Southbourne hotels and lodging houses to inquire if any suspicious behavior or abrupt departure had taken place on the night of the murder. But it looked now as if the murderer had not panicked to the extent of throwing away his weapon. Thorne's hunch that it might be a political affair, though he played it down in the Chief Inspector's presence, was not weakened by anything yet discovered, and he had asked the Special Branch for a dossier of the Princess.

The only positive gain so far, and it was a very small one, was the evidence of the Brighton shopkeeper. He had identified the cap as one from the consignment which had come in a month ago; up to the date of the murder, he had only sold four—three to men and one to a girl. He might or might not be able to identify the male purchasers, but the girl—a striking young blonde, and pregnant—he would recognize again anywhere.

"So we're back to the old 'on information received,'" said Thorne.

"Not a very hopeful prospect," the Chief Constable remarked.

"Oh, you'd be surprised, sir. Sooner or later, somebody talks—

maybe the criminal himself can't keep his trap shut. Ninety-nine cases out of a hundred, that's how we get the first break."

"Nobody in Southbourne's talking about anything else. But it doesn't seem to have got us any further." The elephantine Nailsworth gave his peaky, perky little London colleague a look, at once severe and faintly jocular, which attested to their improved relations.

"If this was a bona fide attempt at burglary," Thorne began. The Chief Inspector raised his eyes ostentatiously to the ceiling, but Thorne pressed on regardless, "—the maid, Velma, is the weak point. She doesn't speak English well, and she's obstinate—peasant type, I should think. I can't get anything out of her, but I feel she's more on the defensive than she should be. Who else could have told our man where the Princess keeps her jewels? And who'd break into a house without knowing that much?"

"The Princess has had other maids."

"Oh yes, sir. And we'll have to check up on them. But Velma's the only one who knew the house would be empty that night."

"She and Mrs. Felstead," the Chief Constable put in. "But I agree. We'd be wasting our time on Mrs. Felstead."

Thorne said his next step would be to interview the Italian maid again. He would try to check her movements on the day of the murder, any telephone calls she had made, and so on. If it could be discovered that she had been in contact with a stranger that day, or before it even, the police would have something to bite on. Tomorrow Thorne would return to London and take over the inquiries, which were already proceeding, into the movements of jewel thieves known to Scotland Yard.

The three men discussed press publicity—further appeals for anyone to come forward who had noticed any suspicious behavior; circulars to pawnbrokers in case the murderer had been foolish enough to get rid of his gun that way—the ballistics experts, working on the bullet found in Stone's body, had now reported on the caliber and possible make of the weapon. The rope and hook discovered in the parcel were new, or at least unused, but no local shop had sold such an article; they had

probably been bought separately, and the rope bent onto the
hook by the purchaser. So the rope provided no · clue worth
following up at present. Had the criminal used it, it would
have narrowed down the police investigations, for Scotland Yard
had records of all criminals habitually employing this method;
but—and this was one of the most baffling features of the case—
the hooked rope had been left on the beach, neatly parceled up,
for anyone to find; there were no scratches on the hook; it had
never been put to any use, nefarious or otherwise.

"Maybe," remarked Nailsworth, in a spirit of unwonted fan-
tasy, "it was mislaid on the beach by a mountaineer."

"Why not a gymnast?" Thorne asked. "Some small boy might
have pinched it out of his school gymnasium, for a dare. These
nippers'll get up to anything."

"Well, gentlemen, I think we'd better dismiss the parade now.
Unless there's anything more—?" Colonel Allison rose to his feet.
As he moved to the door, a police constable entered.

"Gentleman wants to see the Chief Inspector, sir. Says he has
information about the Stone case."

"Another of these lunatics, I suppose," muttered Nailsworth.
He had been pestered enough already by the cranks, crackpots
and zealous nitwits who always spring up on the track of a
murder investigation and cling like brambles to the policeman's
boots.

Colonel Allison passed to his Chief Inspector a visiting card
which the constable had handed him.

"Dr. John Jaques. Never heard of him," said Nailsworth. "Well,
I suppose we'd better see him, sir? Bring him in, my lad. And
the shorthand wizard."

14 The Kiss of Death

NAILSWORTH and Thorne gave Dr. Jaques the policeman's look—
the leisurely, ruminant, top-to-toe gaze, neutral yet oppressive, by
means of which, had some supernatural agency whisked him
from sight after five seconds, they could have catalogued him
down to the last button on his coat sleeve. The Chief Constable
introduced himself and his colleagues to their visitor, invited him
to sit down, glanced at the Chief Inspector.

"I understand, sir, you have some information to give us about
the death of Inspector Stone," said Nailsworth. It was like a
machine talking—a machine adjusted to an endlessly repetitive
ritual.

"Yes, I think I can—"

"Your name and address, sir."

"You have them on that card in your hand."

"You are a doctor of medicine?" Nailsworth went on, ponderous as a steam roller, undeflectible from his routine.

While the ritual questions proceeded, Colonel Allison studied
their visitor. His first impression, when Dr. Jaques entered, had
been of a man uncertain of his welcome yet sure of his status: a
photographer, as it might be, at a society wedding—not exactly
obsequious, but not brashly pushful either—ready to play a
needed part unobtrusively and professionally. There was nothing
obviously offensive about him; yet Colonel Allison found himself thinking, "impudent fella—a bit smooth." Perhaps it was the
man's eyes: a hint of mockery behind their deference. He looked
sane enough, anyway, which was more than could be said of most
of the funnies who had bowled along to assist the police. No, not
a photographer, thought the Colonel now; an actor. The glib

speech, quick on its cues; the rather theatrical fluff of white hair
(cast him for the benevolent if eccentric uncle, back from Australia, his fortune made, ready to help out the struggling young
couple); above all, the face was surely an actor's, with its mobile
mouth and loose flesh—a face which, by rearrangement of its
fluid planes, could become a different face, or at any rate the
face of a quite different character.

The Chief Constable pulled himself out of these unprofitable
musings. Or rather, he was abruptly jerked out of them by the
doctor's replying to some official phrase of Nailsworth's, "No, no,
I've not come here to make a confession." It was not the words
so much as the light, amused tone in which they were spoken that
gave Colonel Allison an obscure sensation of outrage. And, as if
Dr. Jaques were instantly aware of this without even needing to
have looked at the Chief Constable's face, his voice changed
color and he went on, soberly, with a worried expression, "I'm
afraid it's a good deal more difficult than that. For me."

"If you will give us your statement, sir, in your own words,"
said Nailsworth patiently. "Keeping to the facts, please—no
hearsay, or theorizing."

"On the morning of October 10th I was rung up in London
by Mark Amberley," began Dr. Jaques, in a manner that might
have been the most delicate parody of a police constable giving
evidence in a magistrate's court. "He told me that his brother had
telephoned to him from Southbourne, asking him urgently to
come down, bringing money with him; he was to ask me if I
could come too. I have known Mark's brother for some time. He
changed his name, seven or eight years ago, to Chesterman—
Hugo Chesterman."

"Wait a minute!" Thorne was snapping his fingers like a school-
boy trying to remember the right answer. "Amberley. Amberley.
Hugo Amberley? No. Chesterman . . . I've got it—Chester Hugh
Amberley. Was that his original name?"

Jacko lowered his eyes, and a look of pain passed over his
face. "Yes. I see you remember. Hugo changed his name after
being released from prison."

"Jewel robbery, wasn't it?"

"I believe so," said Jacko, inclining his head. "I traveled down here with Mark. We read about the death of your Inspector Stone in the morning paper. When we got to Hugo's lodgings"— Jacko gave the address—"he'd told Mark, by the way, to ask for him by a different name, we found him and Daisy in a very agitated state. Daisy Bland, I should have said, is a girl he has been living with for some eighteen months."

"Would she be a striking blonde?" asked Thorne, with a flick of the eye at Nailsworth.

"I suppose you could describe her that way," replied Jacko coldly. "She is a patient of mine. She will become a mother toward the end of December. Hugo told us that he had run out of money, and was frightened of the police connecting him with the murder, being a man with a police record, if his presence in Southbourne were discovered. He said he must go into hiding for a bit, till the fuss, as he put it, had blown over."

Nailsworth drew in a sharp breath, clenching his fist.

"We gave him some money, and I agreed to put up Miss Bland in my own house. She's there now. Mark returned to London with Hugo, and Miss Bland and I followed by a later train."

"Did it not occur to you and Mr. Amberley that you might be compounding a felony?" asked the Chief Inspector.

Jacko made a little grimace. "I really don't remember. I'm fond of Hugo and Daisy, and they were in trouble. One does what one can for one's friends, under such circumstances." He took out a clean, folded handkerchief and dabbed his lips. "Besides, Hugo swore he had nothing to do with the crime. I did try to impress on him that, if he ran away, it would look like a confession of guilt, but the poor old boy was too panicky to see reason."

The doctor paused—for so long that Nailsworth at last prompted him. "Well, sir?"

"Well?"

"What account did Mr. Chesterman give you of his movements?"

"Oh. I'm sorry. I thought you wanted no hearsay evidence."

Nailsworth's lips tightened. The Chief Constable put in curtly, "You may tell us that, Doctor."

"He said he just happened to be somewhere else when the crime was committed, but couldn't prove it."

Nailsworth leaned heavily toward him, his face redder even than usual.

"Do you say you were 'satisfied' by *that*? Went round the corner to see a man about a dog—that's what it amounts to, eh?" The Chief Inspector was evidently holding himself in by a mere thread.

"One believes one's friends," replied Jacko, not without dignity.

"When they are convicted jewel thieves? You are not normally in the habit, I take it, of consorting with—"

"Steady, Nailsworth," warned Colonel Allison.

"I know it must sound pretty impossible to you chaps," said Jacko, with a pleasant, open smile. "I can only say that I believed Hugo had been going straight, recently, and I'm naïve enough to imagine that a conviction for robbery doesn't turn a fundamentally decent young chap into a murderer."

"But, since then, you've changed your mind, sir?" Thorne's colorless expression—he might have been a clerk in a booking office discussing a destination with a traveler—betrayed nothing of the excitement throbbing within him. He remembered now that Amberley, alias Chesterman, had been a cat burglar of phenomenal agility: it was all fitting in.

Dr. Jaques made a deprecatory gesture, his open hands pushing away something from before him; he's like a dog, thought the Chief Constable, sitting up begging, its fore paws scrabbling at the air.

"You changed your mind," Thorne repeated.

The doctor's features fell, or rearranged themselves, into an agonized expression; he seemed to be having difficulty with his voice.

"I'm afraid so. Yes. Last night I had a long talk with Miss Bland. She was in an overwrought condition, on the verge of collapse. I thought it would be good for her to talk it out of her system—what had happened down here." He gulped. "Look here, must you have all this?"

"It's what you came down here to tell us, isn't it?" Colonel Allison tried to conceal his growing distaste for the man, but not altogether successfully. He was startled by a dart of rancor, really venomous, from the doctor's eyes.

"It's not very public school, I agree," said Jacko. "But one's public-school code—my friends, right or wrong—doesn't seem to me altogether adequate when a policeman has been shot in cold blood."

The Chief Constable frowned. This damnable fellow had gone right to the spot, like a mind reader: the public-school code, that the only unforgivable sin is to betray one's friends, was exactly what had been coloring the Colonel's mind during this interview. And worse—the doctor's last remark had adroitly driven a wedge between the Colonel and his two subordinates, who were unhampered by this sort of gentlemanliness.

"Can we keep to the point," he said. "Your talk with Miss—er —Bland."

Jacko related it, at full length and with little hesitation, to the continuo of the stenographer's pencil. When he had finished, there was a brief silence.

"Have you seen this revolver of Chesterman's? Do you know what make it is?" the Chief Inspector asked.

"I don't."

"But your private opinion is that he did not get rid of it, as Miss Bland wished you to believe, after the altercation at his brother's house?"

"That is my impression. I only hope I am wrong."

"You know Chesterman's present whereabouts, I take it?"

Jacko's eyes flickered. Then, a little too quickly, he said, "No, I'm afraid I don't."

"That is unfortunate. Most unfortunate." Nailsworth's tone conveyed somehow that it might be even more unfortunate for Dr. Jaques than for the police. "But surely Miss Bland is in touch with him?"

"Not to my knowledge. Of course, you can ask her."

"We shall, sir. And now, perhaps you will give us a description of Chesterman."

"But Scotland Yard will have that on its files."

"You can bring it up to date for us. If you please, sir," Nailsworth relentlessly pressed him.

"Oh well, if I must, I must."

The Chief Constable abruptly rose. His Intelligence work during the war had involved him in some pretty unscrupulous transactions; but they had never caused him the physical nausea which he felt in Dr. Jaques' presence. Nailsworth and Thorne had stronger stomachs—best leave it to them.

"Just remembered. An appointment with the Town Clerk. Will you carry on, Chief Inspector," he said; and with a curt nod he strode briskly from the office.

As the door closed, Thorne observed a queer little grin on Dr. Jaques' face—a grin of relief? satisfaction? or was it just a reflex to the Colonel's brusque treatment? The atmosphere in the room was more relaxed, at any rate, after his departure—so relaxed, indeed, that when the doctor's description of Hugo Chesterman had been taken down, Thorne suddenly poked his long nose at him, saying in a tone of complicity, camaraderie almost:

"Now, come off it, Doctor. Don't tell me you don't know where Chesterman is hiding up. You must have some channel of communication with him, anyway?"

The expression of disapproval on Nailsworth's huge face faded into one of crafty alertness. All right; if that was the way to take this medico to pieces, he could do his share of the bouncing. He made a little sign, dismissing the stenographer from the room.

"Look, you've got that description," said Jacko. "You really can't ask me to do more. It's—"

"I beg your pardon, sir, but we *are* asking you. This description is all very well; but we don't want Chesterman slipping out of our hands. We've got to find him at once."

"You're talking as if he—as if the case was already proved against him," Jacko protested.

"You've certainly convinced me, sir, that there is a strong case against him theoretically, on our present evidence." Thorne spoke without apparent irony, still in that tone of something like matiness. Watching the two, Nailsworth was astounded to find himself thinking "birds of a feather."

"If he is innocent," Thorne continued, "he'll be able to prove it—and the sooner, the better. His young woman must be in great suspense. Bad for her. But you're a doctor—I don't need to tell you that."

"Yes, that's true," said Jacko, with a sort of eagerness, as though this consideration, presented to him for the first time, offered him an honorable way out.

"This girl now, Daisy Bland—was she an accomplice of his, in his jewel robberies?" asked Nailsworth heavily.

Thorne could have kicked the Chief Inspector. After playing the doctor so skillfully, and all but landing him, to have the line snapped by this clumsy intervention!

Dr. Jaques froze up. "Really, Chief Inspector, what an extraordinary question! How should I know? I assure you I was never in their confidence to *that* extent. Apart from anything else, my professional—"

"Quite, sir, quite." Thorne attempted to close this exhibition of huffiness. "As we were saying, it's simply a matter of getting in touch with Chesterman as soon as possible. If he's innocent, well and good. We're only asking you—"

"I've already told you. I don't know his whereabouts."

"Then I advise you, for your own good, to find out," said Nailsworth menacingly. He had had enough of this velvet glove stuff; an obscure resentment smoldered in him at Thorne's making all the running; and his anger over the killing of Inspector Stone was implacable.

"Are you threatening me?" said Jacko. "I come here to help the police, and—"

Nailsworth's huge fist crashed down on the table. "You're in a

very awkward position. I'm warning you. You've already com-
pounded a felony, it may be, by assisting this man to escape from
Southbourne. You are harboring a woman who is very likely his
accomplice."

"Oh bosh!" exclaimed Jacko, quite unintimidated. He might
have been trying to goad the Chief Inspector into violence.

"Don't you take that line with me!" Nailsworth made a powerful effort to control himself. "I'm just telling you. Ask yourself
how it'll look when the case comes into court. A doctor's professional reputation is easily lost, eh? A doctor who is on intimate
terms with a jewel thief and his mistress; a doctor who helps a
murderer and obstructs the police—oh yes, it'll all come out."

"I can see why you sent away your stenographer. Didn't want
him to hear you blackmailing a witness—sorry, putting pressure
on a witness sounds better, doesn't it?" Jacko appeared to be
enjoying himself hugely.

"Come now, sir, do you wish to co-operate with us, or not?"
asked Thorne.

"I've given you a statement. Don't you call that co-operation?"

"Should Chesterman get in touch with you, before we've found
him ourselves, are you prepared to communicate the fact to us?"

"Well," said Jacko guardedly, "that's asking a hell of a lot of
me."

"I'm asking you to do your duty as a citizen."

Oh God, thought Nailsworth, the double-talk again!

"You realize, sir, of course, that we may have to inquire into
your own bona fides?" Thorne smoothly proceeded. "Just the
usual routine inquiries. You have a partner, I suppose?"

"No." For the first time, Jacko looked uneasy.

"Must be awkward for you, then—these visits to Southbourne?
Canceling your appointments at such short notice?"

"My appointments?"

"Your patients. You did say you were a doctor of medicine,
didn't you, sir? You are in practice?"

"Oh, yes. Private practice. I take a few patients. I've money of
my own."

"Ah. I see." Thorne made it sound uncommonly sinister. "Well, sir, if you'll read and sign your statement, we'll not keep you any longer from your professional duties."

There was silence till the typewritten sheets were brought in, silence while Jacko read through them and signed his name at the end.

"If you'll also initial each page, please, sir," said Thorne; then, "That will be all. For the present. You may be hearing from us. Good morning, Doctor Jaques."

Was there the faintest stress on "Doctor"? Nailsworth didn't know what his colleague was up to, but he'd let him play it his own way. The two police officers appeared to have lost all interest in their witness: Thorne even turned his back as Dr. Jaques went to the door; and it was Thorne's back which, from the doorway, Jacko addressed:

"Look here. Supposing Hugo does get in touch with me—what line am I to take?"

Nailsworth expelled a long, slow breath. Thorne, speaking over his shoulder, not looking at Jacko, said, "That's up to you, Doctor. You could make an appointment to meet him, in some public place probably. And you have our telephone number."

Jacko came back a little way into the room. "Are you suggesting I should be actually present when you arrest him?"

"We should detain him for questioning. We could detain you too, if that'd make your mind easier, Doctor."

"But, damn it, he's a friend of mine."

"Very painful for you, sir, I realize. Well, it's up to you. Oh, one thing more, Doctor," said Thorne when Jacko was at the door again. "This girl, Daisy Bland. Was Chesterman intending to marry her? In the near future?"

"I—I really don't know. Why?"

"Just wondered. Her health good?" Thorne's voice was cheerful and detached.

"Oh yes. She's quite a robust young woman. But I don't—"

"Rather an ordeal for her, giving evidence in court. Think she'd stand up to it, in her present condition?"

"My dear chap, there's no question of her giving evidence against him."

"Why? She's not his wife."

There was the briefest pause, before Jacko replied, "Oh, I see. . . . What I meant was, she's devoted to him. She wouldn't do it."

The door had hardly closed behind Doctor Jaques when the Chief Inspector was giving instructions on the internal telephone that he should be shadowed.

"And now, my lad," he turned formidably to Thorne. "*You've* got some explaining to do."

"Sir?" asked Thorne innocently.

"Oh, come off it. You as good as tell that blighter to arrange a marriage pronto between Chesterman and his girl. A wife can't give evidence against her husband. And without this girl's evidence we shouldn't have a hope in hell. You must be off your rocker."

"No, Chief. What I was conveying to the doctor is that he should damn well see to it they *don't* get married."

Nailsworth stared at him incredulously. "You really think?— But he's fond of them—must be, to help Chesterman out and take the girl into his house."

"Maybe he's fond of the girl. Maybe he's too fond of her by half. So he comes in here, oh, ever so reluctantly—it's a painful business informing against your best friend, but every right-thinking citizen must assist the Law—and puts the spot on this Chesterman. No doubt he'll be comforting the girl on the morning of the execution. Nothing like a good solid family friend when you're in trouble." Thorne spoke with a raging bitterness that Nailsworth had never encountered before.

"Draw it mild, old man. He's a queer cuss all right, but—"

"He's rotten from top to toe. It'll take me months to wash him out of my system. He plays it dirty. And this Chesterman, if he did it, he played it dirty too. So I've got to play dirty. Sometimes I wish I was in some decent clean job—like sewage tasting."

15   An Arrest in London

Two days later, Jacko was sitting alone at a table in the buffet of Charing Cross station. He sat with his elbows on the table, which he had carefully dusted off with a clean handkerchief, in the attitude of a chess player who has made a strong move but will not relax his attention, is already thinking ahead to guard against any unexpected reply of his opponent. From time to time he raised his eyes to the door which faced him, but absently, as though he were more interested by his own thoughts than by the imminent arrival of the person whom he awaited. He wiped the rim of his coffee cup daintily before taking a drink, then, head in hands again, resumed his meditative pose. No one observing him could have guessed the extraordinary exhilaration which was flooding through him.

On his return from Southbourne two days ago, he had written to Hugo Chesterman at the accommodation address which Hugo had given him, to make an appointment; if Hugo could not come, he was to ring Jacko at his own house; he had not rung yesterday, so no doubt he'd be turning up here any minute now. Jacko paused to recall admiringly the finesse of the letter he had written: without committing himself to anything he would not be able to explain when they met, he had hinted that there were new developments which made a meeting imperative. Silence on Hugo's part meaning consent, Jacko had rung up Inspector Thorne at Scotland Yard yesterday evening, to inform him of the assignation: "Of course," he'd said at the end of their brief conversation, "you'll go through the motions of arresting me as well."

It was pleasant to sit gloating over his dispositions. He almost hoped that Hugo would not arrive too punctually and interrupt his thoughts. He did not hate Hugo, any more than a tarantula hates its natural prey. Not now, at any rate. There had been times in the past when Hugo got beneath his skin—"Oh, Daisy's safe enough with you"—that sort of thing had rankled for a moment; but Jacko had sealed off those light, deadly barbs at once, being able to contemplate, even to relish any aberration of his own except his physical impotence. No, the pleasure he now felt was unalloyed by hatred—the pure pleasure of power. He had played with human lives before, but never to such purpose. The sensation of controlling Hugo's destiny, and Daisy's, was almost physical—a heady, stimulating pleasure better than any drug; and the risk he himself ran seemed to increase the area of this delicious sensation.

His thoughts wandered to Daisy Bland. Her beauty, like Hugo's careless taunts, had exacerbated him from time to time. Her trust in him made a piquant addition to the cold, reckless game he was playing. Oh yes, he could lust after her all right; he found no trouble in admitting to himself that the sight of her distress was sexually agreeable, as it would be agreeable to torment her physically; but he was quite capable of subordinating his lust to the power game which he found so much more satisfying.

A small child, passing, stumbled over his outstretched foot. He picked the child up, brushed her coat, made a few engaging faces at her, and restored her in good spirits to her mother. His mind returned smoothly to the problem of Hugo and Daisy. Their love for each other, so ardent and exclusive, had always irked him; he felt an obscure need, not vindictive but dispassionately compulsive, to defile it—bring it down to his own level, as a hooligan may be driven to shatter a stained-glass window or a beautiful image, the mere existence of which he resents because it reproaches him with a kind of truth quite beyond his understanding. It occurred to Jacko now that, if Daisy Bland could be persuaded to give evidence against her lover, voluntarily, with no pressure from the police, their love would be brought down to the dust more effectually than by any other conceivable method.

For this, Hugo would never forgive her, nor Daisy forgive herself.

Jacko contemplated the idea with the awed fascination of an artist who imposes upon himself a task of almost impossible difficulty, knowing that if he succeeds the result will be his masterpiece. He must persuade or coerce the girl into believing that, unless she gave evidence against Hugo, she too would be charged with murder. She was stupid enough, docile enough, to believe it. But—here was the appalling obstacle—would the infatuated creature care? Might she not prefer to die with Hugo, as a convicted murderess, rather than to live without him? There was the baby, of course; Jacko had forgotten the baby—that'd be the best way to undermine her resistance. And if he could convince Daisy that Hugo himself wanted her to give evidence, so as to save the baby's future and her own, there was quite a chance that he could break her down.

The intricacy, the subtle irony of this scheme made Jacko rub his hands. The besotted girl, with her ridiculous passion for Hugo, was quite capable of believing that he would make a heroic gesture like this; and anyone with that amount of credulity ought to pay for it. The prospect of innocence overthrown and outraged thus by its own hand appealed to Jacko as the spectacle of rape might appeal to a man of less complex viciousness. Not for a moment, as he meditated his scheme, did Jacko conceal from himself, with so much as a wisp of hypocrisy or self-deception, the enormity of what he planned. One could hardly say that his exhilaration had carried him beyond the sense of good and evil, for he had no moral landmarks at all.

It was the motivelessness of Jacko's behavior which would most shock those concerned in the Chesterman case; for the presence of motive, however wicked in itself, makes evil recognizable, tolerable, human. The more simple-minded tried to explain Jacko's gratuitous betrayal of Hugo and Daisy by his desire to take the girl away from her lover, ignoring the fact that, after what he had done to them, nothing on earth would induce Daisy to see him again, and that he was quite intelligent enough to have

realized this. Psychologists, in well-paid articles for the popular
newspapers, working on the scanty information about Jacko's
past which reporters had been able to dig up before he was
smuggled out of the country by the police, discovered an explanation in Jacko's childhood: he was the only son of a dissipated,
neurotic woman, who had alternately spoiled him and treated
him with freezing, contemptuous indifference, dragging him
round Europe at the heels of herself and her current lover, or
depositing him for periods in boarding schools—a piece of un-
wanted human baggage. To this regime the psychologists attributed his jealousy of normal human happiness, his pathological
need to impress himself upon the lives of others, his plausibility
and adaptability in doing so, and the profound hatred of mother-
hood which directed his talents into the practice of abortion.

But it may be that Inspector Thorne came as near to it as anyone when, after the case was over, he told Nailsworth, "Jaques
ought to be put in a glass case, in a museum, with a label underneath—*The only known specimen of a totally irresponsible man
outside the loony bins.*"

Looking up, Jacko noticed Nailsworth and Thorne pacing
amidst the crowd beyond the buffet door. He glanced at his
watch: Hugo was already five minutes late. This did not disturb
him unduly, for it seemed impossible that the curtain would not
rise upon a play he had so carefully written and rehearsed in
his own mind.

The door opened. Hugo Chesterman, looking cool and wary as
ever, but not at all the hunted man, stepped through. He glanced
round the buffet, waved gaily to Jacko, then, after buying himself
a cup of coffee, came and sat down beside him.

"Well, old son, fancy meeting you here," he said. "How's the
family?"

Jacko gave a little, deliberate pout of the lips before replying.
"Daisy hasn't been in very good shape."

"Oh? I'm sorry to hear that. Nothing seriously wrong, I hope?"

Jacko detected, with pleasure, the sudden anxiety behind
Hugo's off-hand tones.

"She's worried, naturally," he said. "And not hearing from you—"

"I've got a letter for her. Will you take it?" Hugo passed an envelope to Jacko. "That'll cheer her up. No repercussions of our seaside visit, I suppose?"

Jacko lowered his voice. "That's what I asked you to come along about. Daisy wants you to marry her."

"I know." There was a faraway look in Hugo's eyes, confident and affectionate, which riled Jacko. "But not just now, surely?"

"That's the whole point, Hugo. Don't you realize—if the police get warm, they'll question her. If she's your wife, she can't give evidence against you in court. If she has to give evidence, she'll crack."

"If, if, if. You worry too much. Anyway, why should the police get warm?"

"Oh well, if you're quite happy about it, that's that."

"You know damn well I'm not happy about it, you old ghoul. But embarking on the state of holy matrimony entails making public appearances, and the fewer of them I make, the better—until they've got someone in the can for that business at Southbourne."

"So you definitely won't make an honest woman of her, yet?"

"My dear Jacko," said Hugo, in one of the rare outbursts of sincerity, simplicity, which seemed to change him into another man, "nothing any of us could do would make her an honester woman than she is. Or corrupt her. She's the gem of them all."

Jacko gave a little shrug, smiling at Hugo. Malice boiled profoundly within him. Seeing Nailsworth and Thorne at the window, he took out his handkerchief and dabbed his lips.

"I suppose I shall never know, Hugo," he said deliberately, his eyes fastened on the young man, "whether you did shoot that policeman or not."

The two Inspectors, summoned by Jacko's prearranged signal, had entered the buffet and, followed by a couple of plainclothes men, were quietly making their way past the little tables.

Hugo gave Jacko a veiled, impudent look. "I suppose you never will," he said. "Very tiresome for you."

At that moment Nailsworth's hand came down on his shoulder. For a second or two Hugo remained perfectly still; then he slowly looked round and up, as Nailsworth said, "Hugo Chesterman, I am a police officer and it is my duty to arrest you on—"

"God damn you!" Hugo swung round toward Jacko, only to see Thorne's hand upon the little man's shoulder.

"This is an outrage," Jacko was exclaiming. "Who the devil are you? How do I know you're police officers? This gentleman is a friend of mine. You're making an abominable mistake."

Jacko looked thoroughly rattled, glancing incredulously from Hugo to the policemen. Really, thought Hugo, poor old Jacko is putting up a marvelous show; but I'm sunk, for all that. His eyes flickered round the buffet, where half the people were already on their feet, staring, or moving toward the center of excitement. He picked out the two plainclothes men between him and the door, and his tense muscles relaxed. Not an earthly of escaping. Oh Daisy, oh Daisy, he said within himself, dimly aware of the other copper doing the palaver to Jacko—"detain you for questioning in regard to the murder of Police Inspector Stone at Southbourne."

Jacko was pretty well gibbering with outraged indignation. It was a good act, and Jacko was doing his best, but Hugo suddenly felt sick of it all. "Better go quietly, Jacko. You can bring an action for wrongful detention later. These police louts are only capable of one idea at a time."

A fierce pain shot through Hugo's upper arm. Nailsworth's powerful fingers were driving into the muscles. Glancing up at the Chief Inspector's large pink face, hard as basalt, Hugo had a foretaste of what was to come. His right arm was temporarily paralyzed by that grip, and he could hardly lift it when the handcuffs were brought out.

That afternoon, Daisy returned from a solitary walk in Holland Park to find Jacko waiting for her at home. Something in his face made her cry out, "What's the matter? Where have you been all day?"

"Daisy, you've got to prepare yourself for some bad news. Sit down, my dear, and try to keep calm."

She sat down, obediently, without a word, going deathly pale.

"The police have arrested Hugo."

"Oh, *no!*"

"The awful thing is—I'm afraid it was my fault."

"They've taken him away, to prison?" Daisy did not seem to have heard Jacko's last words.

"They must have been shadowing me—heaven knows why." Jacko peered through the muslin curtains. "There's a man outside now."

"I don't understand."

"You see, Hugo asked me to meet him this morning. At Charing Cross station. And—"

"Oh, you never told me! Why didn't you *tell* me?" Daisy's rough deep voice came out as if her heart were overflowing.

"He didn't want to put you in any danger. I must have been followed from here. Because we'd only been talking for a few minutes, in the station buffet, when the police—"

"Is he well? How was he looking?"

"Yes, my dear. Quite well."

"Did he give you a message for me? A letter?"

"He sent you his love. He's not a great one for writing letters, you know. He told me to tell you, if the worst should happen, not to keep anything back from the police—"

"I must go to him at once. Where is he?" the girl broke out wildly, half rising from her chair.

"Daisy, please! Do calm yourself! I'm trying to think what's the best thing to do. It's terribly difficult. You see, the police arrested me too."

"But—they let you go?"

"Somehow they must have got onto my visit to Southbourne—when Hugo sent his SOS. Anyway, I was detained for question-

ing. They kept me for hours. Of course, I didn't give anything
away."

"Oh, I knew this would happen! I knew it would happen!"
Daisy sobbed, burying her face in her hands. "What will they do
to him?"

Studying the girl's bowed head with satisfaction, Jacko pursed
his lips. Then deliberately, as if dropping the words between the
fingers which covered her ears, he said, "I suppose they'll take
him down to Southbourne for an identification parade. And then
he'll be charged at the Police Court."

Daisy's body quivered. "What are we to do? Oh, I'm so useless
to him! If only we hadn't gone to Southbourne! And we were so
happy there."

"You'll be allowed to visit him soon, I'm sure. And if the case
does come into court, we'll get a good lawyer."

"But I want to do something now."

"Steady, old girl. It's all just a bit ticklish. For me, I mean.
The police don't like it at all—my having helped Hugo to get
away from Southbourne. And doctors have to mind their p's
and q's."

Daisy threw up her beautiful head. "*I* know! Mark."

"Mark?"

"His brother. He must help. I'll ring him up now."

Jacko put up a hand, as if to restrain her; but Daisy was
already hurrying out into the hall. He could hear the leaves of
the telephone directory being ruffled, then Daisy's voice: "Mark?
This is Daisy . . . Daisy Bland. Something awful has happened
to Hugo. I must see you at once. . . . No, when I see you. I'll
ring for a taxi straight away."

Two minutes later, Daisy was in the drawing room again,
having fetched her coat from upstairs. With the sightless, single-
minded look of a woman driven by her strongest instinct, she
brushed past Jacko and drew aside the curtain.

"He won't stop me, will he?"

"Who? Oh, that plainclothes chap. We can but see."

Daisy was fumbling in her shabby purse. "Jacko—I'm afraid I haven't enough money for the taxi. Could you—"

"I'm coming with you."

"Oh, you are good to me! I was terrified of meeting Mark's wife again. Can you really spare the time?"

"I wouldn't miss it for worlds," replied Jacko, chuckling.

A taxi drew up outside. As Jacko handed Daisy in, the plain-clothes man came up and showed his card.

"May I ask where you're taking this lady, sir?"

"To her brother-in-law's house."

Daisy heard no more, for the two men moved away a little from the taxi driver's inquisitive ears. Presently Jacko got in, and they started off.

"Fixed him all right," he remarked cheerfully. Daisy was in far too great agitation to wonder how it had been done so easily. The long drive to north London was passed almost in silence, for Daisy was rehearsing the appeal she must make to the Amberleys, while Jacko was thinking out how best he could turn the meeting to his own advantage: Gertrude Amberley's personal dislike of him, he reflected, would be his trump card.

Mark Amberley led them into the drawing room, where Gertrude was sitting with books littered on the floor around her. She rose to greet Daisy, but only gave Jacko a cool nod. It was noticeable, during the conversation that followed, how her eyes seemed unwillingly drawn to the girl's swollen figure, flinching away from it, then returning to it.

"Hugo's been arrested," said Daisy. "For that murder at Southbourne. He didn't do it. You must help me."

"Arrested? Good God!" Mark fumbled with his fingers, throwing an agonized glance at his wife. "When did this happen?"

"You tell them, Jacko."

Jacko gave his account of the scene at Charing Cross. "They released me after a few hours," he ended. "I'm rather surprised they didn't charge me with being an accomplice after the fact."

"Because you gave Hugo money to get away from Southbourne?" Gertrude asked incisively.

"Yes. And I suppose because I didn't inform the police immediately, on hearing Hugo's story. But, as I told them, my professional reputation—"

"And what about Mark's professional reputation?" said Gertrude, her light, high, school-mistressy voice a little shrill. "Hugo dragged him into this. I was against your going down to Southbourne, Mark, even though we'd no idea then what it was all about. And now you've put yourself in a position where you'll have to give evidence in court that you helped a criminal to escape. I've no patience with—"

"Now, Gertrude, that's a bit hard," Mark protested with unusual firmness. "You've no right to prejudge the case against Hugo. The evidence against him may look bad, but the police do make mistakes."

"How can you talk like this?" cried Daisy. "Hugo's your brother. You're both talking as if he was—was somebody you'd just read about in the newspaper. I *know* him. He's done wrong things, but he'd never shoot a man like that. You must believe him. If we don't, nobody will. We've got to help him, not discuss him like a stranger." The girl had quite forgotten her prepared speech. And now it was not her words but the white-hot faith and love behind them, the tragedy of her pale, pleading face, which made the impression.

Gertrude Amberley was not a fundamentally bad woman or even a cold-hearted one, for all her intellectual pretentiousness, her puritanism, and her neurotic fear of those cruder manifestations of life which lay outside her experience. Her chin jerked up impatiently now, and flushing as though she had been caught out in some lapse from her rigid critical principles, she said, without any of her usual aggressive self-defensiveness:

"You're quite right, Miss Bland. It's not an abstract problem. I'm afraid Mark and I do tend to—well, take rather an intellectual line about things. And I can't pretend that I approve of Hugo. But of course we want to help. Only I don't quite see—"

"I knew you would!" Tears had started in Daisy's eyes at this unexpected change of tone. "I'm so ignorant. But we can get a lawyer for him—isn't that what we should do first?"

"Certainly," said Mark, following his wife's lead. "That's the least we can do."

"And I'm so worried about what happened here. You know—when Hugo took out that pistol. It'd make things so bad for him, if—"

"One only hopes the police won't ferret it out anyway," Jacko broke in—a pious hope, since he had already informed them of the episode. He had been glancing from Gertrude to Daisy, with a worried, sympathetic expression which effectively concealed his real anxiety lest Daisy should be winning the older woman to her side.

Mark said, "I don't see how the police could hear about that—"

"Unless you or your wife volunteered the information," Jacko put in smoothly. "I'm glad to think Gertrude's public-spiritedness doesn't extend that far. After all, it was only a harmless prank of Hugo's, from what I heard, and far too much fuss has been made about it already."

It was neatly done. The half-glance at Daisy on "from what I heard," implying that it was she who had minimized the incident to Jacko; the light, contemptuous tone: they stung to life again Gertrude's antagonism, reminding her of that occasion when she had groveled before Hugo, utterly terrified and humiliated, and of her neurotic outburst against Daisy which had led up to it.

Gertrude's voice became cold and brittle. "You have curious ideas, Dr. Jaques, about what constitutes a harmless prank. Perhaps, if you had been present, you might speak with more authority about it. I was threatened with a revolver and my brother-in-law clearly meant mischief. Mark will corroborate me. Miss Bland's account of the episode is hardly reliable, it seems."

"Oh, don't be so stuffy, Gertrude!" Jacko spoke with calculated impudence. "We all lose our tempers at times, and you can hardly blame Hugo for it after you'd made such an exhibition of yourself—calling Daisy a tart and I don't know what else."

"So Daisy—Miss Bland has been spreading it round to all and sundry!" Gertrude furiously exclaimed.

"Oh, please don't let's quarrel now! What does it all matter? Hugo's in terrible danger—don't you understand?" said Daisy.

"I understand perfectly. I'm not a moron. And I've no intention, Dr. Jaques, of running off to the police with the squalid little story."

"Of course not," said Mark fussily.

"But, if I am questioned about it, in court or elsewhere, I shall feel bound to state the facts. Quite objectively."

"'Objectively'? Lord love us!" exclaimed Jacko, throwing up his hands.

"Oh, Gertrude! Please! You don't mean that? When it might help to—to hang him?"

"Nobody is hanged for *not* firing a revolver," Gertrude replied, with a little twitch of her mouth.

"You know that's not what I mean." Daisy had struggled to her feet, and stared at Gertrude with a wild expression which gradually set into one of despairing calm, as the woman would not meet her eyes.

"The point, surely, is this," said Mark—the lecturer getting a discussion onto the right rails again. "It would be unthinkable to offer this information to the police gratuitously. But, if they should ask us whether we have any evidence of Hugo's violent temper—"

"Then little Gertrude cannot tell a lie," said Jacko, with a fine assumption of disgust.

Daisy swung round upon Mark, standing over him, a lioness in her beauty and anger. "Do *you* believe he did it?"

"But really, Daisy, that's not the point. I—"

"Do you believe your brother shot that policeman?"

Mark Amberley turned his head away, as if her incandescent blue eyes were scorching his skin. "I don't know," he said miserably. "How can one be sure?"

Daisy, in a quite different voice said, "It's no good, Jacko. They don't want to help us." And before the Amberleys could speak, she was out of the room. On the pavement, she turned to Jacko, who had at once followed her. "You're the only person Hugo and I can trust now." Her eyes searched his face under the street lamp. "*You* believe in Hugo, don't you?"

"Of course I do, you silly old goose."

They walked away toward the main road. Presently Daisy said, "I can see Mark's point of view. He was trying to be honest. It's very important to him to be honest, isn't it? even when it's his brother?"

"Oh yes," replied Jacko, with an involuntary, furious grimace which was his sole reaction to his own infamy, "you could say he makes a profession of it."

16   Fair Enough

THE next morning, Saturday, Hugo Chesterman was taken down to Southbourne. The preparations for his arrival, almost unprecedented in criminal history, were the result of a conference between the Chief Constable and Chief Inspector Nailsworth the previous evening. Colonel Allison, though he had bowed to the necessity of using Dr. Jaques as a decoy, none the less felt qualms about it, and was determined to give the accused man a scrupulously fair deal from now on.

"A lot depends on the identification, Nailsworth. Southbourne's not a big place, and there's very strong feeling about poor Stone. Everyone here knows a man has been arrested. You're going to get a crowd of rubbernecks waiting at the railway station for his arrival tomorrow morning. Now then: I don't want any of our witnesses to see Chesterman, or a photograph of him, or to be told by a bystander—at the station or when he's brought in here—what he looks like."

"Chuck an overcoat over his head, sir. That'll do it."

"I'm afraid not. It might fall off. Some enterprising pressman might snatch it off. We've got to make dead sure that, when the case comes up in court, the Defense can't say the witnesses might have been prejudiced—even by hearsay about Chesterman's appearance. You realize, Nailsworth, that if Jaques goes into the witness box, there'll be rumpus enough about the police methods anyway?"

"I was only acting in accordance with—" Nailsworth began stiffly.

"I'm not criticizing you, my dear fellow. I'm warning you that we've got to take extreme precautions."

"What do you suggest, sir?"

"I want the whole station and the yard cleared of the public until Chesterman is off the train and safely in the police car."

"Good lord, sir, there'll be a riot!"

"Then you'll have to deal with it," said Colonel Allison, smiling. "He must have some sort of hood over his face, of course, as you suggested. Same procedure when he arrives here. Cordon to keep the crowd right back. Anyone trying to take a photograph gets his camera confiscated."

The Chief Inspector rubbed his chin dubiously. "Very well, sir, I'll do my best."

"I know you will. Now, about the identification parade."

Colonel Allison pointed out that, in a town the size of Southbourne, local men picked for the parade might well be recognized by the witnesses, and automatically eliminated, which would be unfair to Chesterman. Ways and means for avoiding this were discussed. Then Colonel Allison said: "What sort of a chap is this Chesterman? What d'you make of him?"

"He's tough as they come, sir. Not a criminal type, to look at. Quiet; public-school accent; quite the gentleman, you'd think. But he's tough underneath it all right—doesn't give a damn for anyone."

"And he's not talking?"

"He's certainly not confessing, sir. We questioned him for several hours. He admitted he was staying here with his girl, but said they were at the cinema the night Stone was shot."

"He did, did he? Very different from the story Daisy Bland told Jaques. Did you confront him with Jaques' evidence?"

Nailsworth looked a bit evasive. "Thorne and I agreed it'd be best to keep that till later, sir."

"I see. What about the girl?"

"Thorne will be interviewing her tonight."

"A great deal depends on her evidence, eh?"

"Just so, sir," replied Nailsworth woodenly. Then, as if he wanted to get off dangerous ground, "Chesterman denied the charge, of course. He said, 'Whoever did it did it to get the

Princess's papers for political purposes. That's what I think anyway. No doubt she's mixed up in some foreign political business.' "

"Thorne's original theory, eh?"

"Yes, sir. We asked him how he knew about the Princess. Said he'd heard about her in a local pub, and read the newspapers later."

"H'm." There was a pause. Then the Chief Constable asked, "You're sure we've got the right man?"

"He's a convicted thief, a cat burglar. He can't or won't give a satisfactory account of his movements during the period in question. That Brighton shopkeeper has identified Daisy Bland as the woman who bought a cap exactly similar to the one we found nearby, and the cap is Chesterman's size. And everything Bland told Jaques—especially the impression he got from her about Chesterman's revolver—supports my belief that he's the murderer."

"But, if our eye-witnesses fail to identify him, we shall be relying largely on Jaques' evidence?"

"And the girl's."

"Suppose she denies having told Jaques this story?"

"I don't see how she can, sir. Not at this stage. Thorne will get it out of her all right. Of course, I'd be happier if we'd found the revolver. That'd clinch it—"

"One way or another. Yes. But you can't expect the girl to help over that."

"Possibly not." Nailsworth's tone was stolid and evasive again. The Chief Constable glanced at him keenly.

"This was a dirty crime. We don't want to make it a dirty case, though, by exercising improper pressure on witnesses."

"No, sir." Nailsworth's huge face was utterly uncommunicative. Then, with a twist of the lip, he said, "No doubt someone'll say we've been roughing Chesterman up, when they see him brought along with his head covered."

"There was none of that, of course." Allison made it a statement.

"No fault of his there wasn't. At times during the interrogation he fairly asked for it, sir. I'd a job keeping my hands off him. Talk about insolence! I'd swear he was trying to provoke us into giving him a clout. First criminal I've ever met who seems really to hate the police like poison. Honestly, sir, I'd almost not put it past him to have shot poor Herbert just because he was in uniform."

The Chief Constable fiddled for a while with his cigarette case. "Hates us, does he? I wonder why."

"No doubt the Defense will rustle up some trick cyclist to tell us," said Nailsworth. "Maybe his Dad gave him a good spanking one day, or his Nanny wore buttoned boots, so of course he isn't responsible for his actions when he shoots a poor bloody policeman."

"He'd like to get his own back for that jail sentence, I dare say. You don't think he's stringing us along?"

"I don't get you, sir."

"Suppose he has a perfectly good alibi, and is keeping it under his hat till the case comes up for trial. He could have told the girl all that story about going to meet a man at the Queen's Hotel—just as an extra bit of bait for us to snap up. We'd look pretty silly. Wrongful detention—the Lord knows what."

"Why, bless my soul, you don't really think—?"

"Forget it, Nailsworth. No, if it's a put-up job at all, my money'd be on that fella Jaques. Oily bit of work. Get Chesterman out of the way, and the girl's all his. I wouldn't like to be in his shoes when counsel starts pitching into him."

Saturday morning was damp and close. A warm sea mist hung over Southbourne, and it was this oppressiveness in the atmosphere which Hugo felt first when he set foot on the station platform—this, and a silence unnatural in such a place. A blue cloth, covering his head and the upper part of his body, prevented him from seeing its cause. Apart from a ticket collector and a uniformed policeman at the barrier, and a handful of porters waiting beyond it, the station was empty.

Traveling in the first compartment of the front coach, Hugo's

escort had hurried him through the barrier almost before the
other travelers had time to alight. The brief silence was broken
by doors slamming farther down the train. Hugo could hear feet
pounding behind him now, and it was like a pursuit, a stampede.
He began to sweat. The cloth over his head entombed him, and
he would have thrown it off but that his arms were firmly gripped
on either side.

When they reached the station exit, he became aware of
another kind of silence—that of a crowd just before the teams
emerge from the dressing room—and then a distant, rising mutter
in which nothing was distinguishable except its note of animosity,
a sort of angry yet gratified susurration. Kept well back by a
police cordon, all that the crowd glimpsed before Hugo was
hustled into the police car was a smallish figure, weirdly hooded
as if it were the high priest or the victim of some barbaric rite
about to be performed, or the "it" in a sinister, new kind of
blindman's buff. As the car drove off, Inspector Thorne heard a
faint sound from beneath the blue cloth: he was not to know
that Hugo was fighting against an agony of claustrophobia; nor,
had he known, would he have cared in the least.

Two hours later, a group of people were assembled in Chief
Inspector Nailsworth's office, eying one another with the furtive
embarrassment of patients in a specialist's waiting room. There
was the cabby, Charles Poore, a rheumy-eyed old man wearing a
high, yellowish, stiff collar with a stock—his tribute to the occasion. There was the girl, a typist at the Municipal Offices, who
had seen the murderer running away up Queen's Parade: she was
manifestly nervous, and from time to time took out her compact,
only to thrust it back unused in her bag, flushing as though she
had been caught making up at a graveside. Next to her sat a
brash young man, with the professionally cheery expression of a
youth club leader. He had been passing through Southbourne on
a cycling tour, and seen a hatless man walking briskly past the
Queen's Hotel from the direction of Princess Popescu's house just
after the time when Inspector Stone was shot; continuing on his

tour, he had only yesterday seen the newspaper appeal for eye-witnesses, and come forward.

Sitting against the opposite wall were the Princess, her companion, and the Italian maid, Velma. Though they had not seen the murderer at the time, Nailsworth wanted them to attend the identification parade, in case the sight of Chesterman should remind them of some previous meeting with him; for the police were still mystified by the would-be burglar's attempting to break into a house as it were on spec. Thorne had elicited no admissions whatsoever from Velma—the obvious suspect as an accomplice of the burglar, nor had the police investigations unearthed any connection between her and Chesterman. But Thorne still hoped that, when she was actually confronted with him, Velma might betray herself by some involuntary reaction. At present, the Italian girl sat there, rolling up her lustrous brown eyes and sighing melodramatically four times a minute.

The Princess, a gaunt, heavily-furred woman, with hennaed hair and an aquiline face as white as enamel, was deep in a book of memoirs; the huge rings on her fingers sent flashes through the somber room as she turned a page; she seemed entirely at ease, dissociated from the proceedings; and when some passage in the book amused her, the deep, baying laugh she gave set up a visible wave of outrage among the trio sitting opposite her. Mrs. Felstead, her companion, fidgeted incessantly with a bead bag until the Princess, not looking up from her book, laid a hand on the bag and firmly removed it from her.

Presently the Chief Constable entered, followed by Nailsworth. He bowed to the Princess, who acknowledged it with an inclination of the head, handed her book to the flustered nondescript little woman beside her, and assumed an attitude of gracious attention. Charles Poore struggled to his feet and stood, wheezing, with the glum apathy of a very old horse between the shafts, till Colonel Allison motioned him to sit down again.

"You know what you've come here for, ladies and gentlemen. I'll just tell you the procedure. You will be taken out into the yard, one by one. There you'll see a file of men. One of them is a man arrested under suspicion of having killed Inspector Stone. I want you to look at these men carefully—take your time about it—walk round behind them as well and get a back view—one of you only saw the man in Queen's Parade that night from behind. They are all wearing cloth caps, and you may ask any of them to remove his cap, if you wish. You must not address any other remark to them. If you spot the man you saw, or in your case"— Allison turned to the Princess's party—"if you recognize a man you had met before, you must identify him—point him out to us on the spot. I must impress upon you all," the Colonel earnestly continued, "what identification means. It means you must be able to swear in court that, to the best of your belief, this was the man you saw on the night of the murder. Remember, you'll be cross-examined on it. If you only think it *may* be the man, but are not sure, would not be prepared to swear to it on oath, that is not good enough for an identification. You'll understand, of course, that when you leave you must not talk to anyone, drop any hints whatsoever, if you identified or suspected one of these men. Well, I think that's all. But if you have any questions—"

The Princess's deep voice, speaking in a strong foreign accent, turned every head toward her: "It is permitted to make them run?"

"I *beg* your pardon, ma'am?" said the Chief Constable, his eyes popping a little.

"This young person"—the Princess flung out a glittering hand toward the typist, who visibly quailed—"has seen a man running away. To identify, the same conditions will be helpful, yes?"

"Oo, I couldn't!" the typist protested.

"My dear young lady," said Colonel Allison, "all you'd have to do is say a word to the Chief Inspector. But not unless you've already seen a likeness in one of these men, and wish to confirm it."

The Princess raised one shoulder very slightly, as if to repudiate the kid-glove methods of the British police, then returned to her book.

In the yard behind the police station, six men were drawn up.

Hugo Chesterman was third from the left. The others chatted in
a desultory way, looking awkward and self-conscious like new
boys at a school. Hugo glanced round at the high wall behind
and to both sides of him: he'd managed worse walls than that in
his time, but there were policemen at either corner, and anyway
it'd be crazy to make a bolt for it now; he remembered what
Jacko had said about running away looking like a confession of
guilt—easy enough for old Jacko to talk—he'd never known the
inside of a cell. He had been told that he could have a friend or a
solicitor present, and could take up any position he liked in the
line when each new witness was introduced; but he felt too
apathetic to bother. A black frost of bitterness, anguish, despair
had come over his mind.

"Now, my lads," Inspector Thorne called out. The file of men
automatically stiffened as Nailsworth emerged from the back
door, followed by Charles Poore. The old cabby trailed lugu-
briously along the line, with his stiff bow-legged gait, pausing to
peer at each man's face. Hugo was standing at ease, his hands
lightly clasped in front of him. The old cabby paused, muttering
something to himself, wrinkling his eyes at Hugo, then shambled
on.

"Just like a General Inspection," Hugo's neighbor whispered,
nervously waggish. "What price Field Marshal Montgomery!"

"Silence there in the ranks," Nailsworth barked.

The typist came next, and the men were asked to doff their
caps as Nailsworth led her round to the rear of the file. The girl
was speechless, and indeed half blind, with nerves. As she stood
there, her eyes returned several times to the back of Hugo's head;
but she'd sooner have died than request the Inspector to make
any of these men run.

So, like some macabre version of a children's party game, the
identification parade proceeded. The Princess walked round with
the dignity of a royal personage reviewing a guard of honor.
The youth-club type, conscientious to a fault, took an intolerably
long time about it. Mrs. Felstead only raised her eyes from the
ground to give each man a furtive and appalled glance, as if their

faces were dirty postcards. When Velma approached Hugo, Thorne could not detect, closely though he was watching, the slightest change of expression on her face.

The parade had been, from the police's point of a view, a total failure.

"So it depends upon the girl's evidence now," said the Chief Constable. "And you say she refuses to co-operate?"

"Not exactly that, sir. When I interviewed her last night, she was so agitated that I couldn't get any sense out of her. She'd just returned from a rather painful visit to Chesterman's brother—Jaques told me this—he went with her; and he warned me it might gravely endanger her health if I pursued the questioning any further."

Thorne had next visited the Amberleys, from whom he took a statement about the revolver episode.

"So Bland went to their house to try and make them hush it up?" said Nailsworth. "We've got good grounds for taking her into custody, sir."

"What do you say, Thorne?" asked the Chief Constable.

"I'd advise against it for the present. I've reasons to think she'll come clean in a day or so. And I'll be interviewing her again myself, as soon as she's in a fit state." Thorne was relieved that the others did not press him for his "reasons," arising as they did from a brief conversation with Jaques after the girl had gone up to bed.

So it was that, when Hugo Chesterman was charged at the Magistrates' Court on Monday, the only witness called was Chief Inspector Nailsworth. He gave evidence of the arrest and the formal charge in London. The prisoner, who spoke no word except to reply in the affirmative when asked if he desired legal aid, was remanded for a week so that the police might pursue their investigations.

17 The Second Betrayal

"But why can't I go and see him?"

"I've tried to explain, Daisy," Jacko spoke patiently, but the solicitous smile on his face was wearing thin. "There'd be a police officer in the room, and he'd report everything you and Hugo said. You can't talk freely to Hugo, don't you understand—especially after refusing to say anything to Inspector Thorne last night."

"But I don't want to talk about—about what happened. I just want to see him, and tell him I love him and believe in him."

"He knows that," said Jacko, rather perfunctorily. He was debating with himself whether the moment had come to turn on the heat. Daisy's obstinacy had become quite trying; and after as good as promising Thorne last night that he would himself take in hand the softening-up process, Jacko was getting impatient for results.

The sound of the evening paper dropping through the letter box took him out into the hall. On his way back he entered the lavatory, brushed back the gray hair over his temples, and gave himself a lopsided experimental grin in the mirror. He knew the girl was waiting, with every nerve stretched, for the news from the Southbourne Magistrates' Court; she can wait a little longer, he thought, as he opened the paper and began to read. Daisy's calm and equable temperament had always irked him; it was pleasant to see that calm shattered and watch her blindly groping to pick up the fragments. " 'Just want to tell him I love him and believe in him!' Silly bitch! A fat lot of good that'd do him!" he muttered, furiously aware at last of Daisy's loving heart as of an antagonist whose strength he had misjudged and whose downfall had become an obsession with him. Jacko stared into the mirror, into the sick, dilated eyes which met him there, as though they were Daisy's and he was hypnotizing her, willing her to share his own damnation.

"He's been remanded in custody for a week," said Jacko, returning to the drawing room. "And they've granted him legal aid, so you needn't worry about that."

"They'll let me see him now, won't they?"

"He'll be allowed to have visitors." Jacko paused, observing how Daisy's face lit up, her whole body seemed enlivened. The throaty, crooning note returned to his voice, as he went on, "But you've got to be sensible about this, my dear. Do believe me, I'm trying to act in your best interests—and it's only what Hugo himself wants you to do."

He had only to say Hugo's name for the girl to vibrate, as if an electric circuit had been completed, and lean forward eagerly in her chair.

"When I saw him, just before he was arrested, he told me to tell you that, if anything happened to him, you must not withhold information from the police." Jacko's brown eyes were fastened upon hers, not compulsively, but with an anxious, affectionate, honeyed look. "He said, if the police ask Daisy about it, she must tell them exactly what happened that night."

"But *why*?" Daisy almost wailed.

"Because—he told me this himself—he doesn't want his child to be born in prison."

"Oh, they wouldn't do that! Why should they put *me* in prison?"

Jacko explained again, with a patience renewed by the fascination of the game he was playing, the significance of accomplice before and after the fact. "Last night," he concluded, "after you'd gone to bed, Inspector Thorne gave me a friendly warning. He said the police would have no alternative but to charge you with complicity if you went on refusing to make a statement. I managed to postpone it for a little, on the grounds of your health; but I shan't be able to hold them off any longer."

"If only I could see Hugo, and make sure that's what he really wants."

Perceiving another opportunity, Jacko moved rapidly in. "I can tell you this, my dear. They certainly won't let you see him unless you've answered their questions first. Once you've made a statement, there'll be no difficulty about visiting him."

Daisy picked at her handkerchief. The streak of common sense, which had come to her rescue before now, made her say, "But look, Jacko. If they really believe Hugo did it, won't I be—what did you call it?—an accomplice after the fact for helping him bury the revolver?"

It was a great moment for Jacko, so rewarding that he must get up and draw the curtains to conceal from Daisy the triumph on his face and compose it to its normal friendly solicitude. Controlling his voice, he said over his shoulder, "The revolver? Well, of course I don't know anything about that. But—"

"I shouldn't have told you. I'm afraid it's putting just another burden on you," the girl said, with innocent compunction. Then, trying to smile, "I suppose that's made *you* an accomplice after the fact now."

Jacko sat down on the arm of her chair, and took her hand. "You mustn't tell me anything you feel you shouldn't. But I know you've been worrying about the revolver. And if it would help—"

Daisy suddenly burst into passionate, desolate weeping, and gripped the man's hand frantically as if she were drowning.

"Oh, Jacko, it was so awful!" she said, when she had got herself under control at last. Then the whole story of that episode on the beach came out.

The bloody fool, Jacko was thinking as he gently stroked the girl's hair—letting her in on it, instead of burying the gun by himself. Such folly of human trustfulness aroused his mind to an ecstasy of contempt, and he saw with beautiful clarity his next move.

"My poor Daisy," he said. "What a horrible business for you. Of course, this does make a difference."

"Hugo was frightened of what might happen if he was found

with the revolver. Not because he shot the Inspector, but because he'd been in prison," she valiantly replied. "You don't think—?"

"It's what the police will think, my dear. No, you'd better not tell them about that." Jacko paused meditatively. "Did anyone see you and Hugo on the beach?"

Daisy blushed a little. "I'm sure no one saw us burying the gun."

"No, but now the police have got a description of you both, they'll be combing Southbourne for eye-witnesses. There's a great danger that someone'll come forward and say, 'I saw them on the beach together the next morning.' Just that would be quite enough. The police will say to themselves, 'What on earth were they doing on the beach? They'd hardly be making sand castles when they were admittedly in such agitation about the murder.' And the answer'd be obvious, even to a policeman's limited intelligence. So they'd go and dig up the beach where you were seen."

"Oh, God! What am I to do? What *am* I to do?"

Jacko pouted his lips and drew them in again. "We must get there first, my dear. Find the gun and put it somewhere it simply can't be found."

"No, Jacko. I'll go alone. Why should you be mixed up in it? I don't want you to get into trouble too."

"My dear child, of course I'll come with you," Jacko lusciously answered. "It's the least I can do, for you and poor old Hugo."

They discussed how they might best shake off the plainclothes man and find their way to the beach unobserved. Daisy's morale was soaring at the thought of doing something at last—since parting from Hugo she had lived in a kind of stupor, broken only by the abortive visit to the Amberleys, her life measured out in rows of knitting—and Jacko made it sound like a delightful, venturesome game. Tomorrow he had patients he must see. But on Wednesday he could cancel his morning appointments. After an early breakfast, Daisy was to leave the house, quite openly, with a shopping basket. If she was followed, she must try to slip the plainclothes man in one of the big Kensington High Street stores; but Jacko did not think she would be, for until her "collapse" yesterday she had regularly taken a short morning walk. Jacko would make his own way to Waterloo. They would travel separately, but get off the train at the station before South-bourne and there hire a car to drive them the rest of the way; the danger of their being noticed at the Southbourne station, by a policeman who had her description or Jacko's, would be avoided thus.

There remained the problem of Inspector Thorne. If he turned up tomorrow to interview Daisy again, they agreed that she must see him, and give him her account of the happenings at South-bourne—except for the burying of the revolver. Jacko said that the Inspector would be satisfied, once he had her statement, and with any luck would not arrest her. The alternative—that Jacko should tell him Daisy was not yet fit to be interviewed—seemed hopeless; for then she could not possibly walk out of the house the next morning.

Inspector Thorne, to Daisy's relief, did not turn up the follow-ing day—for the very good reason that Jacko had given him on the telephone a résumé of this conversation with the girl. Hardened as Thorne was to the ways of normal malefactors, he found Jaques' cynical treachery almost more than he could stomach. But, unless the weapon was discovered, the case against Chesterman would remain so flimsy that the Director of Public Prosecutions might well refuse to take it up. What riled Thorne especially was Jaques' increasing impudence: the man had the audacity to suggest that, in return for his co-operation with the police, they should withdraw the plainclothes men who were keeping his house under surveillance—it was bad for his profes-sional reputation to have busies hanging around, he outrageously complained. Moreover, Jaques made it quite plain to Thorne that he considered himself indispensable, as a sort of expert consultant: only Daisy Bland, he told Thorne, knew the precise spot where the revolver had been buried, and he himself was the only person who could persuade her to reveal it. Thorne had seen enough of the girl, during his brief interview with her on Sunday, to realize that this at least was true. What had not occurred to the bastard Jaques, in his insensate egotism or hatred or power mania, Thorne grimly reflected, was that mine detectors could now do the job; but it would take a deal of time and organization to sweep a two-mile-long beach with mine detectors; and besides, if the girl herself were caught in the act of recovering the revolver, her resistance was bound to break down all along the line. This, no doubt, was the conclusion which Jaques had intended him to reach. Thorne felt a new wave of disgust as he realized it; however, he had touched so much pitch already, there was no point spoiling the ship for another ha'porth of the filthy stuff. So he fell in with the tactics which Jaques had suggested.

Wednesday morning was bright and fresh. Daisy's natural elasticity of temperament had not been destroyed by the events of the last week. Like all sanguine characters, she was revived by activity: it made her seem more real to herself, in full possession of herself again. Now she was doing something for Hugo, and happy. She knew there were dangers attached to this enterprise; but, if anything, the knowledge braced her. Never an easy prey for doubts or suspicions, she was not at all disquieted by the smoothness with which she had got away from Jacko's house and from London.

Houses, trees, fields whisked past the carriage window. Every telegraph pole was bringing her nearer to Hugo. Her thoughts so tenderly strained toward him that she felt he must know in his heart she was coming. It did not even matter so terribly that this time she would not see him; there was only room for one sensation in her mind—the sense of getting nearer and nearer.

At Stenford, the last stop before Southbourne, she alighted. There, outside the station, Jacko was waiting for her. He gave her a gay, confidential wink and took her arm. Everything was going beautifully. They had a cup of coffee, then walked to a garage where they hired a car to take them the remaining five miles to Southbourne. As they approached the town, a little cloud came over Daisy's mind. She was remembering the last time she and Hugo had gone to the beach; an unlaid ghost was awaiting her there, and she knew she must face it alone.

"I want to go down on the beach by myself first," she whispered to Jacko. "You hang about for a few minutes."

A few hundred yards from the bandstand, they stopped the taxi. Jacko paid off the driver and helped Daisy out.

"We'll meet again presently, then," he said.

Daisy, her bright hair concealed by a head scarf, moved off along the promenade with the brilliant, unseeing eyes of a woman going to an assignation. Jacko lit a cigarette, gazed leisurely for a while toward the harbor wall, then strolled after her. A stalwart young man, in flannel trousers and an open-necked shirt, who was vigorously inhaling the sea air nearby, decided that he too would stroll along in the direction of the bandstand, and followed Jacko.

Daisy moved carefully down the steps onto the beach. There were a few late holiday makers about, enjoying the crisp October sunlight. With her shopping bag and head scarf she looked like a holiday maker too. It was just here, she thought, bravely scrutinizing the pebbly expanse beneath the sea wall. Hugo said, "Shall I make love to you, darling?" A phrase from a hymn, heard long ago in the village church, sang through her head. "My pillow a stone." And suddenly the ghost was exorcised. What had happened here was horrible no longer. Stretching herself out where they had lain, she felt nothing but the remembered warmth of his arms, his lips, his body half covering hers. For a timeless moment, she forgot that she was alone and what she had come here to do.

Presently her fingers, as if of their own volition, began to prod and poke among the stones; but her mind felt no urgency yet—it was occupied with Hugo, and basking in the delight of a memory which had miraculously become pure, shedding its anxiety and shame. The open-shirted young man, leaning on the esplanade railings, caught an expression on her face, when she chanced to look up in his direction, so purely beautiful, so ecstatic that he was reminded of some poems he had been made to read at school—what were they called?—*Songs of Innocence;* they would make sense to him now, he found himself thinking. Innocence! And this

was the mistress, maybe the accomplice, of the man who had
shot poor old Stone! The young man moved away a little. He felt,
irrationally, that he had no right to be witnessing the scene; but
his training mastered his feelings with no great difficulty, and he
continued to keep Daisy under observation.

Jacko descended the steps. The girl's face was growing anxious,
as she turned over the stones more hurriedly.

"Can't you find it?" he asked. "Are you sure this is the place?"

"Yes, I know it was here. Just about here."

How could she possibly forget that? But, even in a few square
yards of beach, there were so many stones.

"How deep was it?" Jacko asked in a low voice.

"About up to my wrist. A little deeper perhaps." She remembered the feel of the big stones and then the shingle beneath
them. She gazed desperately around, as if trying to recognize one
stone among the multitude, and her hands began to move
feverishly. Jacko's impatient look flustered her.

"Lost something, dear?"

A young woman with a child had approached them, unheard
by Daisy in her agitation.

"N-no. It's nothing—" she began.

Jacko cut in smoothly, "My spectacle case. I may have mislaid
it here yesterday. Always leaving it about."

"Now, Desmond," said the young woman. "You help this lady
and gentleman."

The little boy gripped his spade and attacked the beach with
frantic enthusiasm.

"Oh, please don't bother," said Daisy faintly.

"No trouble at all, dear. He likes it. Desmond's a great one for
digging."

"Are you *quite* sure—?" Jacko said, and began to ransack
Daisy's shopping bag, from which, by neat legerdemain, he
presently produced a spectacle case he'd just slipped into it out
of his own pocket, and held it up triumphantly. "It was there all
the time. You just don't look for things properly, Daisy."

After mutual civilities and congratulations, the woman led her child off, to sit down against the sea wall twenty yards away. Daisy stared miserably at Jacko. "We can't go on looking now."

Jacko, resourceful as ever, strolled down the beach, built up a cairn of stones and returned. He began to pick up pebbles and throw them at it, then bigger stones. The nightmare was moving in on Daisy again. Thousands of stones where she and Hugo had lain; how much of the beach would they have to throw at that cairn before they found the gun? She'd never thought it would be so difficult. And Jacko was looking peevish, throwing the stones more and more viciously.

"You must have got the wrong place," he said. "We're just wasting our time."

After a pause, Daisy muttered, "D'you think?—Perhaps it's not here any more."

"Don't be ridiculous! If the police had found it, it'd be all over the newspapers."

Jacko was getting bored. For a moment he wondered if the girl had been deceiving him, playing some crazy game of her own; it was a thought which would inevitably come to a mind so tortuous as his. But a glance at her face, cold with despair, reassured him. Well, the police would know where to look now: there was no point in protracting the farce.

"We'd better be going, Daisy. It's a washout, I'm afraid."

"Do you think Hugo might have come back here and taken it away, before he was arrested?"

What bloody silly questions women do ask, he thought. He said, "I doubt it, my dear. It'd have been too dangerous."

Presently he pulled her to her feet, and they climbed up onto the promenade. The young man in the open-necked shirt followed them at a discreet interval, noticing how the girl's steps dragged and how she kept turning her head to look back at the beach where she had been sitting, like a child saying good-by to its seaside holiday.

"If we can't find it, the police certainly won't," said Jacko—not from any wish to comfort Daisy, but because he wanted to get her along faster to the station and bring down the curtain on this act. In London, they had decided to leave Southbourne by train, after walking to the end of the harbor mole and dropping the revolver into the deep water there; or rather, Jacko had decided it, having arranged with Thorne that they should be arrested immediately after leaving the beach, should their search have proved successful. Otherwise, they would go to the railway station, where a reception committee would be awaiting them.

The stalwart young man, who had been keeping them under surveillance, knew they had not found the revolver. He therefore allowed them to proceed.

"Where's the police station?" Daisy suddenly asked.

Jacko began to point inland, toward the clock tower, then killed the gesture at birth. He had nearly given himself away; a girl quicker on the uptake than Daisy would have asked, "How do you know? Have you been there? Why did you go there?" Rather disagreeably he replied:

"The police station? What on earth do you want that for?"

"Hugo's there."

"Oh, I see."

"Will they let me see him soon?"

It was on the tip of Jacko's tongue to reply, "You'll be visiting the police station very soon, my dear." But such ironies, with a slow-witted girl like Daisy, lacked savor.

"Do hurry up, my dear, or we'll miss that train."

So they walked up the station approach, and the trap was tactfully sprung.

"Miss Bland? I must ask you to step this way. And you, sir," said a large, round-faced man who confronted them just inside the entrance.

Fatalistically, Daisy allowed herself to be led to the station-master's office. She was beyond feeling shock or terror: it was as though, all along, this had been going to happen, and she was prepared for it. When the train had left, and the station was empty again of travelers, Nailsworth took them outside to the police car.

18   From Evidence Received

FOR two hours, Daisy was questioned by Thorne and Nailsworth. They did not bully her: indeed, she was treated with a certain humanity; sandwiches and tea were provided halfway through the interrogation, and from time to time the police officers asked her if she would like to rest. Thorne had only seen her for a few minutes on Sunday, when she was in a state of collapse. Nailsworth was seeing her for the first time; having expected a brassy, pert delinquent, he was taken out of his stride by this girl—so quiet, so amazingly beautiful, mature beyond her years. She made him feel almost paternal, and there were moments when he inwardly cursed that young ruffian in the cells for having dragged such a girl into his disreputable life; when she spoke of him, her voice took on a tenderness, an eagerness which pierced Nailsworth's official hide. It was clear that she believed passionately in Chesterman's innocence. All the time she was making statements which were so many nails in his coffin, this faith shone the brighter. Even Thorne, a harder, more cynical man than Nailsworth, was affected by it. After half an hour's questioning, both officers had mentally acquitted Daisy of any complicity in the crime.

At the start of the interrogation, she had shown considerable reluctance, or rather, it was as if her mind were on something else; and indeed it was—she could only think of Hugo, so near that if she called out he might be able to hear her. Thorne, who at this stage was standing no nonsense from her, hinted pretty broadly that, unless she made a statement which satisfied the police, they would be compelled to arrest her as an accomplice of Chesterman. Whereupon, coming out of her dream, she had said with a spurt of animation, "Do you think I'd mind that, sir?" But then, remembering what Jacko had told her—that Hugo wanted her to tell the truth—she said, "Very well, I'll answer your questions."

When it was over, and the stenographer had taken out his sheets to type the material in the form of a statement, Daisy felt a strange mixture of relief and vague disquiet. She was so exhausted, physically and emotionally, that at first she could not trace the disquiet to its source. Then it suddenly broke upon her that no questions had been asked about what she and Jacko were doing on the beach this morning. Perhaps the London Inspector, who had just left the room, had gone to question Jacko about it. Wearily she tried to think what she should say, what Jacko might be saying now; they had never discussed what account they should give; they mustn't contradict each other. But perhaps they hadn't been seen on the beach at all—yes, how stupid I am, she thought; if the police had seen us, it's the first thing they'd have asked me about. And a little hope glowed in her heart again.

But not for long. Thorne, appearing at the door, beckoned Nailsworth out. Daisy sat on the hard chair, looking, with her shopping bag and head scarf and dumb, forlorn air, like a displaced peasant; a parcel, bearing no label, at some lost luggage office of human souls. When the door opened again, she started up from her apathy, saying, "Can I see him now?"

"Dr. Jaques is engaged at the moment," said Nailsworth.

"No, I mean Hugo—Mr. Chesterman? Please may I?"

Nailsworth turned his head away: he was unable for a moment to master the feelings which must be showing through the official severity on his countenance.

"Now that I've told you everything you wanted to know?" the girl persisted.

Nailsworth, clearing his throat, faced her across the desk.

"Certain new evidence has come to light, Miss Bland, and I shall have to ask for your explanation." He rang a bell: the stenographer appeared, followed by Inspector Thorne, who placed a cardboard box on the desk in front of his colleague.

"Now, Miss Bland," said Nailsworth, restored to his official self again. "From evidence received, we understand that you and Dr. Jaques were on the beach between 11:50 this morning and 12:35. Will you please tell us for what purpose?"

"We—I came down to try and see Hugo."

"On the beach? Come, come, Miss Bland," said Thorne; "that won't do."

"I wanted to go to the beach first, because—because it was the last place Hugo and I—"

"What were you searching for?"

"Searching?"

"You were seen turning over stones, looking for something."

"Oh," said Daisy desperately, "it was Jacko's—Dr. Jaques' spectacle case."

"Are you quite sure?" Nailsworth was relentless now. "Were you not looking for something you and Chesterman had hidden there?" He removed the lid of the cardboard box, took out an object wrapped in a handkerchief, and laid it on the desk. "This revolver?"

"You never asked me about that," was all Daisy could say.

"I'm asking you now, and I want the truth."

With the weapon which he believed had killed his friend lying before him, Nailsworth was again in a vindictive mood; but he was also fair-minded enough to know that, in this mood, he should not continue the interrogation, so with a movement of the hand he turned it over to Thorne.

"Do you identify this revolver as having been in the prisoner's possession?" Thorne asked, his long nose directed upon Daisy like a probing finger.

"I don't know," she faltered. "He had one rather like it."

"The one with which he threatened Mrs. Amberley?"

"He didn't mean any harm."

Thorne questioned the girl for some time about that incident, then abruptly asked: "Surely you can recognize a gun you helped the prisoner to hide away?"

"I didn't look at it very hard, I was too frightened."

"You admit, then, you helped the prisoner to bury it?"

"I—no, I don't."

"If you didn't help him, how did you know the exact spot on the beach where it was buried?"

Daisy could say nothing to this.

"Would it surprise you to know that Dr. Jaques has identified the weapon?"

Nailsworth gave his colleague a glance of some consternation. Surely it was a mistake to let that cat out of the bag so soon? But the girl did not seem suspicious; she only said: "If he has identified it, why do you ask me?"

"Confirmation, Miss Bland. Dr. Jaques might be mistaken. . . . Mightn't he?" Thorne added, after a slight pause.

"I suppose so."

"What did you propose to do with this revolver, if you found it?"

"I don't know."

"Hand it over to the police?"

"Don't be daft," Daisy answered, with a flash of spirit.

"Why not, if you are convinced that Chesterman did not use it to shoot Inspector Stone?"

Again Daisy made no answer. Inspector Thorne slowly wrapped up the revolver and replaced it in the box, which he handed to a constable he had summoned. "Fingerprints first. Then the bullet," he said.

Daisy made an involuntary movement. She believed that scientific experts could tell if a bullet had been fired from a particular gun. For a week she had been evading the question— why did Hugo want to hide it if he is innocent? She could evade it no longer. And now, as if voicing her own thought, the Inspector said, putting a still worse edge on that terrifying question:

"Would you not have supposed, Miss Bland, assuming Chester-

man to be innocent, that he would have handed his revolver over
to us at once? To prove that the bullet was *not* fired from it, and
clear himself of suspicion straight away?"

"Hugo was in a—very upset—he couldn't think straight just
then, I mean. He believed—didn't trust the police to be fair about
it—because he'd been in prison for theft, and it was a policeman
who'd been shot," the girl jerkily answered. She was at the end
of her tether, and Thorne pressed her no more. When she had
signed her statement, they told her she was free to go, but would
be required to give evidence in Court when the prisoner was
brought forward again.

"Have you no relative you could stay with till then?" Nailsworth asked, not unkindly.

"My mother won't have anything more to do with me, since I
went to live with Hugo. Dr. Jaques is the only person who's
stood by me."

"I see. Just wait here a few minutes, will you?"

Nailsworth and Thorne retired for a brief discussion. It seemed
highly undesirable to them that the girl should remain in Jaques'
house; Thorne disliked the idea for purely tactical reasons—the
danger of her prematurely discovering the part Jaques had
played, while Nailsworth was revolted at the thought of any
further human contact between the two.

When they returned, Daisy's eyes lit up. But they had not
come to tell her that she might see Hugo at last. They had made
arrangements for her to board with a retired police matron in
Southbourne for the next few days; they would have her belongings fetched from Dr. Jaques' house. Daisy put up little resistance
to this proposal: at least it meant she would be nearer to Hugo,
even if she might not visit him; and, although Jacko, her only
friend, had done his best for her, his house was tainted with her
misery and she dreaded returning there.

Hugo Chesterman was brought forward again at the Magistrates' Court two days later. He was represented by Bruce Rogers,
partner in a local firm of solicitors. Charles Brownleigh, Q.C.,

appeared for the Director of Public Prosecutions. The Chief Constable had again taken steps to ensure that no cameras should be used when Hugo was being brought into the Courthouse.

Most of this Friday morning was occupied with Mr. Brownleigh's outline of the case. He gave an account of the actual crime, then turned to the prisoner's movements during the period preceding it. He related how, on the evening of the murder, the prisoner had left his lodgings with Daisy Bland, walked to the esplanade, given her a brown-paper parcel to hold, then gone off alone in the direction of the Queen's Hotel, returning half an hour later. Next morning, he said, the accused had cleaned his revolver in the bedroom of his lodgings, and with Bland's help buried it on the beach. He added that, last year, the accused had produced a revolver during a quarrel and threatened to shoot his brother's wife.

Mr. Brownleigh then began to call his witnesses. Princess Popescu, her companion, and the cab driver gave evidence about the shooting. The typist who had seen a man running along Queen's Parade was also called. None of these was able to identify the accused. The Police Surgeon described the results of the post mortem, and a detective sergeant told how a squad of police under his charge had dug up the beach in front of the bandstand and found the revolver. The rest of the day was taken up with the evidence of two landladies, at whose lodgings the accused and Daisy Bland had been staying; the second of these was questioned in some detail about the prisoner's movements and demeanor on the night of the crime. Mr. Brownleigh said that one of his chief witnesses, Miss Bland, was ill, and her evidence would therefore have to be taken later, out of order. The prisoner asking no questions, the case was adjourned till the following day.

On Saturday, the stream of witnesses for the prosecution continued. Mark Amberley was called, and after being questioned about the quarrel between his wife and the prisoner, described how he had come down to Southbourne at the latter's request and given him money; he also described, with some reluctance, how his brother had reacted so violently during a conversation they had had on this occasion about the crime. A picture of Hugo as a man of uncontrollable temper and brutal character was beginning to emerge. Dr. Jaques, who was called next, confirmed Mark Amberley's statement about this interview, and told how he had accompanied Miss Bland back to London. As a result of what she told him later, they had returned to Southbourne on Wednesday to look for the buried revolver, but had failed to find it; they were arrested, and released a few hours later. Dr. Jaques, on being handed a revolver in court, identified it as the property of the accused.

It was noticeable that Chesterman, who up to this point had seemed to take little interest in the proceedings, followed Dr. Jaques' evidence with great attention, scrutinizing him thoughtfully, his expression rather puzzled. However—it may be to Mr. Brownleigh's relief, for he well knew what dangerous ground he was treading—Hugo's solicitor did not rise to cross-examine. Jaques had given his evidence with the frankness he could so readily assume, but cautiously confined himself to plain yea and nay in answering counsel's questions.

His evidence was, of course, extremely damaging. And when he was followed by the ballistics expert who gave his technical reasons for believing that the bullet found in Inspector Stone's body had been fired from the revolver exhibited in court, it seemed all over with Hugo. Bruce Rogers got the expert to admit that such revolvers were common enough in England, and that the bullet was not the normal type used for this make of revolver. But it did little to dispel the impression already created. And worse was to come. The prosecution could not, of course, make any reference to the accused's prison sentence or his criminal career; so the motive for a well-dressed, presentable young man's having attempted to break into a house remained obscure. Mr. Brownleigh delivered himself of no theories on this point. Instead, he called a Detective Sergeant Mann, who deposed that, a few hours after Chesterman had been arrested, and acting on the usual "information received," he had gone with another police officer to a lodging house near Russell Square, where the prisoner had recently been staying, and discovered in his room a kit bag; it contained a leather belt with holster attached, a steel chisel, a file, two pairs of jewelers' forceps, a jemmy, and a photograph of the accused and Daisy Bland.

Bruce Rogers questioned this witness, as he had questioned the police officers who gave evidence of the arrest, on the statements the prisoner had made to them. They all agreed that he had protested his innocence throughout, claiming he had been at a cinema with Daisy Bland at the time when the murder took place.

It was not till the following Monday that Daisy was put in the witness box. Reaction from Wednesday's ordeal, and her advanced state of pregnancy, had made her ill. She lay in bed, comatose at first, under the police doctor's sedative drugs, then passively yielding to the despair which came flooding back as the effect of the drugs wore off. She felt there was no fight left in her, even had she known how best to fight for Hugo. The doctor and the landlady were kind, but kindness could touch her no longer. Time stretched around her like an ice age, obliterating not only all the features of hope but her happy memories too; Hugo seemed infinitely remote.

Newspapers had been kept from her while she was in this condition. On the Monday morning, however, while preparations were being made to take her to court, Daisy was left for a few minutes alone in the parlor. The end of a folded newspaper protruded from behind a cushion where it had been hastily concealed. With a strange expression, both guilty and reluctant, Daisy took out the paper. Her eye lit at once upon a paragraph reporting Bruce Rogers' examination of the police witnesses. She had no time to read more: hearing footsteps in the passage, she thrust the newspaper back where she had found it.

The police doctor, entering with the ex-matron, observed a blind, staring look on the girl's face.

"Are you sure you feel up to it, Miss Bland?" he asked gently.

"Yes, thank you. I only want to get it over." Her voice was low and dull.

The appearance of Daisy Bland in the witness box caused a great stir. It was not only that the Press had been playing up the "mysterious woman in the case," and even the magistrates were improperly eager to set eyes on her. But her pallor, her pregnant state, and the beauty which neither of these could impair sent a vibration of sympathy through the courtroom. Daisy then proceeded to hand the newspaper tribe another gift, dear to their sensation-loving hearts. She fainted. Or, as several reporters were to cautiously phrase it, "On entering the box the witness fell down, apparently in a state of collapse." The doctor who, with Inspector Thorne, had led her in, at once—as the newspapers said—"applied restoratives." While the two men bent over her, slumped in her chair, Bruce Rogers, who had been coldly eying this new and most dangerous witness against his client, felt a curious pang; the scene suddenly took on a macabre quality for him, becoming a scene of torture: he saw Daisy as a victim being revived for further agonies. Bruce was not a highly imaginative man, and therefore all the more shocked by this unpleasant picture which had risen into his mind.

Presently, Daisy was recovered. She heard herself swearing the oath, heard the chairman of the bench saying she could give her evidence seated. Mr. Brownleigh, as he began to question her, treated Daisy with almost exaggerated deference and solicitude; she might have been the widow of a national hero, not the mistress of a suspected murderer.

"I want to cause you as little distress as possible, Miss Bland. I shall try to word my questions so that you can answer them briefly, yes or no. If you feel, at any point, the strain is too much for you, just tell me."

Daisy smiled wanly. There was only one strain she felt, and that was the terrible struggle between fear and desire—the desire to raise her eyes, look round the courtroom and find Hugo, and the fear which prevented her so doing; for she dreaded what she might see upon his face.

Automatically she answered Mr. Brownleigh's questions, re-
tracing the course of events which she had already worn thin
in her own mind. The walk to the esplanade that night, the paper
parcel, the agonized waiting, Hugo's return—it had all become
unreal for her, like a thing she had read about long ago. So she
gave her answers in a dazed, mechanical manner which affected
rather uncomfortably some of those who were present. At one
point only did she come to life. A green cloth cap was handed
up to her, and counsel asked if she could identify it.

"It's like one I gave Hugo," she replied. Throughout, she was
unable to call him "the prisoner" or "the accused," nor did the
Bench rebuke her for this breach of etiquette.

"The one you bought for him in Brighton?"

"Yes."

"If you will look at the label inside—is that the name of the
shop where you bought it?"

"I'm afraid I didn't notice the name of the shop."

"When the prisoner left you on the esplanade, was he wearing
a green cap?"

"Yes."

"And when he returned, was he still wearing it?"

"No."

"Did you make any comment on this at the time?"

"I asked had he lost it."

"And what did he reply?"

"He said it had blown off."

"Were you surprised that he had not retrieved it—a new cap,
one you'd recently given him?"

Bruce Rogers was on his feet, protesting, and Daisy's low-
voiced reply was lost. During the mild wrangle that followed,
Bruce's eye caught Daisy for a moment; her thumb was gently
stroking the cap, and a tear fell upon it.

When Mr. Brownleigh indicated that he had finished with the
witness, Bruce Rogers did not rise to cross-examine. His client
had made it very clear that he did not want the girl to be
badgered any more than was necessary, and Bruce had no wish

to disclose at this stage the line which the defense would take at the trial. As she turned to leave the witness box, Daisy made a great effort and looked, for the first time, straight at Hugo. Almost imperceptibly, he shook his head; then smiled at her—a smile of such warmth and tenderness that she felt as if her heart were dissolving. She tried to smile back, but her lips were quivering uncontrollably, and the next moment she was led out of Court. Hugo had forgiven her. Hugo loved her still, in spite of what she had done. And she knew now that she had done wrong: that little shake of the head had told her everything. From now on, there was only one purpose in her mind—to undo the harm.

At the end of the day, the case for the prosecution was closed. In reply to the chairman of the magistrates, the prisoner said, "I'm innocent of this charge. That is all I have to say." He reserved his defense, and was committed for trial at the next Assizes. So much Daisy read in the newspaper next morning. She then left the house, telling her landlady that she wanted a breath of air on the sea front: but it was not toward the sea front that she made her way.

19 Daisy Consults a Solicitor

BRUCE ROGERS was a conventionally-minded young man. Born and bred in Southbourne, he had never had ambitions beyond the partnership in the family firm of solicitors which would follow his legal training, after a decent interval, as night follows day. This training was interrupted by the war, during which he did his bit, and a little more, surviving it by exercise of the caution so necessary both to the lawyer and the fighting soldier. His experiences in the Normandy and Dutch campaigns, far from unsettling him, made the cozy billet at Southbourne, the protective routine of a lawyer's office, seem more desirable than ever; he had returned to them with all the relief of a hunted fox going to earth. In due course, the partnership was his. He married, furnished a pleasant little house on the outskirts of Southbourne, played bridge and an occasional round of golf, was solicitous about his own health and conscientious over the affairs of his clients. He loved his wife; but for the Law he had a special feeling—an almost filial devotion—as well as a natural aptitude.

His uncle, the senior partner—a somewhat Dickensian character running to madeira, snuff, and calculated eccentricities in dress and manner—considered young Bruce to be a stick-in-the-mud. A young man whose mind had already developed a middle-aged spread, who positively relished the minutiae of the legal profession, and whose only use for wild oats would be as a breakfast cereal, needed shaking up, so Uncle Percival thought, fortified by the recollection of a brief affair with a barmaid forty years ago, which time had transmuted into a fling of Antony-and-Cleopatra-like splendor. So when the defense of that plausible young ruffian, Chesterman, was entrusted to his firm, Uncle

Percival put Bruce onto it. His laudable object, to shake up his nephew's ideas and enlarge his horizons, was now being fulfilled in ample measure.

Bruce had three main obstacles to contend with—the Southbourne public, the Press, and his own client. Local feeling had run so high over the murder that even the prisoner's legal representative moved through troubled waters; without putting it into so many words, some of his acquaintances made it clear that they deprecated his connection with the case, while others, equally ignorant of legal etiquette, were offended because he would not gossip about it and give them the lowdown about his disreputable client; and once, leaving Court, he had been booed by a group of bystanders. Bruce, who had plenty of courage with his integrity, felt all this as no more than a minor annoyance.

The Press was rather more of a nuisance. As the case proceeded, reporters swarmed over Southbourne, attracted by the smell of a *cause célèbre*—the nature of the crime itself, the figures of the accused and his mistress, were sufficient to excite special interest. When it became evident that the public-school type in the dock was not only a probable murderer but a professional burglar, things began to hum. While the case was *sub judice*, little but the bare facts from the Magistrates' Court could appear in print; but reporters were busily unearthing background material, interviewing Hugo's smarter acquaintances in London, pestering his brother, and so on, for the pulsating human-interest stories which could be released when the trial had run its appointed and inevitable course—stories through which the word "Raffles" would run like a signature tune. Bruce Rogers, who had been at first aware of all this merely as a distant if offensive odor, was soon brought into much more disagreeable contact with it. To be starred in one paper as "War Hero Defends Accused in Police-Murder Drama" was repugnant enough; but when Press men buttonholed him in the street and even badgered his wife for interviews, things had become intolerable.

However, these were little troubles compared with the difficulty presented by Hugo Chesterman himself. First, there was

Hugo's personality. By turns evasive or candid, sullen or charm-
ing, lively or sunk in a kind of stubborn, lethargic moodiness,
Hugo was an extraordinarily difficult client to deal with. Bruce
felt, now and then, that Hugo was secretly laughing at him; as an
officer, he had come across the old sweat's brand of mulishness
and covert derisiveness, which could never be quite pinned down
to insubordination, and now he was meeting it again. Gradually,
during their conferences, he realized that Chesterman was a
natural anarchist, despising, or perhaps incapable of responding
to, the social values which he himself took for granted. Throughout, Hugo insisted that he had been at the cinema with his "wife"
at the time of the murder, and that the police had framed him.
When Mr. Brownleigh, in his opening remarks, had indicated
that he would call Daisy Bland and outlined her story, Hugo
told Bruce afterward that she had "got it all mixed up" with the
events of the previous night—or else the police had bullied her
into it. But Bruce could obtain no confirmation of this alibi from
the cinema attendants; and his client would not allow him to
cross-examine Daisy. This recalcitrance nearly made Bruce throw
up the case there and then, but he was restrained by his con-
scientiousness and by the prisoner's evident devotion for the girl.
Also, since it was a certainty that the case would be sent up for
trial, there was little point in divulging more of the defense at
this stage than the alibi on which it would rest.

This morning, the day after Hugo had been committed for
trial, Bruce Rogers was gloomily contemplating his resources.
He had tried to keep an open mind about his client's innocence
or guilt, but the weight of evidence against him was overwhelming. In his favor there was nothing but an unsupported alibi, the
fact that none of the witnesses had identified him, and a vague
story about a Joe Samuels who had made an appointment with
him for—so Hugo declared—the night before the murder, and
then failed to keep it. Joe and two other men, known to the
police, had certainly been staying at the Queen's Hotel that night;
but their subsequent movements had been traced, and Chief

Inspector Nailsworth was satisfied that they had been on their way back to London when the murder was committed.

Bruce could hire a private detective to investigate Joe Samuels' alibi; but, if the police had found no flaw in it, a private operative would be unlikely to do better. On this point, Uncle Percival vigorously disagreed with him. "My dear boy," he had said, "the police have built up a strong case against our client. Why should they start knocking it down? Do you suppose they'd work *really* hard on the Joe Samuels line when they've got a perfectly good suspect in the can?" This argument shocked Bruce, who had the conventional middle-class attitude toward the police, as incorruptible guardians of property, law and order. He said something about the expense that such inquiries would involve.

"Expense? Damn that!" remarked Uncle Percival, feeding an enormous pinch of snuff into his nostrils. "It's all good advertisement for the firm. Put it down to that, if you're fussed about the expenses. There's only one slogan for our profession—'My client, right or wrong.' Are you going to fight the case or just go through the motions?"

"Well of course, uncle—"

"Then fight it to a standstill, my boy. We'll brief Henry Jervoise for the defense—he was a great friend of your father's in the old days. And don't tell me we can't afford him. That stick, Mark Amberley, is contributing to the legal costs, isn't he?"

"Yes. Extremely generously."

"Generous my foot! The least he could do, after blowing the gaff about his brother. Conscience money, eh? That girl—what's her name?—Daisy Bland—ought to stump up too."

"She hasn't a penny, I believe."

"She could get it on account, son. Think what one of those Sunday rags would pay her for a story—My Life with Hugo Chesterman."

Bruce Rogers was indeed thinking about this now. Daisy's evidence in court had proved even more disastrous than he had anticipated. It flatly contradicted the cinema alibi, and this was bad enough; but far worse was the impression of candor and

honesty which the girl had given. No one could be more effective
than Sir Henry Jervoise at turning inside out a prejudiced or dis-
honest witness; but what would he be able to do with a girl who
was so patently neither? especially when her condition meant
that she must be handled very gently if the jury's sympathies
were not to be alienated?

Interrupting Bruce Rogers' thoughts, a clerk came into his
room.

"A young lady to see you, Mr. Bruce. It's Miss Bland."

"Has she an appointment?" Bruce automatically asked; then,
"*Who* did you say?"

"Miss Daisy Bland."

"Good lord! What on earth?—well, show her in."

Daisy bore down upon him like the figurehead of a ship in full
sail. He was immediately aware of a purposefulness, a strong
impetus in her, for which her passive, woebegone appearance at
Court had left him quite unprepared.

"What can I do for you, Miss Bland?"

"I've come to help Hugo, sir. What I said in the Court yesterday—it wasn't true. They frightened me into it. I—"

"Just a minute, please. This is most irregular, you know. Do
please sit down, and let's get this straight. Are you telling me you
committed perjury?"

"They said I'd be accused of the murder too, if I didn't tell
that story. You see—"

"*Please,* Miss Bland. If you gave false evidence under oath—I
take it that's what you are trying to tell me—you should at once
inform the magistrates or the police—"

"But it was the police who made me do it, sir. Them and Dr.
Jaques. Hugo and I were at the cinema, like he said, when it
happened. They got me so muddled. It was really the night
before the murder that he left me on the sea front."

As she spoke, the Gloucestershire accent coming out stronger,
Bruce felt overawed, diminished by the intensity of passion she
conveyed. The wan candor which had struck him in Court was
changed now to an incandescence, a positive fury of conviction;

and it was almost with the panic of a man faced by a galloping heath fire that he rang the bell and told the clerk to ask Mr. Percival if he could spare him a few minutes.

Uncle Percival greeted Daisy with the old-world courtesy he reserved for attractive women, and with no apparent surprise at finding her here. But he eyed her shrewdly enough as she repeated the reasons for her visit.

"My dear young lady," he said, "are you asking us to believe that the story you told in Court was a pure fabrication? Why did you give that evidence, when you knew it would be so damaging to our client?"

"I was frightened, sir. Jacko—that's what we call Dr. Jaques—he said the police would accuse me of being an accomplice if I didn't. And he said Hugo wanted me to save myself by telling it that way. That's why Jacko and I came down here to try and find the revolver."

"One thing at a time, madam," said Uncle Percival, rather frostily now. "I still can't understand why you should have thought it safer for you, if you were trying to save your own skin, to tell that story about being on the sea front than to tell the truth—that you were at the cinema with Chesterman."

Her blue eyes blazed at Percival Rogers, like fires of self-immolation. "I know it was wrong of me. But I was ill. I couldn't think properly. I did what Jacko said was best. Can't you see that I'm telling the truth now?"

If Uncle Percival could see it, he gave no indication. He proceeded to put Daisy through a questioning so merciless that Bruce almost interposed; but soon he perceived that his uncle was testing the girl, to see how she would stand up to hostile cross-examination at the trial. Daisy, though flustered at times, came through it pretty well. To Bruce, at any rate, her manner carried more conviction now than the dazed, mechanical way she had told her story in the Magistrates' Court: Sir Henry Jervoise would no doubt make the most of her having been subjected to undue pressure by the police.

"Well, young lady," said Uncle Percival, with a grunt when he

had finished, "let's hope the harm hasn't gone too far. You realize
you'll be treated by the Crown as a hostile witness, if you give this
new evidence? And I suppose you know the meaning of perjury?"

"I don't want to tell anything but the truth now," Daisy replied, her fists clenched as if anticipating the ordeal to come, and
that blind, fanatical expression in her eyes still. Bruce fidgeted
with his papers. Uncle Percival took a meditative pinch of snuff.

"What are you going to do now?" he asked.

"I want to see Hugo. Surely they'll let me see him now?"

"He's been moved to Oakhurst Jail—that's the Assize town, you
know. We can arrange for you to visit him." Percival Rogers
paused. "You realize that a warder will be present during the
interview? What I mean is—you'll have to watch what you say
to him. No cooking up a story between you."

The girl did not seem to have heard. She was glowing with an
emotion which Bruce found almost intolerable to contemplate;
it was as though a creature out of a fable had walked into his
drab little room.

"How soon?" she asked. "Tomorrow?"

Bruce explained the formalities that were necessary and
promised to put them through immediately. Daisy listened, glowing at him, as if it were the key of paradise, not of a prison cell,
which he was offering her.

"Are you all right for money?" he then asked.

"No. I haven't any. But I expect Jacko would lend me some
more."

"It is quite out of the question that you should see Dr. Jaques
till after the trial," said Uncle Percival. "Have you no relatives
who would help you?"

"My mother won't have anything more to do with me—not since
I went to live with Hugo. I've an auntie in London who—"

"You must write to your mother," said Percival Rogers firmly.
"Make it up with her, eh? And in the meanwhile we'll advance
you a little money to be going on with." He winked at Bruce,
adding, "Without prejudice, of course."

"Oh, thank you, sir. We'll pay it back when—when Hugo is

free. He was going to get a job, and marry me. They won't
convict him now, will they?"

Her ingenuousness was heart-rending. Bruce felt again that he
was in the presence of a being from a legend, from some simpler,
more luminous world where right and wrong had a different
meaning and legal textbooks were unknown.

"My dear child," Uncle Percival was saying, "we're nothing
like out of the wood yet. We mustn't live on false hopes."

"Hope is all I've had to live on ever since they took Hugo
away."

She said it simply, unaware of her eloquence; the emotion
behind her words seemed to overflow the room, and even Uncle
Percival was momentarily silenced.

"We'll do our level best for him, Miss Bland. You can rely on
that," said Bruce.

They discussed plans for a while, then Daisy left. Bruce would
go with her to Oakhurst Jail tomorrow. When the door had
closed behind her, Percival Rogers gave his nephew a quizzical
glance.

"Bowled you over all right, didn't she, eh?"

"She's a remarkable girl."

"You look as if you'd enlisted for a crusade, my boy. Starry-
eyed."

"Oh nonsense!" replied Bruce testily.

Percival Rogers took a pinch of snuff. "Two things are quite
evident. Dr. Jaques is an unmitigated scoundrel; and that charm-
ing creature you've fallen for was lying her beautiful head off."

"But I thought you were satisfied that—"

"I'm satisfied that she'll stand by this new story at the trial. And
I dare say she'll have the same effect on the jury as she had on
you. But the Judge—oho, Prentiss J. is another matter. Sourpuss
Prentiss. Helen of Troy couldn't put anything over on him."

"I'm sorry, Uncle, but I can't accept your position. I find it
perfectly credible that Miss Bland should have been forced into
giving the evidence we heard at the Magistrates' Court; she was
misled by this man Jaques—I quite agree with what you say

about him—and then intimidated by the police. They got her in a thorough muddle between them, and she mixed up the dates."

"Bless your innocent heart! She's deeply in love with young Chesterman—you grant me that much?"

"It seems obvious enough."

"And she's no fool, for all her naïveté. Do you really suppose she could ever have been persuaded or bullied into giving that evidence about Chesterman's leaving her on the sea front just at the time of the murder, if in fact they'd been at the cinema together, as she now claims? No, no, no, it won't wash. I've no doubt in my own mind that Jaques told her she'd got to come clean—that it was Chesterman's wish she should come clean. So she did. And then she realized the damage she'd done. She'd only got to glance at a newspaper yesterday to see that her young man would be putting up the cinema alibi. So she comes to us with this new story, backing him up."

"That's a pretty cynical interpretation, I must say."

"Cynical my foot! I admire the girl. I think she's a heroine. I know she's been done down by that scoundrel Jaques. But all this doesn't alter the facts."

"The probabilities."

"The simple fact that, if you really *were* sitting in a cinema with your young man at a time when a murder was committed, no power on earth is going to make you get up in Court and invent a story about his leaving you on the sea front and walking off in the direction where the murder took place. Miss Bland's evidence in Court would be preposterous, insane, inconceivable, unless it was the truth."

"So the case is hopeless?"

"I never said that. The case can be fought. But it'll be decided now on a tricky point of law. Jervoise has got to argue that the evidence Miss Bland gave at the Magistrates' Court is inadmissible. If he can convince the Judge of that, we've got a fair chance. If not"—Percival Rogers snapped his fingers—"good-by to young Chesterman."

20 Trial and Verdict

A LATE-AUTUMN mist hung over the hills round Byworth in the Cotswolds. The village was silent; its stone houses seemed to be huddling closer together in the hollow where it lay, as if for warmth against the coming winter. Smoke rose up straight from the chimneys, and a few lights already showed in the windows. Walking slowly down the hill, past the dun fields which she remembered from childhood as yellow with charlock, Daisy felt like a ghost returning. The events of the last fortnight washed aimlessly to and fro across her mind, circling and jostling together like flotsam in a back eddy; she could see no pattern or sense in them: she was a piece of driftwood herself, at the mercy of currents, pushed for the time being out of the main stream into a deadwater creek where all activity was suspended.

And indeed there was nothing more she could do now till the trial. Seventeen days to go still. She did not know whether she wanted them to crawl or to gallop. In retrospect, the first ten days after her visit to Bruce Rogers seemed to have flicked past so quickly that her impressions of them had run together into a blur. There had been further meetings with Bruce and his uncle; a change of lodgings; visits to a new doctor; several attempts by the Press to interview her; lonely walks on the sea front at Southbourne, during which she was followed by curious gazes, neither hostile nor sympathetic but speculative and almost timid, as though she were a walking riddle, an animal of some unknown species. And then there were the journeys to see Hugo.

Three times Bruce Rogers had taken her to Oakhurst Jail. They were memories she found difficult now to face with equanimity. Her passionate longing to see Hugo had become an obsession

with her during the period after they had parted. Bruce had tried
to prepare her mind for the physical conditions she would meet—
the cheerless room, the grille, the warder attentive in the background. But it was not these which, looking back on it now, Daisy
was desolated to remember. Something in Hugo himself had
come between them far more effectively than any grille; he had
looked at her and spoken to her tenderly; but each time she
visited him she received a stronger impression, accentuated by
his prison pallor, that he was living in a world which she could
not, with all her love for him, enter. He was like a mortally sick
man who was training himself to renounce all claims upon her,
upon life itself. He talked in a quiet, subdued way, as a sick
child might or an old man, seldom taking his eyes from her face,
sitting very still and self-contained. His attitude toward the
coming trial seemed quite fatalistic; and had Bruce not expressed
to her several times his admiration for Hugo's courage, Daisy
might have interpreted this fatalism as a cowardly resignation.
She soon found out that Hugo wanted her to talk about herself,
the coming baby, what she had been doing, the projected visit to
her mother and the memories of her own childhood which this
evoked—anything rather than the trial.

On one occasion only did he show a flash of his old spirit.
Daisy had received a letter from Jacko, inquiring most solicit-
ously whether he could do anything to help Hugo and expressing
mild sorrow that she had not got in touch with him since leaving
London. When she told Hugo about this, his face darkened and
he said, "If I had Jacko alone for a few minutes, I'd give them
something to hang me for." The chill anger in his voice startled
Daisy, who was not yet altogether aware of the vileness of Jacko's
conduct. She began to defend him, but Hugo cut in harshly,
"Don't talk to me about that ——. He put the police onto me. He
helped them find the revolver. He bounced you into telling that
story in Court. I suppose he never even gave you my letter."

"Your letter, darling? Did you write me one? I felt sure you
would."

"I wrote to say I'd marry you—asking you to make the arrangements—just as soon as we could. The little —— must have been laughing up his sleeve all right, knowing he'd got the police lined up outside waiting to nab me."

"But he could have given me the letter. It'd have made such a difference." It was Jacko's wanton destroying of the letter, not his betrayal of Hugo, which struck Daisy for a moment as the worst infamy of all.

"He gave you no message at all from me that day?"

"He said you wanted me to—" Daisy glanced uneasily round toward the warder—"to give that evidence in Court. Otherwise I'd never have—"

"I know, love. Rogers has told me about that. You mustn't ever blame yourself for it. Promise?" He said it so kindly that her heart overflowed with gratitude and she could not speak. Yet there was something remote, abstracted, in his kindness which made him a stranger; the old Hugo, selfish sometimes and brusque and thoughtless, would have been preferable. When Daisy's mother wrote, asking her to come home, Hugo thoroughly approved the plan.

"But then I shan't be able to come and see you any more," Daisy had said.

"Well, it isn't very cozy here, is it? What do we get out of it? Two people trying to keep up a conversation through a grille."

His reply had hurt her bitterly at the time, though she knew she must make allowances for him in his present state. But today, walking down the hill toward her mother's cottage, Daisy felt light breaking in on her: Hugo had only been trying to spare her; the withdrawal which she had sensed in him was deliberate—he would not let her share his own suffering or his forebodings, would say nothing to increase her agitation. It was almost as if he had been gently loosening the bonds between them, doing what he could to soften for her the ordeal of their final parting.

"You're a good man, my Hugo," she muttered. "You couldn't have done it. You didn't do it, did you, my dear?"

She often asked him in her mind this question which she had never dared ask to his face, and the lover in her mind always answered No. Not even to her mother would she admit the possibility that Hugo might be guilty.

Mrs. Bland had turned out a good refuge in trouble. She offered no recriminations, received Daisy as if she had only left home a month or two ago, and was evidently looking forward to the baby's arrival. Daisy was not to know it, but her featuring in the Press had on the whole proved no disadvantage to her mother. The whole village had been agog about it, of course; but Daisy had always been popular with the villagers, never committing the one sin they considered unforgivable—that of becoming stuck-up. The Chesterman case provided them with drama, a source of endless gossip, and a vicarious sense of being front-page news themselves. Mrs. Bland, so the general opinion went, was taking it very well: she was neither defiant about it, nor cowed. And when Daisy arrived, looking so sad and frightened and appealing, so entirely different from what might have been expected of a girl who'd gone wrong in the big city, it silenced all but the most censorious gossips. That she was going to bear a child out of wedlock meant little in a community where such events were quite traditional. For the first few days, she kept herself to herself, which was considered right and proper under the circumstances. Then one or two neighbors, compelled by ungovernable curiosity, dropped in at Mrs. Bland's cottage. Once the ball had been set rolling thus, any fears Daisy might have had that she would be treated as an outcast were set at rest; her demeanor satisfied the sternest critics, while her predicament—however much the village may have gloated over it privately—gained her much kindness from those she met.

Daisy was determined to work her passage. She spent the mornings, while her mother was out at work, dusting and polishing in the cottage; she gave her two youngest brothers midday dinner when they returned from school; and in the afternoons she took her little solitary walks, for Hugo had told her she must have plenty of exercise, and during these walks she could think about him without interruption. She walked slowly and carefully, since her most immediate fear was lest the baby, due to be born only a week after the trial opened, should arrive prematurely and prevent her from giving evidence. Every day the neighbors saw the girl stepping with her heavy, somnambulist gait along the road which led out of the village; the older ones recalled how, as a child, she had skipped along that road with her companions, bringing back armfuls of cowslips in the summer, returning in autumn wreathed with berries and the cobweb trails of old-man's-beard. She had been a wonderful pretty child, they remembered—a proper little Queen of the May.

And for Daisy, too, these days meant a return to childhood. Her mother, with a countrywoman's instinctive tact and emotional reticence, never referred to Daisy's life in London or to Hugo. They talked instead about the remoter past, about village affairs—anything but what was most on Daisy's mind. Mrs. Bland, having made it up with her daughter, was determined to put the cause of their break out of her mind forever; her manner implied that Daisy had learned her lesson and finished with Hugo, and the girl did not mind keeping up this polite fiction; for she sensed it as part of a healing process, which was strengthening her for the ordeal to come—the two ordeals.

On the afternoon before the trial, Bruce Rogers met Daisy at the station at Oakhurst and drove her to a small hotel on the outskirts of the old country town. A sleepy, genteel place normally, Oakhurst presented today an indefinable atmosphere of excitement, anticipation: people lingered in the main street, talking, forming groups which dispersed only with reluctance, as it might be on the eve of some civil disturbance; and there was a noticeable influx of strangers into the town.

All this mounting tension seemed to tower up like a wave and break into absolute silence when, the next morning, after counsel for the Crown had outlined the case against Chesterman, Daisy Bland was at once called to the witness box. Her evidence, owing to her delicate state of health, would be taken out of order. The purity of her features, the beauty and transparent candor which emanated from them, strangely contrasting with the girl's blurting, countrified accents as she took the oath, made an extraordinary impression in the Court. It often happens in criminal trials that the prisoner, after the spectators' first curiosity about his appearance is satisfied, becomes almost a lay figure, all attention being concentrated upon the counsel who are dressing him in the robes of guilt or innocence. But Daisy's appearance had the effect of turning attention as much upon Hugo as upon herself. It was not only the look of love which passed visibly between them when she stood up in the box; Bruce Rogers could feel a stir among the spectators, could almost hear them thinking, "How could a girl like that get mixed up with a burglar, a murderer?" He saw the jurymen's eyes move back to the figure in the dock, as if seeking there an answer to the riddle; and he guessed that Hugo, looking so calm, so manly, so gentlemanly indeed, was appearing to them in a new light—a light reflected, as it were, from Daisy.

But, if the girl's beauty made a strong impression, her first words rocked the Court to its foundations. Mr. Brownleigh, leading for the Crown, had made it quite clear in his opening remarks that the prosecution's case would rest very largely upon Daisy Bland's statement. He had even asked the Court to extend toward her the greatest possible indulgence, in view of her condition and her relationship with the prisoner. So her reply to his first question gave the unfortunate Mr. Brownleigh the sensation of walking through a familiar door and finding a completely unknown room beyond it. Gripping the edge of the witness box, and speaking in her clearest, most forthright tones, Daisy said:

"I'm sorry, sir. I can say nothing. I can't give evidence. I don't know anything about the murder at all."

The whole Court buzzed and rustled, and there was a restless flashing everywhere, like the stir of silver-poplar leaves in a wind, as faces turned this way and that to observe the Judge, the prisoner, counsel, the witness, and the reactions of other spectators. Mr. Brownleigh's mouth hung open for an instant; then he recovered self-command.

"Are you feeling quite yourself, madam?"

"Oh yes sir, thank you."

"Do I understand that you wish to retract the statement you made in the Magistrates' Court?"

"Yes."

Mr. Brownleigh at once asked the Judge's leave to examine Miss Bland on the deposition made before the magistrates. There was nothing for it but to treat her as a hostile witness, now. Point by point he took her through the deposition; in every case she admitted that this was what she had said, but claimed that every word she had said was untrue. Mr. Brownleigh paused; then, regarding her sternly, said:

"Will you please tell the Court why you made this statement, which you now claim to be a complete fabrication."

"I was forced to make it."

"Are you suggesting that the police put pressure upon you?"

"No, sir. It was Dr. Jaques. He told me that unless I made that statement, I should be charged with the murder."

"You believed him?"

"Yes. I was ill. I couldn't think straight."

"I suggest to you that your original statement was the truth, and you made up this new story about being at a cinema with the prisoner at the time of the murder—made it up when you realized what harm your deposition had done him."

"No, sir," replied Daisy, with a sob.

Mr. Brownleigh's voice remained polite and dispassionate—to bully this witness would infallibly alienate the jury—while he probed all along the line of her new evidence. She could neither be shaken nor tripped up about her movements on the night of the murder: she and the prisoner had been at a cinema from 5:15 to about 7:45 o'clock; they returned to their lodgings, and went to another picture house a quarter of an hour later.

Daisy, to the disappointment of the more ghoulish section of the spectators, maintained her composure throughout this examination. But when Mr. Brownleigh began questioning her about the visit to Southbourne with Dr. Jaques, it was evident that the girl became deeply distressed.

"Will you tell the Court why you paid this visit?"

"Dr. Jaques said the police would start looking for the revolver on the beach, and it must be hidden in some safer place."

"In fact you knew the revolver was incriminating evidence against the prisoner?"

"I beg your pardon?" For a moment there was a stupid, groping expression on Daisy's face.

"I will put it this way," said Counsel patiently. "If the prisoner had not used the revolver recently—used it to shoot Inspector Stone, how could its discovery do him any harm? What, otherwise, was the point of your plan to hide it in a 'safer' place?"

Daisy's lips trembled. "You're trying to catch me out," she cried.

"I'm trying to get at the truth."

Daisy burst out sobbing. "I won't say anything more to anybody—only the truth."

The crime reporters scribbled busily. This was more like it. *Scene in Court. Woman Breaks Down in Witness Box. I Only Want to Tell the Truth.*

When Daisy had recovered, Mr. Brownleigh pressed the matter no further. He went on to the arrest of the witness and Dr. Jaques, obtaining from her an admission that, during her subsequent questioning at the police station, no undue pressure had been exercised, and sat down.

Sir Henry Jervoise, a tall, lanky man with a monocle and quizzical eyes which could set suddenly into a pebbly and incredulous stare, vastly discomposing to opposition witnesses, rose to his feet. His first words sent another *frisson* through the Court.

"Miss Bland, forgive me if I ask you a personal question. You are deeply in love with the prisoner?"

"Yes." She said it in a low voice, bowing her head, but it sounded thrilling and clear as a distant trumpet call.

"You are soon to become the mother of his child."

"Yes, sir."

"You would do nothing, willingly, to incriminate this man you love so deeply?" Sir Henry's slight emphasis on the fifth word of this question indicated the line his questioning would take. He was going, not merely to grasp the nettle boldly, but turn it against the prosecution.

"Indeed I wouldn't," was Daisy's answer; and again a tenderness breathed from her voice which for a moment turned the Court, the wigs and gowns, all the paraphernalia of the Law into an insubstantial pageant.

"I'm sure you wouldn't. What is puzzling us all"—Sir Henry ran a confiding eye along the jury—"is how you came to make your statement to the police and the deposition before the magistrates —a statement so much more damaging to the man you love than the truth would have been."

"You must not make speeches, Sir Henry," interrupted Mr. Justice Prentiss with a dyspeptic primming of the lips.

"I am coming to the question, m'lord," Sir Henry blandly remarked. Then, turning back to Daisy, "Would it be fair to say that you were trapped into making that statement?"

Mr. Brownleigh was on his feet, protesting.

"I will rephrase the question. When you made the statement you have since retracted, was it because you had been led to believe it was in the prisoner's interest to do so?"

"He told me to."

Sir Henry's monocle dropped from his eye. "I beg your pardon? Who told you?"

"Dr. Jaques gave me a message from Hugo—from the prisoner —saying I was to tell that story."

"Ah. I see." Sir Henry gave a strong rendering of a man to whom abundant light has at last been vouchsafed. "And naturally you would do anything which Mr. Chesterman asked you to?"

"Yes."

"You trusted Dr. Jaques implicitly?"

"Yes. He was our closest friend."

"Would it surprise you to hear that Mr. Chesterman gave him no such message to pass on to you?" asked Sir Henry, after a pregnant pause to warn the jury that something important was coming.

"Yes. Well, perhaps not now."

Sir Henry labored the point no further. And just as well, thought Bruce Rogers, knowing how thin was the ice upon which Sir Henry had been cutting these fancy figures.

"Now, Miss Bland. After you and Dr. Jaques had failed to find the revolver, and been arrested, you made this statement to the police. Entirely of your own free will?"

"I was frightened. The Inspector said I'd be charged as an accomplice if I didn't make a full confession which satisfied the police."

"So it wasn't altogether of your own free will?"

"Well, of course, I'd had that message from Hugo—"

"Yes, yes," Sir Henry broke in swiftly. "And what happened next? After you'd signed the statement?"

"The Inspector said he'd make arrangements for me to stay at Southbourne. I had hardly any money."

"To stay with Mrs. Chance?"

"Yes."

"You knew that she had been till recently a police matron?"

"Yes. They told me so."

Sir Henry's eye twinkled. "Made you feel as if you were still under arrest?"

"Don't lead the witness, Sir Henry," said the Judge sternly.

"I apologize, m'lord," counsel replied, in a far from apologetic tone. "Did you ask to see Mr. Chesterman?"

"Oh yes, sir. Several times. But they wouldn't let me."

"Did you try to get in touch with any of your relations, or friends?"

"No, sir. I wasn't well. I didn't want to see anyone except Hugo."

"But the police doctor visited you?" Sir Henry faintly emphasized the word "police." In these questions to Daisy, and later in his cross-examination of Crown witnesses, one line of the defense became clear. Sir Henry, using all the latitude which is commonly allowed to defense counsel in a capital trial, was aiming to suggest to the jury that, apart from her retracting of the

deposition, Daisy Bland had given it under duress. The picture
he wanted them to see was of a sick, desperate and innocent
girl forced to make a false confession and incriminate her lover
in order to escape being charged with murder; and then an
unseemly scramble by the authorities to get an indictment before
the girl retracted her statement, as well she might. Miss Bland
had been virtually held incommunicado, under supervision of a
police doctor and a retired police matron, thus cutting her off
effectively from outside influence. Chesterman had been brought
at once before the magistrates, in spite of the failure of any
witness to identify him; and instead of formal evidence of arrest
alone being given, as is normal, Miss Bland was hustled into
Court the first moment her health permitted it, and taken through
her statement by Treasury counsel.

What all this implied, as Sir Henry would bring out in his
closing speech, was that—since the authorities had made such
extraordinary (and at times dubious) efforts to get the girl's
deposition—the Crown case, apart from her evidence, must self-
admittedly be of the flimsiest. And it was Sir Henry's contention
that the jury were not entitled to treat as evidence one word of
a deposition which had now been retracted.

Although he well knew that the verdict would depend upon
the Judge's direction on this point, Sir Henry contested every
other one that offered him the least purchase. He got little change
from the two Inspectors, who were old hands in the witness box
and flatly denied putting any undue pressure on Daisy Bland; he
did, however, obtain an admission from Inspector Thorne that,
after his arrest, the accused had stated he was in a cinema at the
time of the murder. Sir Henry made great play with the failure of
any Crown witness to identify Chesterman; but he had more
trouble with a new witness—a holiday maker who believed he
could identify Daisy Bland as a woman he had seen under a
lamp on the esplanade just at the time of the murder. When the
medical evidence had been given, Sir Henry cross-examined the
police doctor on Daisy's condition in the Magistrates' Court. He
was seeking to impress upon the jury that Daisy had given her

evidence there in a dazed, mechanical way suggestive of utter
mental exhaustion, the result of pressure applied by the police.
The doctor agreed she had been extremely agitated, and said he
had recommended a rest owing to her condition; he cautiously
admitted that Daisy's demeanor before the magistrates would not
be inconsistent with the theory that her "confession" was in fact
a false one. Re-examining the doctor, Mr. Brownleigh asked:

"Have you any reason to think that Miss Bland had actually
undergone, as my learned friend seems to suggest, a brain-washing process?"

There was a small diversion while counsel explained to the
Judge the meaning of "brain-washing," a phrase which Mr.
Justice Prentiss professed himself unfamilar with. Then Mr.
Brownleigh repeated the question, and the doctor replied: "No.
She was agitated. But in my opinion she knew perfectly well
what she was saying."

On the second day of the trial, after a few minor witnesses had
been called, Dr. Jaques' evidence was taken. Mr. Brownleigh took
him through the events from his arrival in Southbourne with
Mark Amberley, the day after the murder, to his second visit
there and the search for the revolver. Mr. Brownleigh's examination was puzzling to the general public, who knew nothing of
the role Dr. Jaques had played in this affair; Sir Henry had
leisure to admire the skill with which Mr. Brownleigh picked his
way through what was a positive minefield; but he himself was
in a difficult enough position, for if he attacked this witness on
character, it would allow the prosecution to bring evidence
proving Chesterman's criminal record.

Discussing the case afterward, Sir Henry said he had never, in
a long acquaintance with the seamy side of life, come across a
more utterly despicable human being than Dr. Jaques. When he
rose to cross-examine, he fixed the witness with a long, cold stare
which sufficiently indicated his contempt. Dr. Jaques met it in
his own way—that look in his brown eyes, at once servile and
impudent, masking a mind warped by its lust for power, for
destruction. A deeper silence fell upon the Court, and it was

noticed that the two warders in the dock moved closer to the prisoner.

"The accused man is your dearest friend, I believe?" Sir Henry began.

"I have known him well for some years."

"And Miss Bland—she is a very dear friend of yours too?"

"Certainly."

"You have been in communication with her fairly recently?"

"Yes."

"Did you write to say, 'I'm doing my best to help Hugo in everything'?"

"I don't think I said quite that. I wrote that, if I could in any way assist him, I should be pleased to do so."

"When you communicated to the police a confidential statement alleged to have been made to you by Miss Bland, was that for the purpose of assisting her and the accused?"

"I considered it my duty as a citizen to help the police when a murder had been committed."

"Your duty as a citizen. I see. And did your conscience also direct you to tell the prisoner or Miss Bland, your dearest friends, that you had given the police this information?"

"I did not tell them. No."

Sir Henry, replacing his monocle, stared distastefully at the witness. "On the day Chesterman was arrested, you had arranged to meet him in the buffet at Charing Cross station?"

"Yes."

"It was your arrangement, not his?"

"Yes."

"Was it to assist him?"

"Well, no."

"Did anyone except him and yourself know about this rendezvous?"

"Yes, Inspector Thorne."

"When you went to Charing Cross station, were you surprised to find the police turning up?"

"No."

"Did the prisoner give you a letter to pass on to Miss Bland?"

For a moment, Dr. Jaques' glib effrontery deserted him. This was clearly a question he had not expected. He glanced at the man in the dock; then, with an extraordinary quiver of the mouth which made him look, for an instant, like a torturer gloating, he replied: "Yes, he did."

"And what did you do with this letter?"

"I destroyed it."

"Did you indeed? May I ask why?"

"Miss Bland was then under my medical care. She was in poor health, and I considered that the contents of the letter would be dangerously disturbing."

"You read this private letter, then, before destroying it?"

"That is so."

"And you formed the professional opinion that a proposal of marriage, made by the man she loved and whose child she was carrying, would endanger Miss Bland's health?"

Dr. Jaques shrugged his shoulders.

"Answer my question," said Sir Henry, scowling at him.

"It would have overexcited her, and raised false hopes."

Sir Henry gave the jury an eloquent look. "Your solicitude for your patient was remarkable indeed, was it not?"

"Does that require an answer, too?"

"Your whole evidence so far has provided the answer. Now then: when the police arrested Chesterman at Charing Cross, did they go through the form of arresting you as well?"

"Yes."

"Did that alarm you very much?"

"I had no reason to be alarmed."

"Quite so. And when you went down to Southbourne with Miss Bland, you knew that you were going to show the police where the revolver was hidden?"

"No, I thought that she would unintentionally show the police where it had been hidden."

"A fine distinction, Dr. Jaques. So you were not surprised to

find the police were watching you both when you went down
onto the beach?"

"No, I was not. When we couldn't find the revolver, I thought
she'd been fooling me."

"At the station, the police went through a form of arrest?"

"I don't know whether you could call it arrest."

"Whatever term we apply to it, it came as a great shock to
this poor girl?"

"Possibly."

"A shock which, as her friend and medical adviser, you might
have considered extremely dangerous to her health?"

Dr. Jaques was silent.

"You did not have time to break to this unhappy girl the news
that she might be arrested?"

Looking full at Sir Henry, the witness deliberately replied, in
the voice which Bruce Rogers was later to compare with barbed-
wire hidden in a saucer of cream: "I had the time, but no
intention."

Sir Henry indicated that he had no more questions to ask.
Seldom has any witness left the box as thoroughly discredited as
was Dr. Jaques now. It was clear that, on his evidence alone, the
prisoner could never be convicted. But, though Jaques had been
shown up in all his well-nigh incredible baseness, Daisy's deposition before the magistrates remained intact; and, as Jaques, bowing to the Judge, left the witness box, Sir Henry was aware of
something damnable in his face and bearing—an expression he
hardly troubled to conceal now, one of triumph, as if, mercilessly
though he had been exposed, his real object was finally and
irrefutably achieved.

After these exchanges, the trial ran its course less dramatically.
The prosecution closed its case that afternoon, and Sir Henry
intimating that he would call no witness except the prisoner, the
trial was adjourned till next day.

Hugo Chesterman was in the witness box for three hours the
following morning. His demeanor throughout remained calm,
subdued, frank. While Sir Henry was taking him through his

story, Hugo never faltered, and it was evident that he was making an unexpectedly good impression on the jury; from time to time now the jurymen allowed their eyes to dwell upon him, instead of, as heretofore, merely glancing at him in a furtive and flinching way. Sir Henry's final question was, "I am going to ask you one thing more. Are you the man who murdered Inspector Stone on that night?"

"I am not," Hugo emphatically replied.

When Mr. Brownleigh rose to cross-examine, however, the balance soon began tilting the other way. Patiently and dispassionately he drew the prisoner's attention to the holes in his own defense, to small discrepancies and contradictions in his evidence, to the fantastic coincidences which it implied. Was it not an extraordinary thing, if he had really thrown away the parcel containing the rope on the night before the murder, that it should not have been discovered till the morning after it? Was it not strange that at the Magistrates' Court he should not have mentioned his having been in a picture palace with his wife at the time of the murder? Was it not an extraordinary coincidence that a hat, purchased for him in Brighton, should have turned up near the scene of the crime? And that whoever shot Inspector Stone should have used a revolver of a pattern identical to Hugo's? Was it not difficult to credit that an innocent man would, simply from fear of the police, take such trouble to remove fingerprints from his revolver and hide it?

So it went on, Mr. Brownleigh chipping away at Hugo's story from this side and that, till it seemed like some plaster construction hollow and empty at the core. The impersonal way he went to work upon it was matched, almost throughout the cross-examination, by Hugo's air of cool detachment; they might have been two experts discussing the merits of some abstract proposition, arguing keenly yet without personal animosity, politely agreeing to differ.

After lunch, counsel made their closing speeches, Sir Henry arguing with all his skill and force that Daisy's deposition at the Magistrates' Court should be ruled as inadmissible at the present trial. Then Mr. Justice Prentiss summed up the evidence. He instructed the jury first in the legal definition of murder. It was very possible, he said, that the man who shot Inspector Stone had not intended to murder him; but if a person engaged in an unlawful enterprise fired at another person in order to facilitate his own escape, and the shot killed, the crime was murder. The judge pointed out the reasons why this should be so, and paid a tribute to the dead man's devotion to duty. There was no direct evidence, he continued, that the prisoner was the man who had fired the fatal shot; but circumstantial rather than direct evidence was a feature of an overwhelming proportion of cases in which nevertheless the guilt of the accused had been sufficiently established. Whereas the Crown had produced no evidence of identification, the jury must equally bear in mind that the defense had brought forward no independent witnesses testifying to the prisoner's alibi.

The prosecution had asked the jury to draw, from the prisoner's conduct after the murder, the inference that such conduct was consistent only with his guilt. The prosecution's case was based largely on the evidence of two witnesses, Daisy Bland and Dr. Jaques. Every citizen, said the Judge, who had knowledge of a crime, was in duty bound to inform the police; on the other hand, one could not extend approval to a man who had given the police information he had received as a trusted friend; and certainly Jaques should not have continued to take advantage of the prisoner's confidence and Miss Bland's, once he had communicated with the police. The defense had severely censured Dr. Jaques' conduct, and also suggested that the police methods of obtaining evidence through him were improper; the Judge saw no justification for criticism of the police; and it was not Dr. Jaques, he reminded the jury, but Hugo Chesterman who was on trial. It was true that one could not have the same confidence in Dr. Jaques' evidence which one would have had if it had been obtained in a different way. However, the jury were entitled to consider it in so far as it threw light upon the evidence of Miss Bland.

She had told two irreconcilable stories, one before the magistrates, and the other in this Court. The original statement, made
to the police, told against the prisoner. How the police had
induced her to make it was not clear. The jury would naturally
dislike the idea of this young woman's being in any way trapped
—even into telling the truth; but they might well wonder what
possible inducement or coercion the police could have employed
which would make such a woman tell a false story against the
man she loved. In this Court, Miss Bland had retracted her
original statement, and given evidence supporting the prisoner's
alibi. It was for the jury to decide which of these two stories was
the more credible.

Miss Bland had referred to the accused several times as her
"husband," though she was not in fact married. The Judge
warned the jury to dismiss from their minds any prejudice they
might have against the prisoner for leading an irregular life with
Daisy Bland. On the other hand, they were entitled to take into
consideration the letter which the accused had written to her,
proposing marriage; bearing in mind that a wife must not give
evidence against her husband, they might or might not draw
certain conclusions from the prisoner's having made this proposal
when he did, a few days after the murder.

The Judge proceeded to remind the jury, at considerable
length and with complete impartiality, of the various other
points of evidence. But, in Sir Henry's view, the case was already
lost; for Mr. Justice Prentiss had given no ruling that the jury
must disregard Daisy's deposition before the magistrates; that he
had not done so would give every justification for an appeal; and
Sir Henry, detaching his mind from the Judge's measured and
droning exposition, applied it to the legal arguments he would
bring up at the Court of Criminal Appeal.

The jury were out for only a quarter of an hour. They returned
a verdict of guilty. The prisoner once again protested his innocence. Then sentence of death was passed.

21 Last Scene of All

HUGO CHESTERMAN awoke, sweating and trembling, from a nightmare. It was a nightmare which had been familiar to him since his term of imprisonment shortly after the war; perhaps it went further back—to boyhood reading of a story by Poe; or perhaps the dream had its source in the rigid and intolerable oppression of his father's personality, or in some remote, buried memory of the womb and the struggle for birth. He had dreamed that he was in a cell, whose iron walls and ceilings began to constrict, moving in upon him with minute and remorseless jerks. He tried to push them away, but they were irresistible; ever so slowly he would be crushed.

"Daisy," he childishly whimpered, "I've had an awful dream!" But Daisy was not there—only darkness, and an acrid fog of anxiety within, and someone snoring. Daisy never snored. So Hugo came fully awake, to the realization that he was indeed in a cell—the condemned cell. And it was not dark: there was always a dim light burning here; and it was his own heavy breathing he had heard—the warder on duty did not go to sleep.

Another panic flooded his mind. Was it this morning? Then he remembered: the execution was fixed for tomorrow; and he smiled wryly at the absurd sense of relief which swept over him. As if twenty-four hours made any difference. But of course they did. Twenty-four hours more of being alive, though the appeal had failed and there was no hope now of a reprieve, meant something all right. A man *could* live without hope, he realized: he could live simply on the wholesome and nourishing fact of not being dead. "Bliss was it in that dawn to be alive," he found himself muttering.

"Anything you want, old man?" asked the warder.

"No thanks. Just reciting beautiful poetry to myself."

They weren't bad chaps, these warders, as warders went. And, considering it was a copper he'd shot, they treated him pretty well. Though why the hell I didn't shoot that all-time-low bastard Jacko instead, God alone knows, he thought; even the cops go white round the edges when they mention him; had to smuggle him out of the country immediately after the trial. I suppose he wanted Daisy. What a hope!

The thought of Daisy sent anxiety swarming over him again. She'd be visiting him today, with the baby, for the first time since before the trial, and for the last time. He must say something to comfort her. It was she who'd have to go on living. But what on earth was there to say? He dreaded this interview more than he dreaded the brief interview he would have next day— with the prison governor, the chaplain, and the hangman. Ever since that morning at Southbourne, there had been a question behind Daisy's eyes, and Hugo knew that he must not leave her without answering it. But with the truth, or with a lie?

He lay in bed now, facing a moral problem. For many years, such problems had meant nothing to him. But he loved Daisy, and once you really loved someone you began to worry about what was best for that person, and this soon got you tangled up in speculations about right and wrong. Hugo knew that, if he swore to Daisy he was innocent, she would believe him; she could go through life assured that little Thomas was not the child of a murderer. But then she would forever carry the terrible burden of having given the evidence which had hanged an innocent man. So might it not be better to tell her the truth, even though it destroyed her illusions about him—darkened, perhaps, for her the memories of their love?

Hugo's mind, turning away from this insoluble problem, drifted back to the events which had caused it. He was with Daisy again in the pub near the harbor, overhearing that conversation about the Princess and her jewels. He was walking slowly past the Princess's house next day, running his eye over

ts possibilities, but in a disinterested way; for at that time he
lmost believed in his intention of going straight, though he
ealized now that it had never been in his nature to do so. But
hen his luck betrayed him—led him beautifully up the garden
ath, only to desert him. Hugo had the criminal's superstitious
elief in luck: when things went wrong, he held it solely respon-
ible and cursed it as a savage curses the wooden god who has
et him down. It was just my bloody luck, he thought now, that
should have met Joe Samuels in the bar at the Queen's and
een given the tip for that ropey horse. And it was just my
loody luck that the Princess should come into the bar and I
hould happen to overhear her mention the dinner date. That's
ne coincidence Mr. Brownleigh didn't know about. The bar was
airly full and the old girl obviously didn't notice me, or she'd
ave been able to pick me out at the identification parade. Then
have to go crazy—put all our money on that horse and lose it.
There was nothing for it then but to lift the old girl's jewels.

Hugo remembered it all with appalling clarity—Daisy's de-
pair, and his own reluctant decision. He could see now that
omething within himself had resisted the plan, confusing his
nind, undermining his nerve, leading him into idiotic mistakes.
What on earth had induced him to take the rope and then leave
t in Daisy's keeping? He had had some vague notion, he remem-
ered, that if he should fail to clamber up onto the porch top,
he rope might come in useful for an attempt to break in at the
ack of the house. But then, when he left Daisy on the esplanade,
e changed his mind—for no apparent reason—and handed her
he parcel. It had all been so fumbling, so indecisive and ama-
eurish. On top of which, he had to go and mistime the whole
peration, arriving on the porch top only to discover that the
Princess had not yet left for her dinner date.

It seemed to him now that his heart could not have been in
he job; certainly his mind had failed to concentrate upon it.
While he lay on the porch top, waiting for the Princess's bedroom
ight to go out, he was haunted by something tragic and ominous
e had seen in Daisy's face. She had called to him to come back;

or was it a voice in his own heart? what his father used to be eternally nattering about—conscience? Well, Daisy was the nearest thing to a conscience he'd had for many years. The web of deception, which he'd spun round her life with him, entangled his own feet now, so that his actions dragged and floundered like the feet of a man in a nightmare.

No less vacillating and half-hearted, he could see now, had been his conduct after the crime. Throwing away the parcel, sending for his brother and Jacko, hiding the revolver, failing to work out an alibi with Daisy, walking into the arms of the police —there had been something more than panic behind all these childish mistakes. The enemy within, the Accuser within, had taken away his strength. Behind his bravado on the day after the murder, behind his fatalistic courage in court, there had been a terrible hollowness: guilt had eaten away his will to live: he had gone through the motions of self-preservation, but feebly and perfunctorily, like a dying man who knows he is better dead.

For Hugo viewed his deed now without self-deception, and its consequences without self-pity. That night on the porch, when Inspector Stone had called to him to come down, he had fired the first shot blindly, not aiming, intending only to frighten the man off for a moment so that he could make his escape. But his luck had sent the bullet into the man's body, and the second shot was fired in sheer panic at the visible result of the first. Over and over again, since, he had asked himself how he came to lose his head and fire that first shot. It had happened in a mindless flash. But his claustrophobic horror of prison, his reckless contempt for the police and the society they represented, together with the idea of Daisy bearing his child in poverty and solitude, Daisy deprived of his presence when most she would need it—these, it seemed to him now, were the motives which had touched off that act of blind desperation. Fear and love between them had pulled the trigger.

Hugo considered coldly the man who had fired the shot, not seeking to exculpate him or find excuses for him. One can hardly say that he felt remorse; vexation, perhaps, at the way he had botched the whole job; but for his victim he felt no more pity than for himself—the Inspector was dead, and tomorrow he himself would be dead, and there was no point in wasting tears on either of them. If you killed a man, and they pinned it on you, they had a right to take away your life in exchange. But it ought to stop short at that; the evil a man did should not live after him; the sins of the fathers should not be visited on the children. It was not the murder, but what it would mean for Daisy and their child, which filled Hugo now with a sickening despair. He had not known the true meaning of love till he met Daisy, nor been acquainted with the burden of responsibility which true love imposes.

When he was taken out to see Daisy, however, a few hours later, the problem which had given him so much anxiety solved itself. He knew suddenly that at this, their last meeting, nothing mattered but the truth. During the earlier stage of their relationship he had deceived her, partly at least through fear of losing her love; and later he had lied to her, though not often. Now, even if it spoiled her image of him forever, the truth must be told.

"Daisy, love," he whispered through the grille which separated them, "I must tell you. I did it. I did shoot the Inspector." Anxiously he searched her face. There was shock there and sadness, but no revulsion. "Will you forgive me, Daisy?"

"I've nothing to forgive, sweetheart. You were always a good man to me."

The gentleness in her voice broke down his defenses, thawing the tough ice which had lain for so long at the center of him. "I'm sorry," he said, and realized that he *was* sorry—not for Daisy only, but for his deed, and its victim. "He'd done me no harm. He was a good chap, they say."

Somehow the air was cleared. This interview, which he had so much dreaded, was nothing worse than sad. Daisy held up the baby for him to see.

"He's just like you," she said.

"Did you have a bad time, love?"

"No. Just a few hours." Her lip trembled; then she said bravely,
"I'm glad I've got him, my darling."

"That's a good girl. You look after him well. Don't worry about
me. I'll be glad to get it over. I'm not frightened—you get used to
the idea after a bit."

At that, she started to cry, but quickly checked herself. Each
of them had courage, and was trying to give it to the other.
Presently, like an old married couple by the fireside, they were
talking quite calmly, with no barriers between them, about
everyday things—Daisy's reconciliation with her mother, her
plans for the future—and about the happy times of their past
together. There was much to say, and little time to say it; but
what needed saying most did not need words—their speaking
eyes exchanged messages of love and gratitude.

"Three minutes more," said the warder.

Daisy went deathly pale. Three minutes—and beyond them a
waste of years to live through. "I'd have waited for you," she
muttered, hardly knowing what she said.

"Yes. But it's best this way. Look, Daisy, you marry some
decent chap. Young Thomas'll need a father. Don't spend the rest
of your life brooding about me."

"Yes." Her voice was submissive and faint. She bowed her
head, and the fingers of one hand stroked the grille between
them. She had Hugo back now; there was no withdrawing from
her, no barrier, as there had been during their interviews in
prison before the trial. Though physically they could not touch,
Daisy was aware of strength flowing into her from him; she had
come here to give him what help she could, but it was she who
was being supported.

"And listen to me, Daisy—you're never to worry about the evidence you gave. It'd have made no difference," Hugo said
urgently. "I had it coming to me. Forget it."

"All right, my dear," she answered, knowing she could never
forget it, but feeling now that one day she might be able to remember it without an agony of self-recrimination.

"It's you who've got the forgiving to do," he said. "I messed up your life."

"You *were* my life," she passionately exclaimed. "And you always will be. No girl was ever so happy."

Daisy's emotion communicated itself to the baby in her arms, who awoke and began to cry.

"There, there, my little love," she said.

"Is he hungry? Does he feed well?"

"He's a good baby—aren't you, my precious?"

The warder said, "I'm afraid time's up, missus."

"Can I say good-by to him?" asked Hugo.

The warder hesitated for a moment; then, taking the baby from its mother, he gave it to Hugo. Hugo held it in his arms, kissed it, gazed down at it with a sort of gentle incredulity.

"He's my first, you know," he said to the warder. "My one and only. Fine little chap, isn't he?"

"Champion."

Hugo opened the baby's fist and put into it a small piece of prison bread which he had been holding in his left hand. "There you are, Tom," he whispered. "Now nobody can ever say your father has never given you anything."

FINE MYSTERY AND SUSPENSE
TITLES FROM CARROLL & GRAF